THE HUSBANDS

How far would you go to find out who killed your wife?

T.J. BREARTON

JOFFE BOOKS

Published 2019 by Joffe Books, London.

www.joffebooks.com

Cover photo: Oakley Clement

ISBN-13: 978-1-78931-083-2

For Oakley

PROLOGUE

How do you feel?

The text message woke him up. His vision was fuzzy, bad dreams chasing him out of sleep. After reading the message a second time, he realized it originated from "No Caller ID."

Gray midday light came through the bedroom windows. The air smelled stale, like bad breath. It was one of the worst times of day.

Actually, they were all the worst. The nights when the house was dead quiet, just the sound of the wind outside, the occasional pop as floorboards and joists contracted. The stolid morning air in the house, no smell of coffee, no foreheads to kiss before work. Noon, with its vast emptiness and aimlessness. He felt dead. Life was a prison.

Ted wiped a hand over his face, sat up and picked up the phone.

How do you feel?

Probably a wrong number. Or someone from the funeral home, though it was too early for that, and too odd a question. Maybe someone from Megan's family with a new phone? But a mobile number would've shown up. It could've been a reporter trying to hide their identity. There was one who'd already published two articles on the so-called Park Killer.

Ted replied: *Who is this?*

He swung his legs out of bed, the floor cold under his bare feet, and the phone vibrated in his hand.

I want to know how you're feeling.

He stared at the words as a new message appeared.

We should talk.

He tapped out a response. *Think U have wrong number.*

The reply was fast: *No I don't.*

Then: *You're Ted Archer.*

Ted felt the blood pulsing in his neck. He punched in another reply but the caller beat him to it.

I killed your wife and son.

Ted dropped the phone on the bed like it was on fire. He stared at it, then he snatched it up and called Detective Severin, but hung up before the call went through. Severin wouldn't do anything.

He paced the room, waiting, trying to think. He typed: *Call me.*

And then added: *If Ur who U say you are.*

The phone rang, the ring tone his wife had given him — "Sharp Dressed Man" by ZZ Top. As a joke. When she was alive. Ted could hardly move.

At last he put the phone to his ear and answered. "Who are you?"

"Ted," a male voice said. "How are you feeling?"

"Who are you?"

"I told you."

Ted's whole body shook. His vision faltered. "What's your name?" This was the guy who'd killed Megan and Colton.

"You'll find out who I am. I promise you. First, listen."

"I'll kill you," Ted said. "I'll kill you." He couldn't think of anything else to say.

"I'll let you kill me," the caller said. "If you want to. That's the point, Ted."

"What point? *What point?*" It was hard to breathe. He looked out the window, not really seeing. "I'll . . . kill you."

"Ted . . ."

"I'll find you."

"Ted! You're not . . . let me say this, because I have to be brief."

Ted took a deep breath. This might be his only chance. "I'm listening," he said.

"Good. I asked you how you're feeling."

On the verge of blacking out. "I don't know."

"Before I texted you. What about then?"

"I was asleep."

"Before that. How have you—"

"How do you think I've been feeling? What kind of — how do you *think?* They're on my mind every second of every day."

"Ah! Let me interrupt you. I don't have much time. Right there — you said it. They're on your *mind* every second. And this is causing you pain. *This* is causing you suffering. There's nothing physically assaulting you — it's all in your mind."

What the hell was he talking about? Hang up. Call Severin. This guy has said all sorts of things that could mean something. Think like a cop. Maybe they can't trace the number but—

Ted pulled the phone away from his ear and stared, wondering if it had something like a call recorder on it. He'd never used one, but he didn't know half of what his phone could do. Maybe something else? There was an old tape recorder around somewhere. He moved into the kitchen and started yanking out drawers.

"Ted, healing is only possible when we stop heaping blame and shame upon ourselves. When we seek to understand the conditions shaping our lives and understand the mind for what it really is."

Listen to the voice — any accent? No. Is he excited? He sounds calm. Listen for background noise.

"Ted, are you there?"

He couldn't find the tape recorder. He scrambled for a pen and paper. *Keep him talking.* "I don't understand what you mean."

"I'm talking about the nature of the mind, Ted. The nature of suffering."

Ted found a pen, yanked off the cap with his teeth and started scribbling on an instruction manual for one of his tools.

"What you're experiencing right now, Ted. The pain you feel — you don't have to."

He tried to listen and write down what the caller had already said at the same time. His writing was a mess. He threw the pen aside. "You sound like a shrink." *Where is he? That's the most important thing.*

Ted said, "Maybe certain people — you know — they get stuff like that, get into these ideas you're talking about. But not where I live . . ."

He waited for the killer to give something away.

"That's a fair point. People go to church. They go to work. They raise families. They're lost in their delusions."

The mention of raising a family produced a familiar sensation, one he'd gotten used to over the past two weeks: an elevator in freefall, stomach floating. It was true he thought about his wife and son incessantly, but it wasn't exactly continuous. He could preoccupy himself for fleeting moments; he could punch the wall, he could run until his chest exploded, or just lose himself for a few seconds in some automatic activity like brushing his teeth, but when reality crashed back in, it often felt like falling. Like dying. Like hell re-forming around him.

Silence.

"Hello?"

Quieter than before: "Ted. I asked you how you were feeling. But I actually know how you're feeling — you feel sick and lost. You were all wrapped up in your family, in who you thought you were, and now that's gone. But you gotta see the bigger picture here. The disease of identity causes more pain and suffering than any pathogen. It promotes hate and greed and war."

Ted was barely listening now. Instinct took over. He headed out of the bedroom, toward the stairs, the basement, the shotgun and box of double-ought shells.

"It's a problem for all mankind," the voice continued. "You know what I mean? What do you think a vaccine is? You have to produce a little disease in order to have the cure. The death of your family will help inoculate the planet."

Ted switched on the light and bounded down the stairs. Feeling better than he'd felt in days. A spark of something. Purpose.

In his ear, the killer kept going. "It will be hard for you — it will be the greatest challenge of your life, Ted, but you've got everything to gain. And really — literally — nothing left to lose. You see what I mean? You're now an empty cup."

"Uh-huh. I get it."

"I gotta go, Ted. But I'll keep my promise. I'll tell you who I am. You'll know — I promise you that. Unless you call the police. If you try anything, you'll never get that chance. It has to be just you and me. If you talk to the police, I'll never call you again. They'll never catch me and you'll never find me or have the opportunity to kill me."

"I don't understand . . . I don't believe you."

"You can believe me because I'm confident. I'm confident because I'm sure that by the time we're done, you'll no longer feel the need."

"What?"

Ted found the shotgun, took it down from the exposed joists. He held it barrel-up in one hand, phone in the other. *Think.* The guy was local to the region, maybe. He was from here.

Ted said, "You're not going to turn yourself in. You can't convince me my family deserved to die. I'll never hear from you again. Just tell me now."

There was a silence. "Ted. If I fail, then my death at your hands is the correct outcome."

Ted sat down with the shotgun across his legs. He felt too heavy to stand. There was a stray sock beside the dryer. His little boy's sock. Ted felt like throwing up. He tried to load a shotshell but his hands were shaking.

The caller's voice was soft now, almost soothing. "Maybe it will help to think of me as crazy. I'm crazy enough to have killed your wife and son and then called you to tell you. You should believe I'm crazy enough to do exactly what I'm saying."

The call ended.

PART ONE

Are you truly a good person, or are you merely afraid?
Maybe it's men with heroic courage who eschew society to become
outlaws while cowards follow the rules.

CHAPTER ONE

Tuesday, November 27

Kelly stopped reading when her phone rang. She thought about letting the voicemail pick up but leaned over and checked the number. Then she took a quick hit of her coffee and answered. "Kelly Roth."

"Good morning," Genarro said. "Got something for you."

She closed the file and sat up straighter. "Okay, sir."

"Good news first or bad news? Well, both could be bad news depending on how you feel about Central New York."

She drew a quick breath. "I feel fine about it, sir."

"Some guys up there have sent information to ViCAP and are looking for a consultation. These are separate homicides and in different jurisdictions. Two women and one woman and child. There's also . . . I'd like you to come in, have a look."

"All right, sir."

"See you in ten, my office."

He hung up. Kelly slowly put the phone back in the cradle. She swept aside the document she'd been reading — a psychopath's mind unspooled on paper. Killers like Billy Bath weren't legally allowed to profit from memoirs or biographies, but Bath had produced copious personal manifestos. Captured after killing eleven women, he'd then felt the urge to write down all his thoughts, and give them to the FBI to study.

She clipped her ID to her suit jacket and grabbed her valise. She took the skyway across to the main building for CIRG — the Critical Incident Response Group — four stories up.

"Come on in, Roth." Genarro was pushing sixty. He wore a spotless dark blue suit, his hair coiffed into a gray-black swoop. He didn't get up.

She sat down opposite him.

"So," Genarro said. He pushed a file across his desk. "I'm going to show you Auburn Police Department first. This was seven months ago."

Kelly flipped through the file. Pictures of a woman, face-down in a creek.

"That's at a spot outside Auburn called Island Park, at the top of Owasco Lake. She was killed late evening, mid-week. There's a gas station about a hundred yards away, attendant thought he heard a firecracker, but it was a jogger who found her about an hour later. CSS recovered a single .30-30 casing about ten yards from the body. Medical examiner extracted the projectile and the ballistics are consistent with the casing. No sexual assault."

Kelly scanned the report, swallowed, and looked up at Genarro. "Victim was pregnant."

"Eight weeks. They went to her husband first — something like this screams husband or dejected lover — but the husband was at work, and it seems solid. He works for a company called Xylem and they keep good records. He's on camera at his job during the shooting. No evident motive."

Genarro pushed another file toward her. She looked at the new photos.

"Second victim," Genarro said. "Three months ago. This is on the east side of Onondaga Lake. Different lake, sounds similar, but you knew that. Crime-scene did an adequate job, bagged the hands, scoured the scene. Once again, found a .30-30 casing nearby, no fingerprints. Otherwise some beer cans and cigarette butts they brought in for DNA. Also no evidence of sexual assault. Apparently some local duck hunter found her."

Kelly looked up from the photos of the dead woman lying in tall grass. "Onondaga Lake is in the middle of the suburbs."

"He's some local guy, that's his spot. Cops know him — he's friendly with Liverpool Police, called them direct." Genarro shifted in his seat. The lines around his eyes stood out against his otherwise smooth skin. "So, at this point, after the second victim, nobody's talking about a connection yet. For one, she's not pregnant. The detective in Liverpool came down hard on the husband, too, grilled him for a couple of days. Multiple witnesses claim he spent all night at the restaurant he owns, but she was found in close proximity, less than a mile away."

Kelly looked at the female victim in the golden marsh grass, face-down with dirt scattered over her. The next pictures showed close-ups of various body parts. Same MO — shot in the head.

"Again they couldn't get anything on the husband so they let him go. With this guy, maybe all the media coverage, I don't know — he took off."

"Took off?"

"He's got a cabin on Green Pond in the Adirondacks. State troopers have been keeping an eye on him up there."

Genarro slid the final file across the desk. "Last one. This is a double. And it's rough — there's a juvenile."

The woman was on the ground, fully clothed, blood matting one side of her brown hair like chocolate syrup.

Beside her was a young boy on his back, small gray face toward the sky, missing an eye.

Kelly put the photos back in the folder, mindful of the slight trembling in her hands, and skimmed the autopsy reports. The woman was forty. Her son was ten.

"This one was in Constantia," Genarro said, "eleven days ago. Similar shots to the back of the head, like a witness execution."

"And with a .30-30," Kelly said. "That's a pretty common load for game hunting. And these hunters keep showing up at the crime scenes . . ."

"Different type though — deer hunters. They made the emergency call and local deputies responded. It crossed my mind for a minute, too — but it *is* deer season, and the mother and son were found along a hunting area, so the coincidence is moot. Plus, the duck hunter who found the other one in the tall grass there — he uses shotshells, not jacketed bullets."

She looked up at Genarro. "So how did they end up finally linking these? I assume if we've been called, someone linked them. Because of the media?"

He folded his hands together. "In part. The police have kept the information about caliber and bullet casings left at the scenes out of any press conferences. But Broward — that's the chief of police in Liverpool — knows a guy from Constantia. Somebody's married to somebody in their families. Broward's sister, I think, is married to a Constantia cop named Severin. Anyway, it came up over Thanksgiving, everybody together, talking shop. They compared cases then did some digging around and found out about the Auburn case — the one from seven months ago. That's when they got together on it and called us."

She went back through each file, checking dates, locations. "So they hadn't connected any of these before Thanksgiving; before the twenty-second?"

"Day after. Broward and Severin were together, talking, and that's when they hit on it. They called to run it through the database yesterday. Media got a hold of the story on the third killing right about the same time, but there's only been a couple of articles, and they focus on similarity of locations, so they're calling him the 'Park Killer' since they all happened in some kind of state or local park."

"There's a direction to it," she said, picturing a map in her mind. "Auburn is southwest of Liverpool, Constantia is northeast."

He lifted his eyebrows and said nothing.

"But they're spread out over time," she said. "So maybe that doesn't matter."

He watched her. "You don't recognize any of the names? You're from the area. Not Haig? How about Payton or Archer?"

"No, sir. I don't know any of the victims or their husbands."

"MO and ballistics match for each victim so it could be four people on one gun. Get the gun, get the perp. But the signature isn't exactly jumping out. There's three women, ages from twenty-one to forty, one pregnant, plus one ten-year-old boy. Nothing in common except that they were in isolated areas. Was it chance? Was it premediated? Is this guy just driving around looking for victims? That's what we need to know."

Genarro got up and went over to the window. "So I'd like you to go up there. You've expressed a desire to get into the field, you're a good researcher and I think you could use the experience. Consult with the lead investigators, offer what you can. There's a federal prosecutor watching, named Starkey. He'll pull up a chair when we need him. In the meantime, I'd start by touching base with Chief Broward in Liverpool."

"Liverpool's tiny. He's a police chief; a paper-pusher. Looks like the County MCU was involved."

"It was their crime scene unit on that second one, but I think Broward is your point person. He's the one who called us."

She stayed sitting. The questions and concerns popped up too fast to inspect them all.

Genarro said, "Broward used Law Enforcement Online to plug in everything from the three jurisdictions — crime scene descriptions, victim descriptive data, lab reports — I'll forward it all on to you. I've talked to Broward, and he seems on the ball, but this is spread out over different jurisdictions; everybody seems friendly and sharing information but they're . . . they punch out and go home at the end of the day." Genarro meant that the people involved had lives. Kelly didn't. She didn't argue. He said, "I need you to analyze, check everything against their timeline and form your own investigative matrix. What do you think?"

Don't hesitate. "I'm good to go, sir."

He gave her a long look, almost paternal. "It's getting cold up there. You still have a thick enough winter coat?"

"I burned everything when I moved to Virginia, sir."

He blinked, hesitating. "I didn't know you joked, Roth."

"There's some truth to it, sir."

* * *

Packing was a pain. She not only didn't have a good winter coat, her buttery-leather boots wouldn't last a day around those lakes and marshes. She took a break, drinking a cool beer on the screened-in terrace. It was warm in Virginia. Ribbons of mist floated beneath the large Laurel Oaks, the air scented with night-blooming gardenias.

She wondered whether to tell her family she was coming. She'd been straight with Genarro — there was no conflict, she had nothing against Central New York, and what had happened to her there could've happened to her anywhere. But she'd chosen to stay in Stafford after completing FBI training and hooked up with the Behavioral Science Unit. One benefit was never having to go back home.

Images from the crime scenes kept surfacing. She didn't know if she was ready for this.

She forced herself to finish packing. She'd buy a warmer winter jacket when she got there, give it away before she left.

* * *

Up ahead of the dawn, into her routine, first push-ups, then sit-ups, then pull-ups on the bar she'd bought for her rented apartment. Her flight was in four hours, it was still dark, but she was wide awake.

She took a quick shower, rubbed the steam away from the mirror and looked at the scar running down her torso.

There were jokes during training that she was out to prove women could do it better. They called her Clarice Starling, even though it'd been decades since *The Silence of the Lambs*. People couldn't let it go, apparently. She didn't look like Jodie Foster anyway, but had full lips, thick dark brown hair and her father's hazel eyes.

It was a breezy morning, climbing to sixty degrees when she boarded American Airlines Flight 4612 out of Reagan National Airport in D.C. headed for Syracuse, NY — a one-way ticket. The FBI was frugal, and she flew coach. The scheduled flight time was an hour and twenty minutes. The cabin was crowded — people still flying home from the Thanksgiving holiday.

She had a seat in the back of the plane, which was quieter, though it smelled of urine. Kelly opened her laptop.

Everything on the murders had been uploaded before she left — digital versions of what cops called "murder books" — copies of field reports, medical examiner's reports, interviews and witness statements, CSS reports and a few crime scene diagrams originally done in pencil and scanned. She also had with her the online versions of the two newspaper articles which had very little to go on besides rumor and fear.

Tammy Haig was twenty-one. Her husband Blake, twenty-five, worked as a Utility Assembler for Xylem, a water technology company. Tammy was a psychology student at Wells College. They'd been expecting their first child.

According to the husband, who worked nights, Tammy often stopped at Island Park on the way home from her evening class. She had entered the nearby convenience store at precisely 8:22 p.m. on Wednesday, April 25, to get something to eat. The jogger who'd found her dead in the creek claimed the Fitbit he'd been wearing had said 9:28. The medical examiner put time of death at 8:30, with homicide as the cause.

The next victim was Danica Payton, thirty-three years old. At age sixteen — then Danica Harbaugh — she'd been top of the swim team at Liverpool High School. As a young woman she competed regularly in the Ironman competition, posting some of the fastest swim times recorded. She was pretty; full lips and broad shoulders, a mass of auburn hair.

After an injury derailed her athletic career, she married Roger Payton, an older man from Baldwinsville. Roger had been working at a restaurant called The Trading Post since he was eighteen, from dishwasher to manager to owner. They went hiking and kayaking and traveled together, married seven years.

Like Tammy Haig, Danica had a habit of spending time in a park near her home. She'd been murdered there, left beside Onondaga Lake among the cattails and marsh grass, hidden from view of vehicles zipping past on the parkway, but not far from them — just seventy yards.

There was no obvious connection between the two women. They never knew each other and were only joined in death.

The Archers were the most recent victims. Mother and son. They'd been shot to death along the edge of a nature preserve. No connections to the other victims.

Megan Archer had been walking her son home from school on a warm autumn afternoon. They did this on days when the weather was good. The husband, Ted Archer, said this was probably the last time they'd walk together before spring. If the weather had been bad, they might not have taken the route. They might still be alive.

Funny, the little things.

In each case, time of death was either pinpointed circumstantially or by physical evidence narrowing it down. Danica Payton had been last seen at her restaurant at approximately six thirty and had been shot between 7 and 9 p.m. on the night of August 18, a Saturday. The murder of the Archers was twelve days ago, Friday November 16. Their time of death approximately 3:30 p.m.

Kelly thought about the times and dates — ages, too — each murdered woman was older than the previous one. She spent a few minutes plugging contact info for the lead investigators into her phone, then closed the laptop and rubbed her face. They were flying above the clouds. The sun was on the other side of the cabin, dazzling above all the white.

Then as the plane descended, the clouds grew thick and dark.

* * *

Raining in Syracuse — nothing new there. The weather people expected it to become snow by nightfall. She picked up the keys for the rental from the Alamo kiosk and walked into the lot, pulling her suitcase behind her and covering her head with a gift shop newspaper, looking for space number 16. The Mazda was the most low-key car they offered — light brown, no bells or whistles, like something her father would've driven. She loaded her bag and drove from the airport to the hotel, two miles away, checked into her room, dried her damp hair, plugged in her laptop, and went out to find some food.

Near St. Luke's Hospital was a Thai place on an otherwise desolate, wet street. It was still early. She found a table in the corner with a view of the door and ordered the Tom Kha Kai, enjoying some peace until the waitress returned and struck up a conversation.

"Are you a medical student?"

"No."

"We get lots of students in here, and nurses and doctors."

Kelly looked out the window. Danica Payton, she thought, the former athlete, would be first.

The waitress hovered by the table, as if waiting for Kelly to keep up her end of the small talk bargain. She tried on a smile for the waitress, who blinked twice and walked away.

Back in the hotel room, she phoned the Liverpool Police Department and left a message for Chief Broward. She took out her laptop and opened the Danica Payton file since Broward was in charge of that case.

Danica's parents lived in the area. She had two brothers, Russell and Matthew Harbaugh. Each with records — both DUIs. They liked to have a good time. There were lots of relatives in Syracuse and its many suburbs and outlying small towns. Her husband Roger, by contrast, was an only child of divorce.

Kelly watched the interviews with Danica's brothers. They were both big guys, beefy and muscular, Russell wearing a leather jacket, Matthew in a nylon zip-up. Talking about their dead sister, the siblings were quiet and attentive. Both had credible alibis.

She watched the Roger Payton tape next. Danica's husband slouched in his seat and buried his head in his hands. He repeatedly wiped at his eyes and looked devastated. If it was a performance, it was a good one. But the interviewing detective was pushy.

Detective Faber had positioned himself off-camera, just his shoulder visible and sometimes part of his head. "I know how it is, right? I got a wife who doesn't work either, you know what I mean? You're out there busting your ass — I mean you and me, we're both putting in long, hard hours, you know . . . and then she asks for *this*, or she asks for *that*. She's got your credit card. And I know your restaurant has been . . . look, we both know about this economy."

Roger Payton kept shaking his head. "No. We're fine. Nothing like that."

"I know what it's like, is what I'm saying. There are days I just as soon cut her loose. Let her see what it's like on her own. She's got nothing to do except spend my money and complain about where I go or what I do. It passes through your mind, you're human — that's all I'm saying. A little insurance money, no more nagging . . ."

"I didn't kill my wife."

And on it went, Faber hoping to lure Payton into admitting something. The tape lasted several hours.

Her phone buzzed on the table. Liverpool Police. She answered, "This is Agent Kelly Roth."

"Agent Roth." He sounded out of breath. "Chief Broward."

"Hello."

"Thanks for getting here so fast. So how do we do this? You want to come down to the station or—"

"I'd like to look at the body and visit the crime scene."

He hesitated. "Well, crime scene's kinda . . . Everything's been photo-docked, everything's been to the lab and come back . . ."

"I'd like to have a look anyway. Will Detective Faber be meeting me?"

"Uh, no. I, ah . . . I'll be meeting you myself, then, I guess. So I'll see you over there and — what else? You said you wanted to view the victim."

"You still have a body, I hope."

"No, no — I mean, yes, we do. Absolutely we do. Just . . ." Broward trailed off and breathed into the phone for a minute.

"Chief Broward?"

"So I thought — I don't know — I thought you were maybe going to, like, teach a class kind of a thing. Tell us what to look out for. You're a profiler, right? You teach a class down there at the FBI headquarters? Is that it?"

Kelly got up from the small table and paced the room. "I did start teaching, yes. I'm not exactly a profiler. There's no real 'profiling division' with the FBI, but what I'm here for, Chief Broward—"

"You can call me Rob, if you want."

"I'm here to help you. Whatever you feel will best serve you and your team, that's what I want to do. We can meet as soon as you can gather everybody up, and I can tell you what I think at this point . . ."

And what did she think? Nothing, not yet, and premature guesses didn't help in a field detractors still called FBI voodoo. There was no clairvoyance. There was analysis, modeling, and prediction.

"But it wouldn't be much more than you already know — I've only seen what you've entered into the system, what you sent my SAC at the BU."

"Um — say that again, now?"

"I mean my supervisor at the FBI." She stopped pacing and shut her eyes, pinched the bridge of her nose between her thumb and finger. Too much time sitting in an office, too much time with her head in books, going from Stafford to her home in Nokesville and back again.

She didn't even have a cat, let alone keep friends. She was rusty with people.

She opened her eyes. "What I mean is, I think I can best help you if I have a chance to look at everything myself."

"I got you."

Take it easy, Kelly-bell.

Her father's voice in her head.

Just go easy. You'll be all right.

I don't know how I'm going to be able to do this. I don't know if I can do this . . .

One foot in front of the other, Bell. Don't overthink it. One foot in front of the other, just like anything else. Same way you've gotten through all the rest of it.

CHAPTER TWO

She drove to Onondaga Park, on the north end of the long, narrow lake, and stood looking out at the smokestacks across the water. Her watch said it was after twelve — Broward was late.

Throughout the park were wooden benches, somewhat randomly placed, each bearing a dedication to a lost loved one. James Axelrod, Beloved Father. Margaret Stone, May She Rest in Peace. Henny McNamara, Who Will Be Missed Forever. The last time she'd been here there'd been a dozen or so benches; there were four or five times that now. Life moved on, death didn't stop.

A Liverpool PD car came in off the parkway, rolled to a stop on the dirt parking area. Broward was younger than she'd expected, tall and fit, dressed in jeans and a white police chief shirt and a thick parka. He smiled as he approached and stuck out his hand. "Rob Broward."

"Kelly Roth," she said.

"Flight okay coming up?"

"It was good, yeah."

His gaze lingered. "It stayed in the air I guess, right? Never been a big fan of flying, myself — like my feet on the ground." He shook his head and then looked toward the water's edge and flapped a hand. "So, over here."

Coming in from the parkway, there was the dirt lot, a short span of mown grass, then a wall of tall, golden marsh grass hemming the lake. The air smelled slightly fishy; a breeze came through, hissing as it ruffled the stiff vegetation. Broward walked a few paces then stopped. "Okay, right in here." He pointed. "Danica Payton was around this spot, face down. Mostly obscured from the road, sort of half in the broomsedge here. The guy who found her comes here in the evenings sometimes around dusk, shoots duck. We all know him — he had us going there the first few times he'd come out — someone reported shots and we come down here, find the guy hunting, middle of suburbia, duck calls and everything. He was all ready for us though — he says, 'Hunting waterfowl is under federal jurisdiction.'" Broward chuckled again and scratched his mustache. "Good guy. He's a good guy, Joel McKenna. Think he just likes to get away from the wife and kids when he can. But he's a real sportsman . . . did you know that — duck-hunting, or, ah, waterfowl — that's a federal thing?"

"I did." She lowered down onto her haunches. Broward was a talker. But that was okay. She could think when people were talking. "Her husband hadn't reported her missing, then."

"No, no. I thought that was in the report."

"Just confirming it with you."

"Yeah — Roger was busy with the restaurant, just expected she'd be home when he got there later."

Kelly touched a stalk of broomsedge, golden grass as tall as she was with a brush-like tip. "And the fact that the duck hunter, Joel, he sometimes fires a weapon down here — that accounts for why no one called in hearing a shot?"

"It might be, yeah. Most likely. We weren't able to find any witnesses, no one who said they heard it. But a .30-30 is pretty loud. At the press conference we announced a hotline and asked if anyone had been driving this route between six thirty and seven thirty on the night of, if they heard anything, saw anything, to call it in. We're a small city but we get thirty-six thousand vehicles passing through here on a daily basis — we got over fifty calls, witnesses described ten different vehicles, including a black van. It's pretty dark over here. And there was no one else in the park, not anywhere near this spot, anyway. Someone was way up along the lake, walking their dog, said they heard something they thought was fireworks; kids shooting off poppers. Even when the park gets a lot of visitors in the busy season, this strip along in here — not so much."

"Just people like Joel the duck hunter. Or kids with fireworks."

Broward looked down at her.

Kelly asked, "Which way was Danica facing? From the pictures it's hard to tell."

"She was, ah . . ." He stepped into the tall grass, pushing it aside, then circled around. He lay down in the weeds, his head toward the water. "She was just like this." He put one arm up above his head, as if reaching for the lake, twenty feet away. His other arm was tight against his torso. His head was to the side.

Broward got back on his feet. "Best I could impersonate a chalk outline."

She paced the area, thinking, seeing what came into her mind. "And no bruising around her wrist, from the ME report."

"No." Broward glanced around. "I'll have to look at it again, but we're pretty sure she wasn't handled, not dragged here or anything. Where she was found was where she was shot. One shot, boom, she goes down."

"There was some dirt on her back." Kelly bent down again and dug through the crushed weeds, finding the loose soil below. She dusted her hands off and stood back up.

Broward was watching her. "We took samples. That all went to the lab, too."

"You think he got out of the vehicle?"

"Well, there's footprints all over here, we took a few castings, but nothing definitive that he approached her after he shot her. Could just be a little dirt got on her when she fell."

Kelly pulled her pea coat tighter. The rain had tapered off shortly after she'd landed but the afternoon temperature was falling. "I'd like to look around a little more."

"Sure. Let's walk down to the lake." Broward took a narrow path in the broomsedge. She followed. She saw the water through the tall golden stalks. She also saw a green plastic bench sitting almost hidden in the weeds. "That's where Joel sits sometimes," Broward said and then lifted his arms. "This is pretty much it. Just a few feet of these big grasses here. Kind of a barrier around the lake. My feeling has always been that Danica Payton was just looking out at the sunset, and that was the last thing she knew."

They walked back out of the tall grass and stood by the cars in the dirt lot. Kelly watched the traffic rolling past on Onondaga Lake Parkway. "I remember this spot. A real speed trap."

"Yeah we post someone here pretty regularly."

"But no one out running radar the night Danica was killed."

"No. No one out."

"And the thinking is that he shot her from over here. Maybe from his vehicle. The bullet entered the back of her head at an angle, suggesting he was lower down, maybe sitting in his car in the dark and she's walking past and he shoots. Nothing to show he approaches her after that — he just drives off." She scuffed some dirt with the toe of her boot. "So I guess the question is, why is there a casing there?"

"Right," Broward said. "That's what we asked. If he's in his car, and he fires, the bullet casing is going to pop out, land somewhere inside the vehicle, most likely. It could have bounced though, maybe off the side of the car, hit the ground. But you figure he'd notice that and pick it up."

Kelly thought about it. People in law enforcement thought about casings. Maybe hunters. Military personnel. The average person? Possibly.

Broward said, "So you want me to gather everybody up? Have that meeting?"

"Tell me more about Joel McKenna, the guy who found her. Does he own a .30-30?"

Broward looked at the ground, put his hands on his hips. "He does. It's a pretty common gun. Very common. We went over everything with him several times, story never changed. He uses a shotgun out here. And he was the one to call it in, even though he was already in the system from some stuff back in the day. Nothing major, though."

"He was in the system, so you checked the body against his DNA."

"We did."

"And you have a good crime scene unit here?"

"They're a county unit. Their best tech was out that day but we recalled him. If Joel McKenna's DNA was on the victim, we would have found it." Broward scratched his mustache again. "But it wasn't. He was cleared."

"How about the .30-30 he owns? What's the model?"

"He's got a Marlin. Lever-action." He gave her a critical eye, probably considering the extent of her firearms knowledge.

She knew that the .30-30 was the most common chambering in lever-action rifles. But just because the recovered casings had '30-30 WIN' stamped on them didn't mean the rifle used was a Winchester. Other rifles were chambered in the same load — Browning, the Savage Model 99, and Marlin. "You did a rifling test on it?"

"We did not do a rifling test on Joel McKenna's gun, no."

The inside of a gun barrel shaped the bullet as it fired, like a fingerprint, every gun different. "Why not?"

"The mushrooming and contortion of the projectile dissuaded us."

A gust of wind hunted the gaps in her suit. "I would strongly recommend you have that done, Chief Broward. With all respect, if the rifling of his gun barrel matches patterns on the projectile recovered from the victim, that's a dead-lock."

Broward gave her a look, a light smile playing on his lips, like he didn't know how to take her.

She'd already profiled him: he wasn't quite tall enough for basketball, broad-shouldered enough for football, but he seemed the outdoorsy type. Probably had gotten stoned a couple times as a teenager. Liked to drink domestic beer. Smoked cigarettes for a few years, quit, started running to keep in shape with middle age coming on, probably wouldn't mind sitting here and doing a little duck hunting himself, if he weren't chief of police. She knew he was divorced, had two kids. She figured girls — daughters softened a man.

"If you think it will help, I'll make it happen," he said.

She looked toward the buildings which formed the downtown area, just over a quarter mile away. "Can we walk over to the restaurant?"

"Roger Payton isn't there. He was here for a while dealing with affairs and then he headed upstate to another place he owns up there in the Adirondacks. He should be back in a couple of days."

"I'd like to have a look anyway. If you don't mind."

"Sure."

They started walking, passing by the memorial benches, avoiding piles of black and white goose poop. She pointed out a bench.

"Yeah," Broward said. "Joe Harbaugh. Her grandfather. Roger Payton said she liked to pay her respects, take her walks here."

"You felt okay letting Payton leave town?"

Broward was quiet a minute, his jaw twitching. "We had nothing to hold him on. And he's got a restaurant to run, so he's not just going to disappear off the face of the earth. The guy had just lost his wife. I figured, pay out a little rope, let him go, but keep an eye on him."

"I watched the interview between him and Detective Faber."

He gave her a sidelong look. "Faber resigned."

"Ah. Okay."

It made sense — his name only showed up on the initial paperwork and he'd been overbearing, bordering on inappropriate, with the victim's husband. But there could be more to it.

Broward said, "Liverpool is just over two thousand people. There's me, there's Sergeant Ridgley, we've got three full-time officers and four part-timers and then there was Faber. Faber was used to burglaries and assaults. Not this. We haven't had anything like this."

"Well you had the County Major Crimes Unit involved."

"For the crime scene work, yeah. And as I'm sure you know, they've got investigators. But Faber was quarterbacking it."

"So do you have a new detective now?"

"We're in the process."

They walked in silence for a minute, Kelly thinking about Danica Payton taking an evening stroll, somebody watching her, waiting for the right moment. The park was huge — a seven-and-a-half-mile linear greenway hugging the shores of Onondaga Lake. Several smaller roads crisscrossed through, accessing the marina and boat launch. At Christmas the roads were used for "Lights on the Lake" when locals and tourists drove slowly through a colorful display of lights shaped into holiday characters — her father had taken them when she was young. Mostly she remembered his swearing and frustration with traffic. Today, the Christmas decorations had yet to come, leaving only sparse trees scrubbed bare by November wind.

To the east, Oswego Street split into Old Liverpool Road and Onondaga Lake Parkway, which passed the spot where Danica Payton had been murdered. The Trading Post restaurant was still ahead, on Sycamore Street, and they were getting close.

Broward kept talking. "You know, the thing with Detective Faber — Faber was old-school — work your suspects by telling them you're trying to eliminate them so you can move on and get the bad guy. Faber liked Roger for it right off the bat."

"But you didn't?"

"We talked to all the staff from the restaurant that night. If he'd slipped out, he'd done it so fast . . . no. And Roger doesn't own any guns. What Faber did was try to trap Roger into admitting he'd hired someone."

"The style of shooting does have characteristics of a contract job."

"Except for leaving behind a bullet casing," Broward said.

"Except for that," she agreed.

* * *

The Trading Post restaurant had been sided with half-logs to resemble a cabin. Kelly opened the thick, wooden door. "Can we get a table?"

"Yeah?"

"Best way to get a look around. Just two people having lunch."

The inside was cozy, wood finishing decorated with faux furs and beaver pelts and Native American blankets. The bar was nearly full, customers chattering and country music playing and everything smelling like fried food and barbeque sauce. A pretty brunette waitress gave the two cops a wary look, then forced a smile and called over. "Sit anywhere. Someone will be right with you."

They took a table in the dining area, where the décor shifted to an eclectic mix of vintage advertising posters. She sat down and looked around the busy scene, picking out an older couple who reminded her of her grandparents and two middle-aged guys in suits, eating burgers with gusto. She asked Broward if he'd change seats. "Sure." Now she had a view of the bar and entrance.

"So," he said. "Quantico. You live there?"

"I live near there."

"How often do you come out into the field like this?"

"Not often. How much was Danica here?"

Broward leaned back, hung a boot from his knee and pressed a thumb to the corner of his mouth, then looked at his thumb. "All the time."

"Did she hang out, sit at the bar?"

"Oh sure. Roger doesn't drink. Or, he didn't. Danica wasn't a big drinker, either. But she'd come in, visit with people, talk to her husband."

"And she had no stake in the restaurant?"

He shook his head. "It's all Roger's. He bought it about ten years ago when it was on its last legs. Smart, though, he's a pretty smart guy — he kept the original name. You see some people they come in and they take over a place and change the name and nobody shows up. Change the menu all you want but don't change the name. It's been The Post for like fifty years."

"Can you walk me through the last time she was here?"

"Okay, well, she was here late that afternoon. Witnesses said everything was plumb. She talked to Roger, had a few laughs, they said, and then she went to the park."

"She told him that's where she was going?"

"I don't think she said it explicitly. But she had her walking sneakers on, and she went over there pretty regularly. She couldn't really run anymore, on account of her blown-out knee, but she walked. So Payton says, so her family says. I guess it was a busy night. Roger pitches in and runs food out of the kitchen when the rush comes. She stepped out just before the rush. He said they'd had a quick kiss goodbye and agreed to meet each other at home. He'd get in late — typically close to midnight on a busy night."

A waitress interrupted, hesitation in her eyes. "Hi. You guys eating, or . . . ?"

Broward said, "Yeah, we'll take those menus. Roger call in or anything recently?"

"Still up at Green Pond. Supposed to be back the day after tomorrow. He called yesterday and talked to Eileen." She studied Kelly a moment, her tongue poking the inside of her cheek. There was something in her eyes, back in the corner of her gaze, like a territorial claim. "Get you something to drink?"

"I'll take a Coke," Broward said.

"Just the water is fine."

"Okay." She gave them a crooked smile. "I'll be right back."

Broward scanned his menu then looked up. "Are you going to eat?"

"I already did."

He closed the menu and looked worried.

"No, go ahead," she said.

"I'm starving." After a moment he looked up from the menu again and spoke in a low voice. "Some people got word about how Faber treated Roger. They said no way was Roger guilty. He was too in love, no reason to hurt his wife. Others thought he was good for it — maybe they'd been trying to have kids or something and he got upset. So neither side was happy with me — mad about Faber or mad I let Roger go."

"And then you made the connection to the Archer murders . . ."

"That's right. Which I guess made Roger Payton look even less guilty, since he was up there when it happened. Far as we know." Broward glanced around and said, "Hey, I'm just gonna wash up. Hit the head. Be right back."

She watched as he crossed the restaurant and said something to the waitress who was getting his Coke from the bar. Then he disappeared into the back.

Kelly noticed the two middle-aged men in suits were sneaking looks at her. She dabbed at her phone with a finger, made a few notes, sneaking looks back. When Broward reappeared, he picked his way across the dining room and headed for the two men. After a moment it was clear they were friendly with the chief. She took another sip of her water. Broward said something and the men looked over. Broward patted one of them on the back and returned to the table

"Those guys — one of those guys sold me my house. They're both in real estate."

She gave them one last look. The one who'd made eye contact with her looked vaguely familiar. "Let's talk about the other victims, okay?"

"Okay."

"So far it seems that no one from this case — not Danica, not Roger, no one from the restaurant — is connected to anyone else."

"Not that we've been able to determine."

"But your brother-in-law is Detective Severin, who's in charge of the Archer case. He's married to your sister?"

"That's right. Eight," he rolled his eyes toward the ceiling, "no — nine years they've been married."

"The Archers are the most recent, killed twelve days ago. Tell me what you know about Ted Archer. He was a husband, he was a father, what else? Did he have any enemies?"

"Well, for that you'll have to ask Lou. You know, Detective Severin. But I think the answer is no. Ted Archer is a well-liked general contractor. Has his own business like Roger, few guys working for him, does some commercial and some residential. Pretty average guy, keeps about his business. He was at work, same as Roger, same as Blake Haig, husband of the first victim."

"And Ted Archer's wife and son were discovered by deer hunters."

"Correct."

"But it's not like they were out somewhere on a game trail."

"No. But they were right along the edge of Wheeler Road, and that borders the wildlife area. The mother was walking the son home from school."

"Borders it, but it's inland a ways, it's not on the lake, not on water."

"That's right. Wheeler is back in a ways. It's McCloud Road that runs along the lake, I think. But Wheeler is up above the green line and there are marshes around there. You think water has something to do with it?" His eyes shone.

"I don't know. Might, might not. And so mother and son were walking along Wheeler . . ."

"And, well, same thing as you thought about Danica Payton — they were shot at relatively close range."

The waitress came back with their drinks. "You two ready to order?"

Broward ordered a short rack of ribs, fries and a side of slaw. Kelly just handed back her menu. "Nothing, thanks."

The waitress left again and Kelly said, "So Megan and Colton Archer were found just alongside the road. The hunters found them around dusk, three hours after they were killed. Just like with Danica Payton, it's a quiet area, not a lot of people around."

"Right. DEC responded to the call because of the wildlife area, so did the sheriff's department."

"The mother and son spent three hours on Wheeler Road, lying there, no one else saw them before the hunters?"

He cocked his head and looked at the wall behind her. "I think — and you'll see it — the way they fell, you'd miss them from the road." Broward's gaze slid back. "It was only because one of the hunters was looking out as they drove past — the start of the game trail is about an eighth of a mile from where the bodies were found — he was looking out of the truck and he thought he saw something. They circled around, found what was there, called 911, hung around until the deputy responded and called in Detective Severin. The hunters gave statements. Neither had fired their weapon."

She let this settle. "What is going on with Ted Archer right now? Did he run off somewhere, too, like Roger Payton?"

Now Broward ran a hand through his dark curly hair. He looked uncomfortable. "No, he didn't. Severin says, you know, Archer is just shut in his house. A total mess. He tried to go back to work a few days ago, fell apart in front of the crew, just collapsed into tears. Went home; hasn't been back to work since. He's got a couple of foremen, though, running his contracts." Broward shook his head, as if imagining the sudden and tragic loss of his own family. "It's just . . . it's just, you can't . . ."

"I'd like to speak to him," Kelly said.

"Yeah. Yeah we can arrange that. Far as I know, like I said, he's just been home. He's just banging around in that house, alone. God what a thing."

CHAPTER THREE

Ted had debated whether to call the cops. Endlessly.

You could conceal a phone number using an app. Ted had searched for similar apps able to do the opposite — unveil a masked number. The *Privus Pack* seemed best. He paid for it and installed it on his phone.

Unable to eat or sleep, he'd waited for the killer to contact him again. If anything, the anticipation distracted from memories of his departed wife and son. The call had been a blur and it took a day just to remember and write down the various things the killer said — *healing means no more blame or shame; suffering is in the mind.* Ted thought he'd gotten most of it, and he studied the words, but he was a simple guy and it seemed like bullshit.

Why even consider it?

Maybe there was a grain of truth to it, something about redirecting his attention, about the promise of revenge, because since the first moment he'd thought of finding this guy and putting a bullet in him, the pain had begun to fade a little. A dark hope had filled his heart.

And then the day itself had passed, and the windows darkened, marooning him in hell once more, and the killer never called. The night which followed was long and suffocating, and when morning finally came with the rain spitting against the windows and a hollow nausea rooting down inside of him, Ted called Detective Severin.

The detective showed up promptly with another cop and peppered Ted with questions while the other cop, Epps, read Ted's notes on the conversation with the mystery caller. They took it more seriously than he'd expected and stood around in Ted's kitchen which used to smell like coffee grinds and ripening bananas and was now rank with spoiled food and cigarettes. Ted had stuck the shotgun away and hid the shells back in the wall, same place he'd kept them when Colton was . . . ah God, when Colton was around . . .

"And this guy said 'attenuate'?"

Ted looked at Severin. "Huh?"

"Your notes. Your transcript of what he said."

"Yeah. I'm pretty sure. Something like that. 'Inoculate.'"

"So he has a little vocabulary," Epps said.

"Why'd you wait a day to call us?" Severin asked.

"I bought an app for my phone that could show me his caller ID and I figured out how to record calls. I wanted to see if he'd call again. But he didn't."

"And there was no way to call him back? No number? You couldn't just hit a call back button or anything?"

"I tried. Nothing went through."

"Huh." Severin glanced at Epps then at Ted. "Will you excuse us for a minute, Ted?"

"Okay."

"We'll step outside."

Epps scrunched his nose. "It's cold and raining out—"

Severin glared at him so Epps nodded, once, to himself. They moved to the door and Severin told Ted, "We'll be right back."

Ted drifted to the window and watched them talk. Severin's wife Leanne was the sister of Rob Broward, the Liverpool police chief. Ted knew Severin and Broward had been talking about the possibility of linked victims — Ted's family and two other women, one of them pregnant. The media too — those articles on the so-called Park Killer. Severin and Epps were probably still wondering why he took so long to notify them. Someone calls you and claims responsibility for murdering your family and you call the cops immediately. Right?

I'll let you, Ted.

I'll keep my promise.

It had to be bullshit. Maybe this son of a bitch who killed his family just wanted to twist the knife. Or maybe it was just some kind of fucked-up joke by someone else.

But he couldn't stop imagining it — finding this psycho, killing him slowly. He'd been telling himself it wouldn't really stop the pain, just mask it for a while.

Right. And killing this guy won't bring them back. Nothing will bring them back.

The door opened and the cold rushed in. There was something in Severin's eyes, like sympathy. "Ted."

Ted waited.

Severin looked into a corner, then his gaze wandered back. "I think you need to consider that this might be someone messing with you. You know, some random person."

"I don't think so. I think—"

"He didn't provide any details of the shooting besides what he could've seen on the evening news. This could be some sicko taking credit for kicks."

"It was him."

"You don't look so good, Ted. You've been cooped up in this house for days. The funeral home says you're not moving ahead with the burial . . ."

"That's my business."

Severin looked away again, put his hands on his hips. Epps blew his nose.

Ted considered what Severin said about the funeral. Meg and Colton had been killed on Wednesday, the week before Thanksgiving. Their bodies were on ice and soon frozen ground would make burial impossible, but like Severin said, he'd yet to move forward. He didn't want to host a funeral in the middle of the holidays, didn't want to see pictures of his wife and son beside two closed caskets while he sat listening to a priest talk about God and His mysterious ways. Didn't want people cooking and bringing their sympathy casseroles to his house.

The dining room table was still dirty, plates covered in old, hard food. No lights on except in the kitchen. Cold, too — he'd been keeping the thermostat down and could see his breath a little bit — the cops' too. It was better cold.

People had been through the house. Severin and others, telling him to leave things as they were while the investigation went on. Meg's family had come; her parents, her sister, one of her cousins. He'd tried to be patient and understanding but hurried them out, preferring to grieve alone. To decide whether to go on.

Since the killer had called he'd felt more focused, even lighter. And now Severin was doubting it all.

"Ted," Severin said, his face twisted with pity.

"It was *him*."

Severin stopped. "Look, I can barely understand what you're going through. But in a situation like this, Ted, the emotion you're feeling . . ."

"You're not going to do anything?"

Severin raised his hands. "Of course we're going to get on this and see if we can nail it down. But we'll need your phone."

"I gotta keep it."

Epps snapped on a pair of rubber gloves and put his hand out. Severin said, "Your phone, Ted. Come on. You want us to help you? Give me your phone, let us work on it."

"I can't do it. I gotta have the phone, guys — please."

Severin exchanged looks with Epps. They both had that face, like they were warming up to arrest him, call in a psychiatrist, something. "He's not going to call again, Ted. I can pretty much guarantee you that. But if he does, we'll have the phone, we'll deal with it. In the meantime, you ought to get some rest."

"I can't."

"Ted." Severin sounded like he was running out of patience. "You called us. Okay? Now let us help you. If there's any truth to it, we'll get to the bottom of it. Trust me."

Ted finally dug out his phone and placed it in Epps' gloved, outstretched hand. Epps then rummaged in the kitchen cabinets until he found a plastic baggie to dunk the phone in and zip it up. Seeing the phone in the bag filled him with dread. Like his last chance at some sort of peace was gone, and he was lost again. This time, permanently.

* * *

Kelly watched the men in suits pay their bill and leave. She'd gone to high school with 400 kids in her same grade so it wasn't always easy to put a name to a face, and it had been more than a decade, but one of them was definitely ringing a bell.

Broward was talking. "Anyway, after Danica Payton and then the Archer killings, I called Auburn PD and asked about the Tammy Haig case from seven months ago. It was pretty much cold at that point, people had moved on, the media had gotten tired of playing with it. But I had Detective Orzo and Detective Ingram pull everything out and when the Haig evidence all matched up with Danica Payton and the Archers, that's when we thought, okay, maybe a series."

"Four different victims."

He glanced up from his meal. "Five, counting Haig's unborn baby. I know we don't have fetal homicide laws in New York, but I consider the fetus a victim. Personally."

She took a sip of her water. It tasted slightly sulfurous. "We'll say three different killings in three different counties. So if the Haig case was cold and the media had left it, where did the new stories come from? Calling him the Park Killer."

Broward scratched his neck. "I mean Three Mile Bay is not really a park, per se, it's a nature preserve, but there's not a lot of homicides around here. Three killings in three counties, like you're saying, and they built their own story out of it. Right when we did, pretty much." He gave her a look. "So now what?"

"I'll want to get everybody together, soon. But I need to see as much as I can before I do that, I need to talk to people. It's better than basing any recommendation off field reports and medical examinations." The way she formed the psychological portrait of a killer was like a Polaroid developing, at first fuzzy and indistinct.

"Sure . . . but isn't that what you do? I mean don't you — I don't know —read up on all this stuff, read about serial crime, look for patterns in an open case, you put together a profile. I know what you said on the phone. But you're in the . . . the behavioral, ah . . ."

She gauged him and decided he was more curious than pushy. "Behavioral Analysis Unit. BAU-5. We look for patterns in MO, in victimology, in signature."

"Signature . . ."

"A signature might be part of an MO, it might not, but it's the same across the crimes. An MO can change based on necessity, like waiting until the victims are in an isolated area, whether that's in a park or alongside a nature preserve. But I think he's carefully selecting these spots after watching where the victims go, waiting until they're most vulnerable. So, that in itself might be part of the signature; part of a psychological need."

"Like, what gets him off."

"Right."

"And what's the other one? You said victimology."

Kelly noticed some other diners looking over, eavesdropping. Broward's volume had risen. She lowered her voice some more, hoping he'd catch on. "Victimology is partly about any relationship between victims and the offenders. Sometimes it might be the relationship of the victims to each other."

"Which could also be part of the signature."

"Yeah."

Only bones remained on Broward's plate and he set down his fork and knife, opened a moist wipe and started cleaning off his fingers. "Listen, I'm glad you're here and we can do whatever you need. We should do the rifling test on McKenna's gun — you're right about that. I overlooked it because I kind of know the guy, and I shouldn't have. And we can interview people again: talk to Ted Archer, Blake Haig, go up and see Roger Payton. I'm just saying that there's a bunch of us eager to hear what you think. Whenever you're ready."

"I'd like to see the body next."

"We can do that. I just need to run back to the office for a few minutes. If there's anything you need to do, you know . . ."

"Nothing I need to do."

Broward snuck a look at her and she wondered if he'd checked into her background, what he might know. She had yet to notify her mother she was here, though her mother lived ten miles from where they sat. Or her brother, even closer, in Baldwinsville — Rick had three kids and a therapist wife named Uschi.

"Well," she said, "I need a coat. Is the Herb Philipson's store still over on Oswego Road?"

"Yes ma'am. You need a coat, huh? Yeah it's still over there. That's where I go."

Outside, it was getting colder. After agreeing to meet her at the morgue in a half an hour, Broward drove off. Kelly sat in the rental car and looked at her phone, thinking about her family.

Then she drove away from Onondaga Lake.

* * *

The assistant medical examiner opened the door and rolled the body out of the cooler. Danica Payton was on her back, bluish in color, face serene, body stitched and scarred from the autopsy. Her organs had been weighed and replaced, stomach contents examined, blood checked for toxicity, pubic hair brushed out and skin swabbed for DNA evidence. Her head was shaved, a stitch encircling the top of her cranium where they had sawed off the top of her skull, removed her brain and extracted the projectile, which was now in a baggie and stored away in Broward's evidence room. The small piece of lead-tipped copper which had ended her life.

The blood toxicology report showed that she'd had a negligible blood alcohol content of .06, meaning she'd had about two drinks at the bar before leaving for her walk. And she was taking the anti-depressant Lexapro. Besides her blown knee she'd been in relatively good shape, a healthy BMI, no signs of chronic illness or infection.

They drove to Broward's police station and he unlocked the room and brought the three large file boxes to a table and set them down. Kelly opened one and went through Danica's clothes. Everything had already been to the lab and back but she put on latex gloves.

Danica Payton had been killed in August, and she'd been wearing yoga pants and a long-sleeved zip-up hoodie, baby blue. She'd had her cell phone on her, her debit card and her license. No wallet.

Kelly held up the bagged phone. "You said this went to the lab for prints?"

41

"Just the victim's prints and Roger's prints and one other person we eliminated — a waitress at The Post. She admitted picking it up off the bar and bringing it into Roger's office after Danica left it there one night."

"Danica left her phone at the bar? When?"

"A week or so before the murder. Detective Faber went through it, followed up on all the recent calls and texts. There were two unrecognized numbers that we determined were telemarketers. Robo-calls."

"I'd like to see a list of all her contacts."

"I'll dig it out."

"Who was the waitress?"

"Um, the one who we just saw. Courtney."

Kelly put the phone away and continued sifting through the box. Danica Payton's sneakers looked brand new, fashionable. She'd been wearing ankle-length socks. A woman in her prime, thirty-three, in good shape, healthy.

"All set?"

She nodded at Broward.

They left and he locked the door. "So, we'll talk later?"

Something Genarro had said about keeping Broward as the point person had been grinding her gears, but she'd spent a couple hours with the chief of police now, long enough to decide he was all right, even if he might be screwing a waitress at The Post. Not that her personal opinion of someone mattered, only whether they were going to be a help or a hindrance. She did her best work alone, but Broward held a few keys she could still make use of.

"I'm going to the other scenes, I'll talk to the lead investigators, and then I'll schedule a meeting for everybody to get together and I'll have something to present. Okay?" She felt slightly anxious about the way he was smiling at her. "What?"

"I don't envy you."

"I'm not sure I, ah . . ."

"Well, it's kind of a takeaway case. These guys are all . . . they're, you know, they're good guys. Just maybe territorial."

She pulled on the coat she'd purchased — short to the waist and with a fur-lined hood. Puffy and warm. She'd also picked up new boots, waterproof logging boots with thick soles and steel toes. "I'm not worried about that."

Which she was.

She was hit with a bright light as she left the station.

"Kelly Roth? Sarah Oxley, Channel Five News." The reporter thrust a microphone forward. Kelly shielded her eyes and looked past the cameraman at a news van. Several pedestrians were gathered along the sidewalk, getting an eyeful. "Can you answer a few questions?"

She proceeded slowly down the steps. "As soon as we're ready, we're going to hold a press conference and I can answer questions at that time. Thank you."

The reporter got in front of her, blocking the sidewalk. "But can you confirm an FBI presence here in Liverpool?"

"I am an FBI agent."

"Is the FBI here because of a serial killer? Are you linking the Payton murder with the Archers and Tammy Haig? Is the Park Killer official?"

"As I said, we'll have all that information for you soon."

Oxley was young, eager, a fire lit in her eyes. "Ma'am, you're Kelly Roth. You graduated high school from West Genesee. Is that why you're here?" The cameraman moved around to get a direct shot.

Kelly squeezed past. "Excuse me, I have to go."

As she walked briskly away, she noticed one of the cars parked across the street contained two men in suits. The ones from the restaurant. Broward's real estate agent and his lunch companion.

Oxley hurried behind her, her heels clicking on the sidewalk. "Has there been a development in the Danica Payton homicide?"

"I can't comment. This is an active investigation," Kelly said.

She heard Oxley address the camera behind her: "That was FBI Agent Kelly Roth, a native of Baldwinsville. It seems the FBI have taken an interest in what could finally be confirmed as a case of serial crime. Liverpool's own Danica Harbaugh, who married restaurant owner Roger Payton, is the first homicide victim Liverpool has seen in decades, and one of several victims in different counties all found with the same graphic bullet wounds . . ."

* * *

Kelly shut herself in the hotel bathroom and leaned against the sink. After a moment she looked at herself in the mirror and stared.

Take it easy. You're all right. You knew this might happen.

She called Genarro at the office anyway. The receptionist said he was gone for the day so Kelly tried his mobile and he answered. "Didn't expect to hear from you 'til tomorrow."

"Just letting you know I've been made, sir. A reporter came at me ten minutes ago, knew who I was, so the story is going to break."

"Okay," Genarro said. "Ah, right now I'm . . . hang on." The call got scratchy and she thought she heard him excuse himself. More rustling and then a door squeaked open and banged shut. She heard street sounds in the background. "Trudy's retiring," he said. Trudy was his wife.

"I'm sorry to interrupt."

"It's okay. I'm having a smoke. Talk to me."

She squeezed her eyes shut. "I went to the restaurant owned by Roger Payton. Think I recognized one of the customers and he must've known someone with local TV. But it could've come from anywhere." She thought again about the waitress, Courtney, the jealousy in her attitude.

"So, just that you're a local girl? Or . . ."

"It's probably a matter of time before they start talking about my history."

Genarro was silent. "Okay. Well, we can deal with it. How you doing? You okay?"

"I'm all right, yeah." She made a fist with her free hand to quell the trembling.

"Kelly, you're one of my best people — you know that. I wouldn't have sent you up there if I didn't think you could handle it. But you've got to talk to me if this thing gets to be too much. This thing you do — and I don't mean to get personal — you put on your armor and . . . I know you a little bit after eight years. Okay? I know what a decent person you are."

"All right, all right . . ."

Neither of them spoke for a while. She heard a horn beep on his end. The sound of him breathing, puffing his cigarette.

"Trudy is going to smell that."

"You get anything so far?"

"I don't know. The man who found Danica Payton never had a rifling test done on a weapon which could match the unsub's." She meant unknown subject. "I'm still on the first victim and I need to talk to her husband, Roger Payton, but he's out of the area."

"Witnesses first, suspects later."

"Well, they handled Payton like a suspect but he's still my best witness for the victim's life, her behavior. I've got her family to look at but they're half the Liverpool phonebook. And I'd like to get over to the other two crime scenes, talk to those investigators."

"I'll call you in the morning and tell you what the deputy director says. If this reporter hassles you, tries to spin things because of your past, we'll handle it. For now, just stay the course. Okay?"

"Say congratulations to Trudy for me."

"Well the retirement is not set in stone yet, but she's carrying bags of mortar. Talk to you tomorrow."

She hung up and tossed the phone on the bed a little too hard. It bounced off with a clunk. She ran the bath, planning to stay in for a half an hour but every time she closed her eyes she was brought back to the past. To five men standing and grinning and smoking cigarettes as she lay on the ground.

Forget the bath. She did push-ups and sit-ups instead.

Afterward, she found the menu on the desk and went through it, then called room service and ordered enough food to put her in a small coma. While she waited for them to bring it up she opened her laptop and confronted the photos: Danica Payton prone in the broomsedge, reaching for the lake. Megan Archer along the edge of the woods, her ten-year-old son beside her, pale gray face toward the sky looking like a flower unexpectedly cut from its stem.

And then there was Tammy Haig, lying beside a creek in another park. You couldn't see it, but a tiny life inside her. Kelly wondered if the killer had known.

No evidence of sexual assault with any of the victims. Execution-style murders, no display on the bodies except for maybe a little dirt. They were shot in the backs of their heads. Crime scene techs had found tire tracks galore alongside Wheeler Road where the Archers had been slain, but it was a popular hunting spot. Nothing to go on.

If it was a series, Haig was the first. There could have been more before her but Kelly doubted it. The killer made no real effort to hide the victims. Didn't cut them up and bury them in pieces. Just shot them when no one was around and drove off. Nothing ceremonious, no ritual.

She'd never really seen anything like it before — the whole thing seemed to have more in common with live shooters and sniper killings than serial murderers; even organized criminals tended to bury or dismember. This was just about the death. As if it were a means to some end.

Maybe that was the ritual in and of itself. The signature.

She started typing her thoughts into her case summary and psychological profile, worked until the food arrived, then ate enough to satisfy. By then it was approaching midnight. Sleep came quickly but only lasted four hours.

CHAPTER FOUR

Thursday, November 29

"Agent Roth?"

She'd been woken up by her phone ringing. "Chief Broward," she said, still half asleep.

"I know it's late. Or, early . . . I just, ah . . . I'm in Constantia."

The hotel clock read 4:18 a.m. What was Broward doing in the town where the Archers were murdered? "Okay . . ."

"Severin called me a couple of hours ago. He had a lot to say. Well, first he told me that Ted Archer had an incident."

"An incident?"

"He thought his family's killer was texting him. Then someone called him, maybe the same person."

She sat up. A light rain ticked against the dark windows. "This just happened?"

"Archer waited a day before calling Severin who then spent time trying to sort through it, he said, see what he could figure out before he called me. He thought maybe some nut was just messing around with Archer."

She got out of bed and feathered a hand over the heat from the radiator.

"Ted Archer killed himself," Broward said.

She froze. "Ahh . . . no . . ."

"They're saying around eleven p.m.. Severin found him. He'd gone over there to talk, I guess tell him what he'd found out, knowing that Archer hasn't been sleeping, you know, was up late." Broward sounded morose and took a deep breath. "Archer did it with a shotgun. Real bad. Real bad stuff."

She didn't say anything. Didn't know what to say.

"Agent Roth?"

"Yeah, I'm here. I'm on my way."

* * *

She pulled up to the little house in Constantia, police vehicles in the road and crowding the driveway. The Archer place was on the outskirts of town, a couple acres at least, views of rolling hills to the south. Dawn was just breaking. It was a pretty place without a caretaker, leaves in the yard, a boy's bicycle fallen against a tree. She parked behind Broward and went in.

The house was cold. Broward came up from the basement and handed her a pair of blue latex gloves. Behind him was an older guy, pushing retirement, his face pockmarked, heavy brown eyes. He stuck out his hand. "Louis Severin."

Severin jerked his head toward the kitchen and they went to stand beside a gas range. "I released the paramedics; county coroner is on the way."

There were dirty dishes in the sink and broken glass on the floor. Plates with congealed food on the dining table. The whole house smelled. There were two holes in the drywall near the table with smudges around them — punches.

Severin saw she'd noticed them. "Ted did that. He's been — well, he's just been a complete wreck. As you'd imagine. CSS is down there finishing up, but it's a pretty straightforward suicide. He tucked the barrel up under his chin and squeezed the trigger with his thumb."

Kelly saw some Lego toys scattered on the living room carpet. She imagined a man, alone in a house that once had been full of life. A husband and father without answers, rattling around in the mess, putting a gun to his head.

"I didn't know Ted's family all that well," Severin said. "I knew Ted a little bit. He was a volunteer fireman for about five or six years, stopped when his son started really getting into sports. He seemed like a good family man. But you never know."

She turned to Broward. "What about this thing with him being contacted by someone claiming to be the killer?"

"I told her about it," Broward said to Severin.

"First I thought it was maybe someone messing with him," Severin said, looking at Kelly. "But now with this . . . I wonder if Ted might've been staging something." He opened his arms. "I'm not saying he didn't commit suicide. I saw the powder marks on his hand with my own eyes."

She considered it. "You think he faked the messages to conceal his guilt?"

"But then the guilt got him anyway. Or he planned this from the outset and faked the messages so he'd seem innocent. You can do it with email. Set it up to send yourself texts that show up as a disposable number, or an unknown number. Right?"

"I think it's possible."

"Ted had multiple jobs going at one time, he went from one to the other. The witness who corroborated his alibi was a construction worker who could've gotten the time wrong. Ted could've easily swung round the preserve when he knew Megan and Colton were walking back from

Colton's school, popped 'em, and driven to another job site."

It didn't quite wash for her — something was missing. "So do you think there's a connection to the other victims? Did he know Tammy Haig or Danica Payton?"

Severin looked at Broward, as if for support. Broward dropped his gaze to the floor. Then he leaned against the counter and looked up at Kelly. "What I think is that this is Oswego County, and here it looks like a possible murder-suicide."

She let that hang in the air as she studied the pictures on the refrigerator: Colton Archer in a football jersey, taking a knee, helmet in his hands, big grin on his face; a science fair certificate — honorable mention; a math test, graded 98 percent with red ink. A big family gathering, Fourth of July probably, Colton and Megan and Ted crowded in with the others. A younger Colton on a bicycle, in motion. Some scenic shots, as if taken on a hike or while camping.

"Come on, let's go down," Severin said.

Kelly followed him down the creaking stairs. Blood and the smell of a gunshot. The basement contained a boiler, a workbench, a pile of materials — cut lumber, siding, sheet metal — sporting equipment, a washer and dryer. Archer's body was in front of the washing machine. The blood was concentrated around the dead man's head. There was more congealed on the floor joists above and what looked like a splash of vomit nearby. Crime scene people were still moving around in white suits and masks. Severin led Kelly and Broward single file and knew where to step and stop.

"He threw up?" Kelly asked.

"Maybe just prior, yeah. Getting up the nerve." Severn pointed up at a spot where the copper plumbing and two wooden braces ran perpendicular to the floor joists in places. Two gun bags were tucked against the ceiling, one of them sagging — empty. "Archer used the shotgun on himself — the other gun tucked up there is a Winchester Model 94. Shoots .30-30.”

He reached up and unzipped the stiff gun bag, enough for her to see an old lever-action rifle.

“If he’s got a box of Federal 150 hidden beneath his workbench, I don’t know what else to say. Too much of a coincidence for me.” Severin zipped the bag and their eyes met. “I don’t know about you.”

She nodded and turned away from the weight in his eyes, watched as a technician took a picture of the body and the room exploded with light.

Say it, Kelly-bell. Go ahead and say it.

“So as part of the initial death investigation for Megan and Colton Archer, you didn’t have a crime scene unit go through the house? Not until now, after his apparent suicide.”

Severin sniffed. He crossed his arms. “I knew Ted Archer was in possession of a Winchester rifle. He volunteered that information during our interview.”

“He volunteered it — but at that point you knew .30-30 casings had been recovered from both the Haig and Payton crime scenes. Did he know about that?” Kelly asked.

Broward interjected, “That information was not reported in the news. They only said ‘gunshot wounds’ — we never released information on the caliber, or the casings left behind at the scenes.”

“But you were talking. You two.”

“You can watch the video if you like, Agent Roth,” Severin said. “Ted wanted to fully cooperate. He’s friendly with some guys on the force, he knows how an investigation goes. Anyway, we came in, we seized Megan Archer’s laptop and her phone and checked to see who might be talking to her. We did the same with the boy’s iPad and phone. I had a look around. No, I did not request a special forensic unit at the house. I came with Detective Epps, we took pictures and measurements of a few things, and we did advise Mr. Archer to leave things as they were while we conducted our investigation."

"You had two deaths, ruled homicides by the medical examiner in each district. Casings with '30-30 WIN' stamped around the primer . . ."

Severin squared off with her, his nostrils flared. "We hadn't completed autopsies, we had no ballistics yet. We weren't even talking about *Haig*. I ran the investigation. I'm sorry if you don't like how I ran it. This was a guy everyone knew with no history of mental illness and no record who liked to hunt deer and small game. In the midst of talking to us, he offered that he had a Winchester 94 among his firearms. For all we know, he confessed it out of a guilty conscience."

"Detective Severin," she said softly. "I'm not judging how you ran your investigation, I'm just clarifying. And now you're planning to search the house and you think you'll find ammunition that's a ballistic match for the victims."

"Maybe — I don't know — but how does this look? Looks pretty cut and dry to me. I regret not finding the box of ammunition before now, but I didn't think Ted would do something like this. Kill himself. No one did."

"Was he ever evaluated?" She looked to both of them. "Did a grief counselor or therapist ever speak to Mr. Archer, assess him, find out if he was a danger to himself?"

"He waived any of that. And we had no grounds to make him do it."

"Can I please see the text messages?"

Severin stared a moment then patted his jacket and dug out a small notebook and flipped a few pages. He handed it to her. "I wrote them down."

"I'll take it upstairs if that's all right."

"Be my guest."

She'd had enough of Severin's testosterone. And it was better to smell the spoiled food in the kitchen than the dead man's vomit and blood in the basement.

Severin's handwriting was sloppy but she made out:

How do you feel?

Who is this?

I want to know how you're feeling. We should talk.

Think you have the wrong number.

No I don't. You're Ted Archer. I killed your wife and son.

That was it. According to Severin's notes, approximately half a minute later Archer had received a call from an unlisted number and the call lasted four and a half minutes.

She left the notebook on the table beside a plate of congealed egg. The boy's room was messy but the bed was made, football trophies on the dresser, a *Minecraft* poster on the wall and a poster of two football players in Syracuse Orangemen uniforms, looking like father and son. She moved into the master bedroom. Ted Archer had jammed two pillows under the bed covers, like he'd used them as a makeshift body to sleep against. His own pillow held a dent in the middle from his final night.

A third bedroom had been converted into an office. She pushed some papers around on the desk, thinking if Ted Archer knew the other victims, Haig and Payton, then maybe Severin was right — maybe Ted Archer was a killer. The idea that Archer had fake-texted himself using a laptop? Time would tell.

But if the texts and phone call were real, she didn't think the tormenter was random. *How do you feel?* It was direct. A killer who possibly got off on the emotions of the bereaved. It might be why the MO seemed almost perfunctory — the real thrill was in the aftermath. Maybe toying with the family members. Watching them suffer. Even make them look guilty.

Amid the paperwork on the desk was a progress report from Colton's first ten weeks of fifth grade. He excelled in Math, not so hot in English. A stack of receipts showed purchases from a local store, and some sporting equipment from Dick's Sporting Goods, more receipts for Ted Archer's general contracting business.

She heard someone coming down the hall and when Broward appeared in the doorway she asked, "Did Archer's call log show a phone call?"

"Yeah, four minutes and twenty-seven seconds. But for that you could use the same burner phone with a blocked ID and let the connection last for a bit. Or there's this thing you can do apparently where you sync a phone with a computer and make calls that way. So your second phone is controlled by the computer. I don't know. Severin can explain it better."

She met Broward in the doorway. "Is that what he's going with, then, officially? Ted Archer killed his family, and then faked communications from someone else claiming responsibility before killing himself?"

"I mean, I know this doesn't line up with Haig and Payton, but it makes some sense. Fake a couple of texts, then say there's a phone call and write the script yourself." He looked past her into the room. "Severin plans to take the gun in and test it. If the rifling matches, then all the speculation is moot."

"The Winchester is a common gun, like you said."

"Probably fifty percent of hunters own a short rancher. I have one. So?"

She took a step back. "So far we've gotten shooter distance from bullet damage to tissue, beveling around the entrance wounds, and patterns in gunpowder residue. A smart killer might know we'll be able to make these determinations, and learn the caliber. But he's left behind the casings anyway — why? That's just icing on the cake. If our guy is in a car, then he's even picking up the spent casings and tossing them out for us to find. No fingerprints, so he's loading while wearing gloves. He could be deliberately leaving the casings."

"To point to Archer, maybe? All victims killed by a gun like the one he owns?"

"I think that's unlikely. I think there's another link, something we haven't seen yet. At least Severin will take the weapon in, shoot it, look at the rifling pattern and compare it to the projectiles from the other victims. But I'd like to call in my own forensic firearm and toolmark examiner. We can use him for Joel McKenna's gun, too." She looked at Broward, waited for the pushback.

"Okay."

The air was heavy, and she let everything settle a moment before she said, "You're right, though."

"I'm right?"

"Things that can happen to a projectile when it hits bone, mushrooming it, misshaping it, could make the striations hard to discern. Just like with Payton and Haig. So I don't want to sit around and wait for ballistics matching. I want to work the people, work the killer." She moved to the office door and had a look, then heard Severin's voice float up from the basement before continuing in a soft voice. "We need a list of everyone who knew Ted Archer. Everyone he worked with, hung out with, his family members. The same for Payton and Haig. Then I want to cross-reference them."

"I've been working on that. I'll hand you everything I got, but there's nothing so far." Broward started drifting back into the hallway.

She followed him toward the large kitchen. Severin came up the stairs as they passed and gave them a look like he'd caught them doing something. "What's up?" he asked.

"I'd like to see Ted Archer's account of the phone call. Chief Broward said there was a notebook."

"That's a waste of time. We work the gun."

"I'd like his phone, too."

Severin grunted a laugh and glanced at Broward before looking at her. "For what? We spent all day on it.

There's nothing you can get, nothing to trace without a number."

"And the texts in the actual phone."

"The phone got sent to the lab."

"This guy could call back, whether or not he's pretending to be someone."

"Oh, come on. No one's calling back."

They fell into an uncomfortable silence. Kelly asked, "Who knows about this?"

"Well, the Shepherd family up the street there are in their windows right now, I'm sure. I already talked with them. They're elderly, were both asleep, didn't see anything."

"I think we should keep it quiet."

"Quiet? Ted has parents. Family members. He runs a business. Even if he . . . I don't see how we can suppress this."

She stepped toward the local detective and Broward jerked into life, as if to get between them. She said to Severin, "He called, after the texts. They spoke. It says in your notes they spoke for almost five minutes. Get me the phone and Archer's notes. Please."

Severin stared down at her with his bruised-looking eyes. Then he glanced at Broward again.

Broward shrugged. "I think we should do it. Can't hurt. If there's nothing there, then it lends to the murder-suicide."

Kelly was still standing very close to Severin. "If Archer fake-called himself like you think he did, he would've used a burner phone account. There will be a record of that. Maybe there's even a prepaid phone somewhere in the house."

Severin waved a hand as if to dispel the tension and stepped back from her. "Ah, he threw it in the woods. Or he smashed it and chucked it in the trash."

"Then we comb the woods, go through his garbage. I don't see the issue — we look into the call he received and either your theory that Archer set it up is vindicated, or we get the service provider, have something to go on if someone else called him."

He walked away with his back to her. "And the service provider gives us thousands of people in the area? Good luck with that." He opened the front door and stepped outside.

When he was gone Kelly asked, "Is he going to do it?"

"I don't know."

"Well, then I need to make a call."

She left him standing there in the Archer house with its pictures of a happy family, the rotten food on the table, the corpse in the basement.

Kelly started up the rental car and blasted the heat, peeled off the gloves and tried to calm her nerves after the confrontation with Severin. Some cops were bullies. He'd tried to bully her in there. But Severin had screwed up. He'd known Archer had a gun which could match the killings but never searched the house for ammunition. Archer claimed the real killer called him, but Severin dismissed it, wanted to bag this case by pinning it all on Archer — to him it was a situation that had resolved itself and she was getting in the way of that tidy explanation.

She phoned Genarro and watched the Archer home in the spreading light as she waited for him to pick up.

"Roth? It's six in the morning. I was going to have a cup of coffee," he said.

"It's early, I know. I'm sorry. I need a couple of people."

"What happened?"

She told him about the phone call and the suicide. "I'm requesting a firearms expert and a skip tracer for the phone."

"We can do that."

"I've got to talk to the other victim's husbands. If Archer was called by the unsub, it's possible they have been too, and not reported it."

"Why wouldn't they report it?"

"I don't know yet. Maybe he's coercing them, blackmailing them. Maybe promising them something."

Genarro didn't say anything so she kept going.

"Severin said Ted Archer had been torqued up. Like he was ready to go out and find this guy himself. Maybe this guy hooks them in and keeps them on the line thinking they're going to get a piece of him. This could be part of the MO, part of the act itself — kill the women and children then mess with the husbands. Get them to implode."

"Severin think that too?"

"No. He thinks Archer set this up. Or, I don't know if he actually thinks that, but he wants to push it that way."

"So how does he reconcile the other murders?"

"He doesn't. Says they're not his problem." She paused. "I think Severin is going to stall on getting me Archer's phone."

"No — you'll get that phone. In the meantime, you go talk to the other husbands. If they admit to being contacted by the unsub then you've got a compelling line of inquiry. I'll see if I can get Cal Wagner to do the ballistics report, maybe Rose or Blanchett for the phone stuff. When Wagner gets there and you're ready, you pull everybody together, all these local departments, and you give them what you've got."

"Thank you, sir."

He paused. "How they treating you?"

"I'm fine."

"You're a thirty-year-old FBI agent there to solve a series of murders they can't. How are they treating you?"

"Broward's not bad. You were right about him. Severin has got a chip on his shoulder. I haven't met any of the others yet."

She saw Broward coming out of the house. At the same time a hearse pulled into the driveway and stopped behind the crime-scene van. "I gotta go, sir. They're taking him out."

"All right. You're doing good."

She got out and went over to Broward and they watched the bagged body get loaded into the back of the hearse. "After we consult, we'll do a press conference and get a new tip-line going, one consolidated hotline for all three killings," she said. "We'll get everything from suspicious neighbors to alien abduction stories but that's what we need."

"Sounds good."

"My supervisor is interceding to make sure we get Ted Archer's phone in case this guy calls back. I'm going to Wheeler Road next where the Archers were found. Then I'm going down to Auburn to look at the Haig case."

"Gotcha."

Broward's jaw was twitching again, circles beneath his eyes. It looked like he hadn't gotten much sleep either.

"Something on your mind?"

He looked sideways at her. "Just wondering if we're going to talk about what happened yesterday afternoon outside the station?"

The remark caught her off guard. "You saw that?"

"I came out, asked them to disperse. You'd already gotten in your car. The reporter said you were a local. I didn't know that. But we're talking about discretion here — about Archer . . ."

"It's nothing," Kelly said. "We can talk about it later. Right now I want to talk to Haig in person and get him to come in for a formal interview. I need you to get Roger Payton back and we'll do the same with him."

He sighed and they watched the hearse drive off with Archer's body.

"Can you do that?"

"I mean, Payton's not going to want to come back. I've tried. We'd have to force him."

"Walk to my car with me?" she said, not looking at him. "That reporter might've been tipped off by the two guys you were talking to at The Post."

"Rutherford? Why?"

"I might've gone to school with him. But this is what I'm talking about, keeping things tamped down. We absolutely should *not* publicize Archer's suicide. Everything we say in the press conference has to be tailored to the idea that the unsub is watching."

"Maybe he already knows. He could be watching Archer somehow, so he knows about the suicide . . ."

She saw a lighted window turn black over at the Shepherd residence. "It's possible."

They got to the car and she opened the door. Broward looked guilty. "Sorry about those guys. If that was where it came from."

"Maybe it was them, maybe not. The press conference will help."

Broward nodded and put his hand on her door as she sank into the driver's seat. He stared back at the Archer house. "How's the guy get Archer's cell number? Maybe he gets out after shooting the woman and her son, digs through her pockets, gets the cell phone and goes through her contacts? You asked about prints on Payton's phone — that what you're thinking?"

"No. He'd be burning time. The whole point of this drive-by method is a quick escape, evade detection."

"So he just looks Ted Archer up in the phonebook or online? Most people don't publicize their cell numbers . . ."

"I think he plans these things out and he gets the number beforehand. If he did this with the others — if he called Roger Payton, he got Roger's number maybe when Danica left it behind on the bar."

"The bar has video cameras."

"Going back to August? Or before?"

He was shaking his head. "You're right. I remember Faber asking about that and they said the video is deleted every forty-eight hours. It's mostly so Roger can keep an eye on his bartenders, make sure they're not giving away the inventory all night long, that sort of thing."

"But she left her phone behind at one point. The waitress picked it up."

"Yeah and she just gave it to Roger. Anyway, that was the victim's phone, not her husband's."

There was more there to mine but she let it go for the moment. "The bigger picture is this — I think our guy scouts these victims, does his homework. These aren't random drive-bys — he's waiting for the perfect moment when the victims are alone and isolated. And if he gets the cell phone number of a husband, he's got to get close enough to do that."

She looked at the Archer house, thought of the cold inside, the life of an entire family stopped dead in its tracks. Over. Gone.

"As far as any information we put out," she said quietly, "we want the killer to think we're fumbling around in the dark. We want it to look like we need the public's help because we have nowhere else to turn. If this guy called the man whose wife and child he'd killed, I want to use that arrogance against him."

"Me too."

He stepped back and she closed the door and drove off into the lightening day.

CHAPTER FIVE

He bought baby powder and a Sprite from the CVS drugstore. The baby powder kept his hands from sweating inside the latex gloves and the Sprite helped him to feel like a normal person.

The mall was a good place. Crowded, anonymous, filled with possibility. He could stroll along and gaze in the shop windows or watch reflections of people in the glass. He could sit on a bench and observe as they came and went from the Apple store, the Build-A-Bear Workshop, the T.J. Maxx.

This particular family was well-dressed. The parents looked older, like they'd had the child late in life, a boy of about three or four who held his parents' hands as they walked down the corridor. The boy kept leaping in the air, but the parents weren't paying attention — he wanted to swing; they couldn't be bothered. The mother was laden with shopping bags. The father squinted at his phone.

They came closer to the bench. He sucked his soda through a straw, watching out of the corner of his eye. The mall was crowded with weekend shoppers but he tracked the family easily enough. The father finally anointed his son with attention, hoisted the boy up, but the mother let go of the boy's hand and hurried ahead.

He let them pass through his field of vision and out of his mind.

Ten minutes later, he was about to find another spot — maybe he would do some more walking first — but a family of four caught his attention. They left the CVS with the two little children chatting away, the mother and father listening attentively. The younger kid had a problem with his Halloween mask and they all stopped.

He sat up a little straighter on the bench and set his empty cup aside.

The father helped the boy with his Casper the Friendly Ghost mask, making sure the kid could see out the eyes. Their laughter drifted over.

He was excited. It was hard to say why, but he just knew it when he felt it — they were the ones. You couldn't think your thoughts before you thought them, anyway, couldn't choose your feelings. These things arose out of the black soup of the mind and anyone who believed otherwise was deluded.

People parted around the family like water flowing around a rock. Finished with the mask, the father picked the boy up and carried him. The little girl took the mother's hand, holding onto her pointed witch's hat with her other hand.

He watched them go. In the river of people, the mother was led by the girl, the father carried the boy.

For a split second he thought the boy had seen him over his father's shoulder — the eyes behind that white ghost mask meeting his own — but then people got in the way and they were gone.

He got up from the bench, threw his empty cup in the trash, and followed them.

* * *

Kelly drove to the Three Mile Bay Wildlife Management Area, where Megan Archer and ten-year-old Colton had been shot and killed.

The crime scene and autopsies suggested the killer had approached from behind them, slowed, shot the boy first, who was facing the road — pop — then the mother from behind as she turned toward her fallen son — pop.

Then the killer drove off, leaving Ted Archer knowing that in her last few seconds alive, Megan Archer had stared down at her dying son. And that Ted hadn't been there to protect them.

Kelly parked the rental car along the dirt shoulder opposite the crime scene. Two white wooden crosses marked the spot. She got out and crossed the road to a wall of trees. No sidewalks, nobody driving through so far. The mother and son had lain just out of sight for three hours while Ted Archer worked late at a construction site. About the time he'd started to wonder why his wife hadn't texted about dinner, the hunters were rolling by.

Flowers, a knitted scarf, and a teddy bear were placed around the wooden crosses, with weather-beaten sympathy cards pinned beneath a rock.

Crime scene tape cordoned off an area about fifty square yards, sagging in places and broken between two trees. She was sure civilians had walked through it — curious kids on a dare and superstitious adults thinking maybe if they could see where it happened, they could keep their families safe.

She matched up what she saw with her memory of the crime scene photos. The victims had fallen just beyond the dirt shoulder where wet, spongey earth sucked at her feet and the air smelled sour. No tracks to be had in the cold ground water. No size ten work boot. Just the two .30-30 cartridge casings found in the road, clean of any prints.

The killer knew the routines of his victims. He killed them in places by water or marsh, not to limit evidentiary material, but because they'd be alone. Perhaps the remote sites served a dual purpose — isolated but also extra psychologically taxing for those left behind. Dying alone.

She pondered what it would take to find just the right victims with routines that fit such criteria. Probably everyone — especially in suburbs or rural areas — found themselves alone at least once a day. But these victims ventured further from the beaten path; Megan Archer and her son Colton had taken a scenic route home from Colton's school; Danica Payton preferred to take walks down to the narrow, lonely section of Onondaga Park; Tammy Haig, the first victim, pregnant, liked to eat her after-class snack by Owasco Lake, perhaps unafraid of the darkness or solitude being that close to home in her quiet, safe neighborhood.

The killer had studied his victims. Learned their habits. He sifted through a variety of potential victims to get down to just the right ones, Kelly was now sure of that.

And he seemed to stick to what he was good at — one or two people only. The women were all married, the Archers were mother and son. Families.

She gave the white crosses one more look and started back to the car, her boots leaving muddy tracks. She wondered if the killer would ever get bored, if he'd need something more — that bigger hit — and widen out, take on more risk. Or if he might eventually get sloppy and screw up. That was how most of them got caught.

But she had her doubts. This guy was too exacting, too much of a planner.

He might never screw up.

* * *

She decided to skip the morgue for this one; nothing to learn from the Archer victims she hadn't seen with Payton. A quick meal would help before talking to Haig.

She ate a poached egg on wholegrain bread at a diner in Auburn, with a side of hash browns she hadn't even asked for. She eyed the greasy fried potatoes warily. She hadn't always been in shape. The diet specialists called it eating your feelings, her therapist had called it post-traumatic stress.

She considered victim traits. Only one was a child — two if you counted the fetus like Broward did. The killer might've known Tammy Haig was pregnant, might've not. Danica Payton hadn't been a mother. It left the question whether child victims were important to the killer, or incidental.

What seemed clear were his criteria for certain locations and schedules — where they went and when. Not everyone took walks alone in remote places. Were there other potential victims he'd dismissed for not checking those boxes? And, if so, what was the pool he selected from?

The killings had all happened within a fifty-mile radius. That was an area of 2,500 square miles. Too big to just come upon people at random and find the right ones. It had to be somewhere more concentrated. A hunting ground of sorts.

She finished the egg, left the potatoes. She called Genarro from her car to run it past him. She wasn't comfortable sharing her developing theories with Broward yet. The police here wanted answers, not conjecture.

"You might be getting ahead of yourself," Genarro said. "You're assuming the victims aren't picked for who they are. Or that there's no other link between them."

"So far, there isn't anything to indicate a relationship between victims. Broward had a list going and I stacked more on top of it with work histories, all known kin, past residences, department of public safety. I've been cross-referencing contacts and there's not even a postal worker between them. They're just too spread out for it to be about them, personally. It's something arbitrary. He's observing people somewhere. Following them."

"Okay, so, you're the local tour guide . . ."

She turned on the wipers to brush away a spittle of raindrops and looked at the diner. A little place like this one wasn't going to offer many possibilities, it had to be something bigger. She thought about movie theaters, stadiums — watching the Orangemen play, maybe — hospitals . . . malls.

Destiny USA had a grandiose name, but it was the sixth largest shopping mall in the country and the biggest in New York State. People visited from all over. And it wouldn't be the first time a killer in the region had used a mall as a place to scout victims. But she needed more.

"I'll get back to you on that," she said to Genarro.

"Where you headed right now?"

"To talk to the one victim's husband either not dead or hiding out."

"Be careful."

* * *

Blake Haig had gone back to work at Xylem Technologies after a mere two weeks of paid bereavement, but he worked a late shift and was still home at ten-thirty in the morning. Cream-white vinyl siding wrapped the single-story house, black shutters framed the windows fronting the street. Haig answered the door, thin and hollow-looking.

"Kelly Roth," she said. "Detective Orzo said I'd be stopping by?"

"Yeah. Um, yes." He glanced at her badge with a kind of disinterest, like he'd seen plenty already. "Come on in."

The place had an aura of stale cigarettes, and something burnt, like an unclean oven that had recooked stray bits of food a few times over.

"Thank you for meeting with me," Kelly said.

"Sure." He led them into a living room with two short couches, a recliner and a big-screen TV. Inlaid shelves held a few books.

Kelly sat across from him. She reminded herself that his wife had been dead for seven months, a good amount of time for accurate recall to fade. "I know you've been through a lot of questions, a lot of interviews . . ."

"I don't mind. Whatever I can do to help."

"Thank you." She looked at the spines of the books behind him. "You like to read?"

"Not really. Well, I read non-fiction. About physics, superstructures, things like that."

"That's interesting."

"Yeah." He kept his gaze direct, his eyes half-lidded, as if sleepy.

"I'd like to talk about Tammy a little bit. Is that all right?"

"Whatever you need."

"It would be great if you could talk a little about your lives, what you liked to do together. Were you more homebodies or did you like to go out?"

He looked away for a moment. "I'd say both. We could stay in and watch Netflix, order Chinese. Sometimes we went out."

"Where would you go?"

"You know, to the Regal for a movie. Or have dinner. Or drag-racing."

"Drag-racing? Really?"

"Yeah we did all that. Went to NASCAR a couple of times. Crash-up derbies. Tammy really liked it."

"Would you say you guys had a lot of friends?"

"I don't know. I think the cops . . . I mean the other detectives talked to all of her friends. Her classmates. Even some people she knew from her pregnancy classes."

"I've been looking through those interviews. Everyone really thought highly of her."

He met her eyes with the same directness but his gaze was lifeless.

"I have an important question to ask you," she said.

"Okay."

"Has anyone ever called or texted you claiming responsibility for what happened to Tammy?"

He smiled for the first time then laughed, just a burst of breath. "Are you serious?"

"I am. Anything? Even a missed call from a strange number?"

"Oh I get missed calls. You can never escape telemarketers. I had one message the other day, some guy pretending to know me — he wanted to talk about some investment opportunity. I can't imagine that sort of thing working, but it must if people are doing it . . ." He looked down at his hands, as if embarrassed about telling her this. "Anyway, I turned my phone over to the Auburn police and they went through it and they have a list of all the numbers and incoming and outgoing calls."

"But since then. Since you got the phone back."

"No. No one has called me."

She gambled. "Because the husband of another victim might have been contacted by someone claiming to be responsible."

"Really." No reaction.

She nodded. Then she slowly got to her feet. "You mind if I have a look around?"

"Sure," he said, rising. "Not much to look at, though. The police took some of Tammy's things and I've given everything else to her family or to Goodwill, that sort of thing."

She pointed at the shelves. "Not the books, though."

"No, not the ones I like, I guess."

It was a sad, short tour. Blake Haig moved at a single unhurried speed, more like an old man than someone just turned twenty-six. He flipped on the lights in each room: kitchen, a bit messy; master bedroom, bed unmade, clothes and boots on the floor and nothing feminine about any of it. She suspected the second, empty bedroom might've once been intended as a nursery — just some baby blue smudges of paint left on the ceiling. The rest had been painted over industrial gray.

He opened a door from the hallway leading into the garage where his Dodge truck sat parked. Tools on the walls, a workbench, some boxes, trash bins. After she said, "Thanks," he clicked off the light and shut the door.

Bathroom next. A rumpled towel hung from the shower door and a single toothbrush on the sink. A small dining room off the kitchen with a farm-style table and hardwood floor, nails jutting from the drywall where pictures had likely hung. There were no traces of Tammy Haig. The place had become a bachelor pad.

"There's one other room," he said, and showed her a pantry, shelves on each side with foodstuffs and a door to the backyard. "That's it." He pulled the string to shut the light. She backed away and let him walk ahead through the kitchen and followed him. He stopped between the couches and waited until she took the couch again before he sat down.

For the first time he looked lost in thought, his eyes unfocused, then he blinked back into the present. "What did he say?"

"Sorry?"

"You said someone might've called the husband of one of the other victims."

"Yeah, we can't be sure. He might've been, ah . . . well, I can't really comment on it."

"You think it was real?"

It was an interesting assumption.

"Like I said, I'm sorry, I can't—"

"I've never heard of anything like that. Someone kills your family and then calls you up — have you ever heard of anything like that?"

"No."

They lapsed into silence, Kelly evaluating how smart Blake Haig was. His interest was piqued, but maybe anyone's would be. She'd dangled as much bait as she could without compromising things. On the other hand, if Haig was in contact with the killer, and he passed on that law enforcement knew or suspected about the phone calls, it might filter out, something might change and confirm the correspondence.

He was looking at her. "Do you, like, study killers and all that?"

"That's part of what I do, yeah. I study narcissistic psychopathic personalities. I try to find patterns that can predict if someone like this might strike again, when and where it might happen."

"You think this is going to happen again?"

"After your wife it happened two more times."

"What are the patterns?"

"Well, the act, the motivation for the act. The *why*." She hesitated, adding, "In some cases a person actually wants to get caught. They can't stop, but some part of them knows that they need to. They might leave something behind that helps the investigation, and it might be conscious or not. They might even reach out."

He'd settled back into his watchful self. Maybe his reserved self. He presented as open and guileless, but she sensed something practiced about it.

Her phone vibrated in her pocket. "Sorry. Let me just see what this is." She dug it out and saw the incoming call was from Detective Orzo with Auburn PD but let it go to voicemail.

She stood up and said, "Mr. Haig, I have to get going." He got off the couch and they shook hands briefly, his grip dry and light. "I may need you to come in, speak to myself and a few other officers."

He scowled. "Today?"

"No, I don't think so. But I'll be in touch and we'll accommodate your work schedule."

"You think it will help?"

"I know you've already spoken to Detective Orzo and his team here in Auburn. And I know when someone like me comes in, it seems like a duplication of efforts. But we want to do everything we can to find out who did this."

She studied his response. Did her being here dredge painful memories? Had seven months of living alone made him numb? Was he hiding something?

She handed him a card. "And if you think of anything in the meantime, or you just want to talk, don't hesitate to contact me. Whatever it is, even if you feel it's unimportant. I'm sure you got the same pitch from the others, but it's true — there are no insignificant details with something like this. And I'm not taking anything away from the other investigators, but they're busy police with multiple ongoing cases — this is all I'm here to do and I won't stop until I have answers."

It was meant to be comforting but she wondered if she'd overstepped. Or even lied. Was she here until the bitter end, or was she still hoping to get just enough to load into a presentation, lay it off on the local police? She burned to be gone from these haunted streets and old memories, back to her quiet, solitary life.

He moved to the front door and opened it up. "Like I said, anything I can do."

Kelly stepped onto the front stoop. She turned back to Haig and said, "I also wanted to let you know I'm going to visit the place where Tammy was found."

"Okay. Good luck."

"Thanks again."

Back in the Mazda, she cranked the heat and called Detective Orzo with Auburn PD.

"I can meet you at Island Park in ten, fifteen minutes," Orzo said. "That work for you?"

"I'm just a minute or two away."

"See you there."

She pulled away from the curb, giving a look back at the Haig house.

CHAPTER SIX

The wind skated over the grainy beach sand at the north end of Owasco Lake, breaking apart the morning mist and carrying scents of fish into Island Park. The creek saddled the park, making it an island, hence the name. Only a dog walker and a couple of teenage kids in hooded jackets. Kelly stood there thinking about being an introvert in a world that idolized extroversion. She wondered if Blake Haig was like she was — seemed so. Or, perhaps also like her, a traumatic event had diverted him onto a different path.

The crime scene was no longer roped off but she had a rough idea where it was. She walked until she was amid a grove of eastern cottonwood with the branches lashing in the strong breeze and looked down at the sluggish creek, the shallow water where Haig's body had been found. The crime scene photos had showed her at an odd angle, upper body face down in the water, legs up behind her on the rocky bank. The spot was less than a mile from Haig's house on Van Duyne Ave. If Tammy Haig had gone home after her evening class, she might still be alive. Or perhaps the killer would've bided his time, waited for another opportunity.

He seemed patient.

An unmarked car pulled in to the parking lot about forty yards away and Detective Orzo got out. He saw her and raised a hand, then ducked back into his vehicle, pulled out a coffee and walked over with his gray tie flapping and dark hair blowing in the offshore wind. A blue suit framed his narrow shoulders, the buttons of his shirt straining against a protuberant belly. Smiling, he extended his hand. "Nice to meet you."

"You, too. Thanks for coming."

The smile faded as he looked around. "Yeah. Well."

"Can you walk me through it?"

He nodded, took a sip of his coffee. "So, this is where she was, right down there. When she was shot she fell forward, tumbled down the bank there and came to rest on the edge of the creek. That's about it."

"How did the jogger find her?"

"He was a little embarrassed. Took some time to get it out of him — turns out he'd walked over to the edge of the creek to relieve himself. You know, take a leak. Then he saw her. So . . . anyway, as you probably know by now, she was taking a night class at Wells, and her professor, guy named Grumett, confirmed she left right at end of class, eight p.m. She's on her way home, stops into the convenience store over there — you can just see it, past those trees." He pointed, took another drink from his paper cup. "We pulled video from the gas pumps and inside the store. Camera inside shows the victim coming in at 8:22 p.m. Went in, bought her donut, came out and walked over here. Clerk at the gas station heard the shot a few minutes later, thought nothing of it — not in this neighborhood. Otherwise no witnesses. We looked at everyone else on video from an hour prior and fifteen minutes after and were able to ID everyone who used the pump or made debit or credit card purchases inside. We talked to all of them — they're on the list. We also had three people that used cash only. Clerk tried to remember the purchases and thought one bought a pack of cigarettes, couldn't remember the other two."

"So no ID on them because of the cash. How about facial recognition?"

"No, not in the system, no records."

"I'd like a look at that footage and that list."

Orzo started for another sip of the coffee, stopped and gave her a look.

"Trust me," she said, "I'm not here thinking I can do anything better. I'm here because Chief Broward in Liverpool called in the request and my job is to take a look at everything fresh."

"No, no, I understand. I was just thinking, there's not much to go on with the MO. There's no display on the bodies, there's a significant age range, there are children involved. How's that work? I thought the FBI had separate units for crimes against children and crimes against adults."

"We do. I'm in both." Close enough to the truth. "That's why they sent me."

"Well, that's good."

She cleared her throat and continued. "You interviewed Haig . . ."

"Correct. Totally voluntary, he waived counsel — we weren't charging him with anything. Blake Haig was at work until midnight. A regular shift. That's why she took night classes." Orzo looked off over the lake. "They were a happy couple."

"You knew them?"

"No, but you could tell. He was just in total shock. He just . . ." Orzo took his free hand and ran it across his jaw. "God he was just beside himself. Could barely bring himself to ID her body, didn't want to discuss the autopsy, none of it. He blamed himself, said he should've made her carry a gun. He'd asked her to, but she'd refused. I told him I doubted it would've made any difference, someone coming up behind you with a rifle."

"He owns guns?"

"One handgun he keeps for home defense. The one he wanted her to take."

"Anyone around here not own a gun?"

"I hear you. That's life in paradise."

Kelly looked over the spot some more thought about a killer pulling up, parked about where they were.

She walked toward the cars and Orzo followed. When she reached the car she turned around, facing the lake. Then she paced it out back to the spot where Tammy had been standing. Thirty, thirty-five yards. He was a good shot. But it was still close enough that she might've noticed someone. Kelly thought again about the killer rolling along behind Megan Archer and her son as they walked along Wheeler Road. "When someone pulls up," Kelly said, "especially if it's at night, you look. Even if it's day. You just do."

Orzo said, "Right, I figure she glances over, notices the car there, but can't really see in. Maybe she pays no attention, or maybe she's a little nervous. If she's nervous she might freeze up, not know what to do. Or, could be she recognizes the vehicle, meaning she knows the person, and it puts her at ease. But I don't think so."

"There's a streetlamp over there — how far does it reach at night?"

"This part is pretty shadowed." Orzo had stopped beside her.

"So she's kind of in the dark. At thirty, thirty-five yards."

He looked around, squinting some more. "I mean either way it's a tough target to hit if you're an amateur. If you're a marksman, that's better. If you're a sharpshooter, ex-military, that's when you've got the confidence to just pull up, take aim. That's been my theory. You probably read that in the report."

"I did."

"Yeah. It's still a risk, though. It's dark, there's a chance she turns and sees him pull up, maybe even hears him chamber a round. Most .30-30s are lever-action, makes a noise when you cock the rifle. So it's a risk. A minor one, but I peg the guy as cocky."

"I might agree with you." She studied the grass, the trees, the creek below. "Something that interests me, though — there's no intimacy with that sort of distance."

"Well, okay I hear that. But hunters will tell you there's plenty of intimacy shooting a big buck from fifty yards. And it's not an easy shot."

"Looking down a scope maybe, brings it closer."

"Could be a scope."

"And maybe he's been hunting her for a while. The intimacy comes from that."

Orzo nodded, and poked at something in his mouth, grimaced like he was in pain. "Could be he gets a thrill being at a distance, too. Maybe the chance he misses, that's part of the high. These guys get some sort of dopamine hit, isn't that it? But he's not gonna miss. He's ex-military, that's my gut. Targets women. Maybe the type doesn't matter. Just finds them alone . . . he's driving around, finds them, follows them a while. If they have children with them, that's collateral, I think."

She tucked her hands in her pockets and gave it all one last look and said, "I've got a firearms expert on his way and I'd like to meet with you and your team and Severin and Broward when he gets here. Does that work for you?"

"Yeah. Works for me."

"While we're waiting, I'd like to look at the Haig interview and the gas station footage."

* * *

She followed Orzo to the Auburn Police Department and waited while a deputy went to the records room and brought out case evidence in a box.

Orzo took her into his office. "You can work here. I'll be gone for about an hour." He poked a finger in his mouth again and made a face. "Gotta get a tooth fixed. Been gettin' bad."

He left and she booted up the video of Blake Haig's interview.

The camera was angled slightly down and the lights shined off the scalp beneath his prematurely thinning hair. Poor video made it tough to read his expressions or be sure exactly what he was looking at but she listened for a while and observed his body language: tight shoulders, everything protectively drawn in. He had on some kind of racing sweatshirt, dark color with red and black checkers down the arms. She made a note that he'd been asked to come in to give his statement but he hadn't dressed smartly. Orzo gave his name and the date and time of day but not his badge number. The woman in the room introduced herself as Muriel Ingram, another detective.

Orzo: "Mr. Haig, first I want to thank you for coming down."

Haig didn't say anything.

Orzo: "I can say that we're all . . . None of us can imagine the grief you've been experiencing. But your being here is a great help to us. The more we can learn about you and Tammy the quicker we're going to find out who killed her and bring them to justice."

Haig nodded, looking down. Kelly leaned toward the screen. She could just make out what looked like a blank stare of shock.

"We have to ask you questions. Certain questions may be unpleasant."

"I understand." Haig was barely audible.

"Were you and Tammy getting along?"

He nodded again. "Of course, absolutely."

"The stress of expecting a child, the money situation, everything okay there?"

"Yes. I was . . . everything was . . ."

"It's okay, Mr. Haig. Take your time."

He lifted his face and looked at the people in the room, his gaze traveling from Orzo to Ingram and back to Orzo. "You need to do something."

"We're doing everything we can. Like I said, we have to ask these questions. So — everything was good between you and Tammy?"

"Everything was good." He looked into a corner, said nothing for a moment and then hiccupped a laugh. "Tammy might get after me because I leave my towels on the floor. We pick on each other for the books we read. She's reading *Fifty Shades of Grey* or something and I'm reading a book on bridges. But we liked a lot of the same movies . . ."

He gave the two detectives another look and then put his face in his hands and his shoulders jumped with a sob. It seemed to finally be hitting him now and Blake Haig fell apart. Kelly made a note about the books, recalling *Fifty Shades of Grey* on the shelf in his living room. From what she'd seen of the house it was the only remaining evidence the victim had ever lived there. There were stages of grief, and people handled it differently. It could be healthy to move on, but it was hard to say what it meant to remove nearly all traces of your departed wife from your home. When her own father had died, what remnants of his existence had her mother kept, and for how long? Kelly turned her mind there only to find a blur of memories. His dark rain jacket hanging on the coat rack in the foyer — how long before her mother had boxed it up?

She returned her attention to the end of the interview, noting Orzo's light touch and Haig's behavior. There was no correct way to grieve, but Haig's initial blankness, followed by his plaintive requests the police "do something" — then the drifting into memories and statements of incredulity — were consistent with bereavement. And either he'd withdrawn from there further into numbness to become the distant, unemotional man she'd met that morning as a natural part of the process, or because there was something else going on. Like the killer was talking to him, too.

She watched the gas station footage next. People came and went. Everything had already been logged — the makes and models of the cars, the identity of the pixelated faces appearing on screen. One customer gave her pause when it looked like he was staring off in the direction of Island Park as he pumped gas. But the time stamp on the video placed the moment at eight minutes after the jogger who discovered Tammy's body had placed the emergency call. The customer at the gas station was probably watching the police arrive on the scene.

She scrutinized the faces of the three unidentified persons for a while, then reviewed the list of those identified. Twenty-six people in all recorded at the neighboring gas station around the time Tammy Haig was murdered.

Her phone rang. Cal Wagner, the firearms expert, had arrived in Syracuse.

CHAPTER SEVEN

A close-up image of a bullet loomed as Wagner took out a wadded tissue from his pocket and blew his nose. Wagner was in his late fifties, mostly bald, fixed with a gray, brush mustache and wearing half-rimmed glasses. He'd worked serial killings in the past and had drafted a presentation on the flight in from Texas where he'd just gotten through analyzing the scene of a mass shooting. Kelly had met his wife, once, in Stafford, at a formal party on Memorial Day, who was lovely, and confessed, after two bourbon pomegranate cocktails, that he was the toughest man she ever met, even though he still cried over their children. After three drinks, she'd told Kelly that his bed farts were loud enough to get their two Foxhounds barking.

"All right. Let's start with some basics." Wagner pointed a thick finger at the screen behind him. "The projectiles recovered from each of the victims are flat-nosed .30-30 bullets. A '30-30' means a 30-caliber bullet using 30 grains of smokeless powder. It's a jacketed or metal-patched lead bullet typically weighing between 150 and 170 grains."

Detective Epps sat at the back of the room with his arms crossed, looking bored. Severin was beside him, listening like he was waiting for just the right opportunity to break open Wagner's analysis. The federal prosecutor named Denis Starkey had joined them with his assistant, Lauren Giovanetti. Broward, Orzo, and Detective Ingram filled out the rest of the law enforcement present in the conference room.

Wagner said, "The conclusion on the make across all victims is Federal Premium .30-30 150 grain Centerfire Rifle Ammunition. The casings are molecular-fused jackets. Its effective range is limited to about 200 yards. When fired, there is a relatively light recoil. The jacket ejected typically flies back and to the side, though it can bounce or behave unpredictably."

"There's a laser pointer if you want it," Broward said.

Wagner shielded his eyes from the projector light to identify who was speaking.

"Right there on the shelf in the podium," Broward told him.

Wagner fished around until he found it then used the laser to trace the shape of the bullet on the screen as he continued. "The projectile is also flat-nosed, which you can see here — you're looking at the copper bullet, the flat lead tip on top. All right: this type of load stands in contrast to spire-point bullets, which can have a flatter bullet trajectory and retain greater velocity downrange. Why am I telling you this? Because a knowledgeable shooter might be forgoing the use of spire-points, confident he'd be at relatively close range to his targets. Or, perhaps like most people, he's not aware of these discrepancies and purchases a conventional load. So at this point it's still unclear whether we're talking about an experienced marksman or an everyday Joe."

Wagner put the pointer away and pressed a button on the laptop, flipped to a new slide showing a box of ammunition. "You cannot ship these in New York State, so no online sales. But you can pick up a box of twenty rounds at Walmart for twenty dollars."

The slide changed to a photograph of a Winchester rifle. Wagner sniffed. "The majority of rifles chambered in .30-30 are lever-action rifles with tubular magazines. What that means is that these rifles are typically very portable, light, with adequate trajectory and wounding at close range. And you can load six shots as fast as you can work the lever."

Severin raised his hand and spoke before Wagner could call on him. "I'm sorry, we're aware of all this. What we're looking for is—"

"I'm getting there." Wagner flipped through slides depicting the various rifles. "Of the lever-action rifles, the Winchester Model 94, the Marlin Model 396 are among the most popular choices for chambering the .30-30. Okay? The Savage Model 99 works with this bullet, though the Savage uses a rotary magazine and is the more likely choice for spire-point bullets, which we're not seeing here in the recovered projectiles, so let's eliminate that." He tapped the keyboard and the first rifle was back on the screen. "My professional opinion is that the shooter is using a Winchester Model 1894."

Kelly watched the smug satisfaction slide over Severin's features. He met her eyes and tilted his head as if to say, *There you go.* Ted Archer had a Winchester tucked up into his basement ceiling. Pretty much all the cops had already been saying Winchester all along, so this was vindication.

Wagner took out a tissue and blew his nose. "Cold and rainy," he said. "Second we touched down, my nose started going."

"At least it's not snowing," Broward said.

"Y'all get some good snow up here," Wagner said, leaning out of the light beam to see the chief.

"Lake effect," Broward said. "Comes down from Lake Ontario. We'll get a couple big dumps this year, three, four feet of snow at a time. It's coming."

"I never could understand living in all that white stuff." Wagner went on for another ten minutes talking about what usually happened to a bullet when it hit a target. His slides showed projectiles in various conditions, misshapen, mushroomed and otherwise.

"People talk about .22s bouncing around in a skull. Let me tell you: I've seen a .22 go clean through a man's chest. We found the projectile on the floor a few feet away and the only marks on it were the rifling grooves. At the same time, I've seen a .38 go into one side of a man's head, travel around his skull beneath the skin and pop out the other side unrecognizable."

Severin muttered and shifted in his seat, making a show.

Wagner continued, "Point being, you hear stories about what this caliber does or what that one does, but bullets can behave unpredictably, and their shape can change. These next images are not for the faint of heart."

New slides alternated between close-ups of various recovered projectiles and the graphic gunshot wounds they'd caused. This up close and personal, victims were reduced to looking like meat. "You can see here, these GSWs are substantial, but the contortion of the projectile is nominal. Now these here, these are GSWs to the head. There's a marked difference and that's because the cranium has altered the shape of the round."

Kelly glanced at Broward. Wagner was confirming his concerns — the contortions to a bullet when it impacted bone. Her phone buzzed in her pocket and she saw a missed call from her brother Rick and a text: *Hey sis. You in town??*

Wagner stepped away from the podium and addressed the group directly. "From what I've seen in these CSS reports, each of the projectiles has endured some contortion. But the ones in the Archer case should stand up to rifling tests, and we're going to try to magnify the heck out of the rest, see what we can get."

She thought about responding to Rick but put her phone away and focused on Severin, who looked like he was getting bad news.

"Finally," Wagner said, "these are narrow wound channels we're seeing here. That means two things. Hand-loaded cartridges have greater velocity and wider wound channels — what the trauma surgeons call 'cavitation.' But these narrower wound channels indicate factory-loaded cartridges, meaning they were purchased with powder loaded in at the factory, and might be easier to trace the sale. That's the one thing. The other thing is when you put this all together, when you consider a shooter opting for flat-tipped, factory-loaded cartridges when he could shell out a few more bucks for the better brand for more secure penetration . . ." Wagner cleared out his throat again. "Well, I've been encouraged to share my opinion, and it is this: this is not an experienced, big game hunter. This is not ex-military."

Kelly glanced at Orzo next, who seemed to be taking Wagner's contradiction of his theory rather well and continued to look on with interest. She figured an experienced detective knew not to rely on intuition, but let the clues and evidence lead.

Wagner continued, "Your unknown subject might have done some target practice and developed a fairly good eye, but he's not a firearms expert. He's using a Winchester 94 with a scope and he's semi-experienced."

Orzo raised his hand. "Either that or he's going for maximum risk, part of the thrill."

Wagner acquired a thoughtful look. "From what I've seen, these are not fly-by-night killings. These are meant to *look* slipshod to some extent — pull up and pop somebody in a drive-by. But they're very calculated and I don't think he's a risk-taker. He's a good shot — not an expert, but maybe he thinks he is."

The killer is arrogant. Wagner made eye contact with her, signaling he was done. She walked to the front. "Thank you, Special Investigator Wagner. I know you didn't have a lot of prep time but that was very informative and I look forward to the final results of your examination."

Broward clapped his hands and there was a smattering of applause. She thanked Wagner again, shook his hand, and smiled as he took a seat. Then she stepped behind the podium.

"So there it is. We're looking for a killer who's using a Winchester 94 and a scope, who has some experience as a shooter. That could be as simple as someone who grew up hunting — maybe he still does — but could also mean target practice, so we're going to want more focus on the regional gun ranges. And we've learned from the autopsies and crime scene reconstruction that a slightly upward penetration point indicates the shooter was possibly seated, perhaps in his vehicle, using the door as an aiming support."

Wagner gave a slight nod, indicating she had it right. She looked at the group. "We know that, with the exception of the juvenile victim, each of the projectiles remained inside the victim's cranium. Like Wagner said, bullets can behave unpredictably inside a body. So, in an oblique way, we've gotten lucky. We have this evidence to examine."

She let that settle and finished up. "Now the elephant in the room — with all of that said, we know the shooter left his casings, or jackets, at each scene. There's no way with all of his other precision that this was accidental, or it's at least a low probability that the casings became irretrievable to him in every circumstance. So this tells us some things. One, with no fingerprints found on the projectiles nor on the casings, the shooter likely uses gloves, and he even uses baby powder on his hands, as particulates were detected on two of the casings. Two, that he's perhaps trying to lead us somewhere, maybe even distract us. What might be said to be a 'calling card.'"

She swept a look over the group and saw she had everyone's attention — even Severin and Epps. "So I want to take a short break, and then I'll offer my own presentation, my profile on the killer."

* * *

During the break, she found Severin in the kitchenette outside the conference room, pouring himself a cup of coffee. Epps was standing with him and saw her coming and left. Kelly poured herself some coffee.

"You're getting Archer's phone and notebook," Severin said flatly. "Should be here within the hour."

"Thank you, Detective."

"Don't thank me — thank your boss, I guess." He showed her his back and left.

* * *

The conference room smelled sweaty and the blinds were drawn. Kelly had put up a large map of the region on the wall. A video camera was recording the presentation.

She stood behind the podium and took a breath, clasping her hands at her waist.

"My job is to look for patterns which form an MO. There's plenty of variation among serial killer cases. Some killers get highly personal — victims are chosen for who they are, or who or what they might represent to the killer — a woman who rebuffed them, a mother who humiliated them, men who undermined them. In your random kill-thrill case, sexual assault or sexual emission is present upwards of ninety percent of the time. But there is no evidence of sexual contact across these cases. These are not random — these are calculated and yet precisely *im*personal — the killing is done from a distance, with a common weapon.

"The times of death vary, the days of the week. Aside from race, the victim traits vary. We're not seeing any evidence so far that the victims knew one another. The locations vary, but share characteristics."

She turned to the map behind her. Red pins marked the crime scenes with a tag hanging from each pin with the date of the crimes. "There is a direction, from the first to most recent killing, and that direction moves northeast, but I don't believe this is a deliberate pattern. And this is a large swath of territory — at least two thousand square miles. The killer's criteria is too specific for these to be randomly selected across that range."

"You don't think he's targeting parks?" Denis Starkey asked.

"He uses empty spaces for the killing but that's not where he's discovering or determining victims. Could be airports, sporting events, malls. High-traffic public spaces."

"Destiny is the biggest mall in the state," Broward said.

"We also need to consider an inciting incident." She took a breath to steady herself. "At the BAU we have what we call the 'Mr. Rogers' effect — you can trace all human behavior to love or a lack thereof. Past trauma — and not always overt abuse, but sometimes neglect — is behind almost every serial killer case we see. Our killer is no different. Somewhere along the line he was abused or neglected or both. And then something set him off."

The room was silent until Starkey spoke up. "So who do we have for suspects?"

No one had an answer.

"I think we work it from the other end," Kelly said. She returned to the podium and clicked her laptop to show a PowerPoint slide. "My recommendation is a three-pronged approach: we run down the list of felons and anyone on watch. We look at possible sighting spots and focus on a central tip-line—"

"We're gonna get thousands of calls through the tip-line," Severin interrupted. "We've already got hundreds on ours and don't have the manpower to follow them all up. People throwing shade on their neighbors because they don't like the neighbor's dog pissing in their yard, now maybe they're a serial killer . . ."

"We'll narrow it down. Our perp is likely male, probably unmarried or divorced, maybe he's suffered a loss—"

Severin made a scoffing sound that reflected her own doubts.

"We look at big, destination stores," she said, "whatever is drawing in people from around the region. Like Broward said, big places like the Destiny mall—"

"Nobody from Auburn goes to Destiny," Severin said.

Detective Muriel Ingram leaned forward and turned her head to look at him. "I do."

"The third approach is Ted Archer's mobile phone," Kelly said. "I'm going to keep it with me and I'll have someone assist me in recording any further correspondence and ping the local towers." She met Severin's hard gaze. "That's why we need to keep Archer's suicide a secret."

"Waste of time."

She ignored him and looked at the others. "You've been focusing on the women and the children, looking at the crime scene, looking at the evidence, which is right. But in order to find the pattern, the signature, I think we need to consider that, to the killer, the women and children are a means to an end. He intends to make victims of the surviving men, too." Still avoiding Severin's eyes, she said, "We have reason to believe that the killer first texted and then called Theodore Archer, husband of Megan and father of Colton."

Severin jumped in to defend himself. "We also have reason to believe that Ted Archer faked this communication in an attempt to deflect guilt."

She looked at him at last. "I understand your position, Detective, and haven't ruled it out. But you haven't been able to produce any evidence so far to support it. And I suspect Blake Haig has been contacted as well, or knows something he's not revealing."

Severin shook his head and sighed. Orzo raised his hand. "Blake Haig denies this, for the record."

"All right," Severin spat, "let's lay it out. Which situation is more likely? That a killer of women and children is going around calling up the husbands for some unknown reason, risking getting caught, or that a man, Ted Archer, choked with guilt, cooks up some story about how he was called up by his family's killer? Obviously you've studied these things, Agent Roth — is there any precedent for this? Any cases like this? Because I'd think there are plenty of examples where killers crack under the guilt. Maybe Ted Archer had a dark side, something he kept hidden." A grin tugged the corner of his mouth. "Maybe he wasn't loved."

"It doesn't explain the other killings," Kelly said.

"It doesn't have to."

Starkey interrupted. "Detective Severin, we've just heard a presentation from a firearms expert with thirty years of experience. We know all the victims were murdered with the exact same ammunition. You called in the FBI because of a series of—"

"*I* didn't call them," Severin snapped. "Chief Broward and the Onondaga County MCU did."

"He teases them," Kelly said quickly. "He teased Ted Archer with the possibility of revenge. The way Blake Haig looked at me this morning, I got the sense he's been given the same promise."

"Oh for God's sake . . ."

"Based on Ted Archer's personal account of his phone conversation, the unsub said he would give himself up to Archer — 'I'll tell you who I am. I'll let you kill me.' Here, see for yourself."

She took a stack of copies she'd made earlier and walked through the room, disseminating them to the group, her anxiety melting away as she found her rhythm with the conflict.

Orzo and Ingram and the two prosecutors started reading right away. Epps seemed interested, too, as if Severin had never shown him this.

"This was written by Archer, based on his recollection of the conversation," Kelly said.

Severin waved the paper. "Or it's completely fabricated B.S. to make himself look innocent. If it was real he would have called us right away."

She took the podium again. "Would he? It's been two weeks since your wife and only child were gunned down, the police don't have any answers, and the man claiming responsibility calls you up and says he'll turn himself in to you, but stipulates that you can't call anyone."

"That's convenient . . ."

"Again, with all due respect, Detective Severin, there are grounds for a man wracked with pain and grief not to entrust the police with this. Not if there's a chance he could find the man who destroyed his life and end him."

There was silence. Everyone in the room was waiting for her next move. She could feel her heart knocking against her ribs again.

Severin's eyes glinted. When he spoke his voice was soft, condescending. "If he actually received such a call, Agent Roth. That's all I'm saying."

"Where is the prepaid you say he used? Where is the proof he used his laptop, synced his phone, *anything* to support the idea that Archer did it all himself?"

"We're going round in circles," Orzo said.

"This is reaching," Severin said, looking around. "Don't you think this is reaching? This is three separate cases where the husbands killed their wives and children using a common gun, a Winchester rifle." He looked at Kelly. "Yeah, okay, your expert said it. But you have copycat precedents in your serial killer files, don't you?"

"But the locations are significant. And I'll clarify that to say it's not so much where the victims were killed, but where they *weren't* killed."

"Knock me over."

"They weren't killed in the home. If the husbands are the perpetrators, why aren't they killing their families in their own homes?"

"Because they don't want it to look like they did it," he said. "That's a no-brainer. And each place was in close proximity. We're talking less than a mile, two miles away from where they lived."

"That may be circumstantial — people sticking close to home, visiting the park nearby. And only Archer owns a Winchester. The other men would've had to obtain one, and would've had to know that the first victim was killed with exactly that type of rifle — but that information *was never released to the public.*"

Severin shook his head. "Why do any of this? What you're suggesting — why go to all this trouble to tease these men with the possibility of revenge, like you say? Lack of love? Give me a break. You know he's never going to give himself up. Right? You know that. We all know that."

"Well, now you're inquiring about the mind of a killer, so we're on the same page." She looked round the room. "In addition to the usual door-to-doors on convicted felons and parolees, we should be looking at sudden death cases — recent events like automobile accident fatalities."

"Right," Broward said, giving her a quick glance before addressing the group. "The killer may have lost someone. He may be acting out because of his own grief.

Maybe he wants to rob men in the same way he felt robbed."

Everyone was getting involved now and Muriel Ingram spoke up. "Agent Roth, going with the theory that the perp wants the husbands to suffer, why *not* frame them for the murders?"

"Exactly," Severin said and clapped his hands once. "Thank you."

Ingram ignored him. "They become the accused and they suffer public scorn and shame. They see themselves on TV and in the news. They have to endure a trial. That's suffering. Right?"

Kelly could feel herself getting flustered. "It's a fair point, but I don't think that's the intent. There could be more that the killer's after which we don't understand yet. Something beyond the promise of revealing himself, or the promise of revenge. That might just be the hook to keep them on the line."

"You think the perp's goal is for the men to commit suicide?" Orzo asked.

"I've thought about that a lot and I'm not sure that's the objective either, though it might be a risk."

"A risk against what?" Severin interjected. "This guy doesn't take risks, I thought. You're saying he's calling up the men to tease them, make them suffer, but that he might actually follow through with his promise? Or he's got some other hidden agenda? Frankly, you're all over the place, and I'm done." Severin stood up. "Because — and let me tell you — aside from all the other shit I disagree with, there's no way someone could call me up and convince me to play along with something like this."

"You asked about precedent," Kelly said sharply.

Severin stopped and looked at her with hooded eyes.

"Psychological experiments have demonstrated how powerful obedience to authority can be. How easily people can be manipulated when certain social pressure is applied," she said.

"Social pressure?" He snorted a laugh and shook his head.

"You're a man — you understand the pressure to protect your family. Don't you? Another man takes everything from you. Takes what you love, then calls you up and promises you a chance to take all that pain, all that guilt and humiliation and sorrow and channel it into settling the score. What's your response?"

"I already told you I'd call the police." He remained just inside the room, looking like he couldn't decide what to do.

"Well, you're police. What did you say to me about Ted Archer? What were your words?" The adrenaline was pulsing through her. "You said, 'You never know about a guy like that.' It took you about five seconds to decide his guilt. So maybe there's something to his mistrust of law enforcement."

The room felt suffocating. Maybe she'd gone too far.

Orzo cut through the heavy silence. "So we got the phone, right? In case this guy calls Archer again?"

"Yes, we have the phone," Kelly said.

Severin swore under his breath and shook his head.

Denis Starkey turned to Orzo. "And your guy, Haig, he denies receiving any calls like this?"

"Denies it, yeah."

Starkey looked at Broward next. "What about Payton?"

"Hard to get in touch with him," Broward answered. "I left him a message asking him to call in. If we need to, we can get the state troopers over to his place."

Severin crossed his arms in the doorway. "It's moot anyway — we can't withhold Archer's suicide. You don't hide this type of thing from family. If this guy was going to call back — and I'm not accepting he called in the first place — he's not going to call up a dead man."

Kelly started to respond but Starkey beat her to the punch. "Then we tell his family, but that's it. We tell them and ask them to keep it completely quiet, completely confidential. No memorial service, nothing."

Severin was already shaking his head. "No way. We might have rights to the body but we can't stop them from grieving, and grieving however they want, even if that means putting an obit in the paper."

"The US attorney's office will make an official request the family not proceed with a death announcement or memorial service until this investigation is concluded," Starkey said.

Severin swallowed hard. Kelly recognized the violence in his eyes. Then he left.

Everyone was rattled from the tension, a bit relieved Severin was gone, but Starkey looked like it was business as usual.

Kelly spoke evenly despite the adrenaline. "One last thing. When we hold the press conference tomorrow, we feed the papers their own preferred meal — that this is the 'Park Killer' and law enforcement is baffled. And when the time is right, we let Archer's family have their service. I'd say we can even watch it, see who shows up, but we've already looked for anyone who knew all of the victims and there's no one. Not a mailman or sanitation worker. Three different counties, three different jurisdictions, three different zip codes. Which is why I think we focus on a central location where the killer is selecting victims."

Epps grunted. "Which location? I've heard a lot of ideas but nothing concrete." With Severin gone, he seemed to have taken over as the skeptic.

"We'll get there," Kelly said. "Just need a little more time."

"Days? Weeks? Let's say we narrow down a hunting ground for this guy, start by picking up anyone who looks shady. We bring them in? We say, can we see your rifle? And they say, sorry, don't have a rifle. Even if we can execute search warrants at that point, let's say there's no rifle in their possession. We ask them a few questions they say, nope, sorry, I'm not killing women and children, and then they go on their way."

"I'll interview them," she said.

CHAPTER EIGHT

Jessica Carter-Spence parked in the large lot of a Walgreens. After she went inside, the killer got out of his vehicle and walked over to hers. He stood there a moment with his cell phone to his ear, pretending to talk. Then he dropped the phone on the ground and bent down, reached beneath the car and felt around until he found the magnetized tracking device and plucked it free. He slipped it furtively into his pocket and then stood up with the phone, dusting it off and muttering. Someone pushed a red shopping cart by, but they didn't look at him. Into the phone he said, "You still there?" and started walking. He carried on the charade until he was back at his vehicle. He put the phone and tracker on the passenger seat.

Tracking was only necessary in the beginning. Once he knew the routine, it was fine.

Honestly, they did the same things every day, went to the same places, saw the same people, said the same things. What was in the book was all too true: people rooted for the same sports teams and political parties, believed in the gods presented to them as children, and all the while clung to the notion they were somehow independent agents making free choices.

Like babies, really.

Of course, there were always slight variations, and you had to adapt. Danica Payton had routinely walked amid the memorial benches beside Onondaga Lake, for instance. She'd sneak her cigarettes there, sometimes talk on the phone, and sit on a specific bench. He'd planned to shoot her on that bench, but the day he'd chosen, she walked over to the tall grass instead. He'd almost bailed right then and there but it was only a slight change and he was hooked. She was too good, the way her husband was ape-shit in love with her, too much to let go.

He remembered her glancing in his direction but she hadn't seen him in the darkness, in the Jeep with the smoked-out windows. She'd turned around to look at the lake and he'd rolled down the window, aimed and fired. She fell into the high grass.

So, a little variation was natural. Megan and Colton Archer walked or drove home from school depending on the weather. Tammy Haig stopped at Island Park after her evening class and had an ice cream or a Reese's. But people were pretty predictable. Minor, unseen events pushed them this way or that. But they didn't make real choices. That was an illusion.

What was happening right now proved it. Constantia had issued a curfew, even though Megan and Colton had been killed in the afternoon. Law enforcement came out of the woodwork like little machines triggered by a household spill. Cause and effect. No choice — conditioned responses to stimuli.

That not everyone was steering clear of parks wasn't evidence of free will — there were always a few tough nuts who held a certain attitude — you know, *don't give in to terrorists*. But they hadn't come up with that on their own, or picked it out of the clear blue sky. They'd learned the slogan from their father or president or some action movie and now that module in their brains had just enough oomph to dominate over fear.

Jessica was like that, still taking her walks, and right through a quiet little section of a quiet little park in a quiet little town. He knew she would be headed there after grocery shopping.

She seemed strong and observant, not easily rattled. But he had another family in his sights after this one, so he had to move quickly. Jessica would pay the ultimate price for thinking she was in control.

* * *

Broward approached Kelly as everyone else was filing out. When they were alone, he said, "That was something. I'm sorry. For what it's worth."

"It's okay." She finished packing up and swung her bag over her shoulder. The conference had left her a little shaken. All she could think about was Nokesville, her home, escaping the hateful eyes of men like Severin, cleansing herself of the idea of a killer for whom killing didn't seem to be enough, just a starting point.

She looked at Broward. "I'll level with you — I usually study cases with a clear picture of everything the perpetrator has already done, their interview tapes, their manifestos. I'm developing this profile as events unfold."

"Listen, you want to grab some dinner?" He focused on her with his gray eyes.

"Thanks . . . but . . ."

"It's because you've seen me eat, isn't it?"

His deadpan delivery made her laugh but she still walked away. Broward caught up with her stride as she turned down the hallway and toward the front door of the police station. "Was that a chuckle? A smile? So you're going to go back to your hotel room to order Thai food, I bet — maybe we could get some together? I like Thai food, too. That's Chinese, right?"

She stopped short of the exit, feeling a tug of loneliness which she instantly regretted and tried to push away. "I've got somewhere to be."

"How long you gonna be? I can wait."

She sighed, her hand on the door. "I really don't know. You shouldn't."

"Well, you know, I'd like to."

She pushed against the crash bar and stepped out into the chill of the late afternoon when the door swung open. "All right, keep your ears on! We'll see."

* * *

She took a hot shower, then dressed in jeans and a white tank-top and the new boots the marines in Quantico would've called "shitkickers." No more pant suits.

She took out Ted Archer's phone and went through the texts and calls that had come in since it had been in police custody. His mother had left a voicemail, the funeral home, and a couple of employees asking work-related questions. Soon people were going to be stopping by Archer's house — you couldn't keep a widower's suicide quiet forever, even with Starkey's order, especially as Archer ran a business. People were going to miss him, and soon. Kelly had the weekend in front of her, buying a little time, not much. If the killer had really contacted Ted Archer, was he stupid enough, or vain enough, to do it again. If it didn't happen in the very near future, it wasn't going to happen at all.

She went through the texts from the unknown caller.

How are you feeling?

A strange opening. Friendly, sympathetic, something people asked each other every day. Then the caller dropped the bomb.

I killed your wife and son.

Any normal person would be provoked by something so blunt, so direct. Even taken out of context, the two messages together could suggest a dark and calculating mind. Or maybe it was all improvised.

Her own phone buzzed on the table. Blanchett, the FBI skip tracer, was here and checking in to the hotel. She let him know she was in her room.

Killers were like artists. A senior agent had told her that in her early days with the BAU. Some artists were spontaneous, he'd said, some more deliberate with their work. Often, you saw an arc — a progression from the seat-of-the-pants method to something more disciplined.

Ted Archer had responded three times:

Who is this?

Think U have wrong number.

Call me.

Right there. He'd been hooked — the caller had reached out in just the right way. Vague, but human.

Witnesses to a crime were notoriously unreliable from a behavioral point of view — people forgot crucial details, skewed the truth, or embellished, but Archer's notes on the call were fairly coherent. Perhaps he was used to thinking under pressure. Archer had tried to pin him down, guessing at the caller's location, his heritage in his notes: *Sounds my age or younger. No accent; maybe from around here, talks like me. If I say anything to cops, he won't call back.*

No way to know what the caller actually said, but Archer's notes had a shape to them: the caller wanted him to listen, wanted to be the only voice to which he paid heed. And there was bizarre stuff about inoculations and the disease of humankind having something to do with identity.

He says he can end my pain. It's in my mind.

Was this planting the suicide idea? Or something else?

The end of "blame and shame" sounded like an incitement to embrace baser instincts — be they to seek revenge, to kill.

The words of Billy Bath, another sociopathic killer, sprang to mind: *Are you truly a good person, or are you merely afraid? Maybe it's men with heroic courage who eschew society to become outlaws while cowards follow the rules.*

Her phone rang: *Laura Roth.*

"Hi, Mom. I was going to call you."

"I saw you on the news."

"Yeah . . . I've just been caught up."

"You looked tired."

Kelly closed her eyes. "Well, that reporter found out I was in town because some guy recognized me in Liverpool."

"Who?"

"He went to West Genny with me, I think."

"Do you know his name?"

"No, I don't."

"Somebody should say something to him. Isn't that a — isn't he interfering with an investigation?"

"He knew someone I guess, maybe he's friends with her. The reporter — Oxley."

"You were trying to keep it quiet."

"Well, we're going to bring out the FBI involvement in a press release tomorrow. But I needed a couple of days to look around, talk to people . . . How you doing, Mom?"

"Have you talked to your brother?"

"Not yet. I've been, you know, working."

Silence.

She repeated the question. "Mom? You doing okay?"

"I'm fine, Kelly."

Typically laconic. Kelly paced the room, feeling fresh anxiety. Her father had been the emotional, chatty one. After his heart attack the house had felt empty. Kelly's mother was self-possessed, never frivolous. Distant.

"I'm going to come by the house, too, Mom. First chance I get."

"It would be nice to see you."

"Yeah. Okay, so . . ."

"Get some rest, Kelly. You're tired, I can tell."

"Yeah, you said. Will do."

"All right."

"Okay. See you soon." Kelly hung up and lay down on the bed and stared up at the ceiling. First Broward, then her mother. They had stirred things up. She saw Craig Danner's face in her mind. The shapes of the other men behind him, blocking off the alley. Danner's hot breath in her ear. His wet, wide eyes.

* * *

Pete Blanchett was tall and thin, dressed in black, carrying two large cases. Looked like a mortician. He'd checked into a room on the same floor as Kelly. She'd never met him before.

"Come on in," Kelly said.

He put his cases down next to the small table where she'd left Archer's mobile. "This it?"

"Yeah."

Blanchett picked up the phone and examined it like an ancient artifact. He opened his cases.

Kelly thought how weird FBI people were, herself included. "Can I get you anything? There's some water in the fridge."

"Uh?"

"Would you like a water?"

"No." He pulled a mysterious-looking piece of equipment out of one of the cases and set it on the table. Then he took out a monitor, set it on the table and connected it to the equipment.

"This will monitor any further contact?"

"Yes."

"And you should be able to get a location if and when he contacts . . ."

"That depends. First we need a phone number."

"The calls came in ID-blocked."

"I'm going to outfit the phone so it unblocks and we can track down and remotely turn on any cell phone if we know the number, even use it as a microphone if we want.

Plus I can watch the towers from here and note any pings from prepaids."

"Good."

Blanchett kept talking. "If there's a new text or a call, we'll correlate tower data so that the reference points will uniquely identify the phone location. And we'll know the exact duration of the call from our end, when it begins, when it ends. Then we can look at all the data from the towers and narrow it down to corresponding times."

"Because the likelihood of other calls originating and ending at the same precise time would be low," she said.

"Very low. But if it's a burner and he's using a new one each time, that's going to make it tougher." Blanchett pointed to the black device. "This is capable of tracking electronic signals of all types, including encrypted cellular. At the very least, we'll get the carrier, contact them, and confirm where the phone was purchased. Once the phone is activated, the chip inside makes it identifiable to the carrier. We'll get one or the other — maybe both carrier and location. But if only the carrier we'll at least get purchase location and can check retailer surveillance video. We put out the purchaser information — give the picture to local law enforcement — and we nab him."

"And if he calls from a hardline?"

Blanchett plugged in a wire. "Traces are instant with the right equipment, and this is the right equipment. You can't hide from Big Brother."

Her gaze fell on Archer's phone. "You said you're able to forward calls?"

"I am."

"So if I leave, and the unsub calls, you can forward it to me."

"Correct."

"And at the same time you can be running your trace?"

"Yes." His eyes connected with hers. "Where are you going?"

"I won't be long."

* * *

Kelly watched from across the street in her rental car, parked in the shadows. It was her brother, no mistaking it.

The pickup truck pulled into the driveway and the light above the garage came on automatically. Rick got out then turned back as if he'd forgotten something. He leaned into the cab, stuck something in his pocket and crossed the driveway towards his house. He was in khaki pants and a dark blue button-down shirt. He looked up.

Kelly sucked in a breath. She got out and called over, "Hey bro."

"What are you doing here?"

She crossed the street. They sized each other up.

"How you doing?" he asked.

"I'm okay. I'm okay. You?"

"Good." A smile flickered across his face. "Where'd you get that coat?"

"Herb Philipson's."

He nodded. "Can you come in?"

"Yeah. Totally."

She followed him into the house. His gait seemed slower, like he'd gotten old. Hard to believe so much time had passed.

Inside was cozy and smelled a bit like pancakes. As he kicked off his shoes, she said, "You're a shoes-off kind of place, huh?"

He chuckled. "Yeah."

She remembered the way he'd been — hunched at the bar, wearing his favorite jean jacket, watching a Syracuse game, drinking Molson Canadian and shots of Cutty.

The living room was dominated by a big flat screen TV and two couches facing each other. Toys were piled in the corner. A child's kitchen set — including stove and sink — sat beside an overloaded grocery cart. Dolls from the movie *Frozen* were buried within the plastic foodstuffs, like stiffened bodies bobbing to the surface.

"This is more the kids' room than the living room. Well, it's my room too if there's a game on. Know what I mean? You want a drink, or something to eat or anything?"

They went through a doorway into the kitchen.

"I'll take something, yeah. You got a Coke?"

"Sure." He opened the fridge. "You don't want a beer?" He poked his head out and looked her over. "Are you on duty all the time or what?"

She leaned against the counter, crossing her arms. "Pretty much."

"I didn't even see you on TV. But Uschi did."

"So did Mom."

"Oh." His crooked grin came back. He elbowed the door shut with a Coke in one hand and beer in the other. "So you got the Mom-call?"

Kelly took the soda from him and popped the lid. "I did."

"We heard about it, you know, when it happened — Danica Payton, right? Everybody was talking about it for two or three days and then it got kind of quiet. But there's more, yeah? That's what the reporter was asking you. They call this guy the Park Killer or something. It's fucking wild. I don't remember anything like this since I was a kid. Remember Billy Bath?" He twisted off the top of his beer and leaned against the stove opposite her. "Of course you probably remember. Who am I talking to?"

"I remember."

He took a pull of beer. "So you talked to Mom, huh?"

Kelly kept her gaze on him. "I was going to call you, Rick."

He looked down. "Yeah . . . No, I know."

"I just had to hit the ground running. I've slept four hours since I got here."

"No shit."

She knew where this was headed and changed the subject. "I like your place."

"Yeah? Shit. I should give you the tour — Uschi would go nuts if she knew you were here. She'd want to scrub the bathroom. She'd want to scrub everything, top to bottom. You know Uschi. Well, I mean, she hasn't changed much."

"It looks nice. Clean. I mean with three kids, I guess. How is everybody? How is Uschi?"

He took another swig. "The kids are good. Mackie loses about a tooth a week right now. Benji is walking, talking. That stuff in there, the kid's kitchen stuff — that was Olivia's old stuff. Ben plays with it now. Loves it." Rick shrugged. "We're modern people, you know? What do they call it? 'Gender-fluid.'"

She just raised her eyebrows.

"Well, shit, you know, I try to get him to watch the game with me and he will, but he'll sit there cooking up a plastic chicken in the oven. Got two older sisters — what are you gonna do?" When he smiled fully, she saw how handsome he still was. The dark smudges under his eyes seemed to fade, laugh lines creased the skin around his mouth and eyes. "I mean I guess there's nothing un-masculine about that anyway. Men cook. Right? I cook. Dad cooked."

"Yeah. Dad cooked."

He took another drink, looked out the window. At the end of the yard were some woods. There was either a clothesline or dog line hanging in the air. He turned his attention back to her. "But Uschi is good, really good. Likes her job. She's at Baldwinsville High School doing guidance counseling."

"Is she really? That's great."

He put his empty beer bottle in the sink. "You, ah, you gonna stick around or . . . ? Hey, how did you know I was going to be home? You never texted back."

"I didn't know what to say."

"Well you just say what's up. I'm in town, I'm busy, whatever."

"I didn't want to make any promises. So I called the store and they said you'd just left. I said I was your sister and they said you had an early shift. What time did you start?"

"I get up at four. Get there at five. So this is like, evening to me. Beer o'clock. You still smoke?"

"No."

"Mind if I have one?"

"Go ahead."

He got another beer out of the fridge. "Mackie and Ben stay at school and come home with Uschi in about an hour. Sometimes sooner. Depends on if she's seeing anyone in her office. Olivia gets a ride with friends after basketball practice. You should see her. Kid's got a wicked jump shot just like her old man."

He opened the back door. "Should be pretty dry out here. You can go back for your shoes if you want."

"Go ahead and puff. I'll just look around. If that's all right?"

"Yeah, sure. Make yourself at home." He flashed her a little smile.

She explored the house. Kelly had last seen Mackenzie when she was a baby. Now she was six and they called her Mackie. God.

She had a fish tank in her room, two little goldfish. The walls were decorated with decals of various birds flitting about. The other half of the room was Olivia's, with a poster of Tamika Catchings, an Olympic basketball star, hanging above her bed.

Benji's room was neater. She'd never even met him.

She went back into the kitchen, looked at her brother on the back deck. Thirty-five years old now. Rick was thirty-frickin-five.

The furniture in the house was decent, everything fairly new-looking. Her big brother was doing all right.

Rick came back in. Half the second beer was gone.

"I don't want to interfere," Kelly said. "Don't want to mess up your routine."

"You're not interfering with anything. I was just gonna get changed. Got a couple things I was gonna do around here before everybody gets home. It's fine." His eyes finally found her. "It's good to see you. You look good."

"I suddenly feel like we're in some TV moment."

He smiled, but it didn't reach his eyes. "Yeah. I guess . . . ah . . ."

"I just . . . I haven't wanted to be back. You know what I mean? But that's not because of you, or Mom. It's just been my life. My work."

He coughed and looked away. "Yeah, I know."

"You talk to Raquel?"

"Little bit. She was just down here a couple months ago. She stays at Mom's sometimes, you know? She stays here. The kids love her. She's doing pretty good. Do you talk to her?"

"We text. Sometimes email. I think we talked on the phone . . . I don't know when it was."

He pulled out a chair and sat down and started to pick at the skin around his thumb. She sat down too and took a drink of her Coke.

The silence lasted until her phone buzzed in her pocket. She checked it, hoping it was a forwarded call or text from Blanchett. *Are we on for a late dinner?* She ignored Broward's inquiry and put the phone away.

Rick was watching her. "So, you gotta go?"

"I'd like to come back. I'll give you some notice next time." She gave him a wide grin. "Uschi can clean if she wants."

You're a peach, Kelly-bell. Her father's voice in the margins of her mind again. Like a coach on the sidelines. *You're my Kelly-bell, right?*

"Yeah . . . We're, ah . . . I mean when were you thinking? We're actually going away this weekend."

"No problem. I'll—"

"We're gonna see Uschi's parents, up in the Adirondacks. We couldn't get there on Thanksgiving — the store was too busy and I had to work. But I do eight days on and four days off so I got the time this weekend, plus Monday and Tuesday, and Uschi and the kids are off."

"How they doing?"

"Uschi's parents? They're good. Dieter is getting a bit senile, but you know, he's still the same old Dieter." Rick frowned. "Did you ever meet Dieter? Or Mischa? I can't remember."

Kelly shook her head, feeling the remorse tighten around her. So much of her brother's life that she'd missed. Uschi's given name was Ursula, and her grandparents were from Germany — she remembered that much. Being here made her feel acutely mortal, like life moved too fast. That's what happened when you came back somewhere. She hated it; it uncoiled inside of her, it itched.

"The kids have a good time up there," Rick said.

She nodded, finished her Coke, and felt the remorse worsen. She stood up a little too abruptly, barking the chair legs on the linoleum floor. "How about tomorrow night?"

He got up, more slowly, a fading hope in his eyes. "Come back tomorrow night?"

"Would that be all right? When do the kids go to bed?"

"Well, you know, Benji's is usually around seven, seven thirty, and we let Mack stay up a little later. Olivia is usually in there reading with her headlamp until eleven — she wants her own room, bad. Yeah, sure, you can come back tomorrow. Of course."

She put on a smile and set the can on the table and made a hasty exit from the kitchen. Put her shoes on beside the front door, thinking, *don't cry*.

Rick followed her. "How are things going with this, ah, the case?"

"Good."

"You being in the middle of this, you don't have to take any more time away from it . . ."

She struggled to lace her boots, feeling frustrated, angry with herself. "No, it's fine. It's good. You're family." When she finally got the boots on, she forced herself to look up at him and saw that his eyes were shining with tears.

"I think about it all the time." His lower lip trembled.

"Don't. You don't have to—" She raised her hand, as if to touch him.

"You'd think it would change with time but I still think about it almost every day. How I should have seen it coming. Or how I should've done something afterward."

"Rick. I don't want to . . ." She felt trapped. A couple of beers in him and her brother was getting emotional. She took her coat and reached for the door.

His eyes grew fierce. "I think about how I should have gone after Danner, went right over to his house and put his head through a wall."

She grasped the doorknob but didn't turn it. She kept one hand up, palm out. "No."

"I still think if I ever see him I'd beat him half to death." The tears spilled and tracked down Rick's contorted face. "One thing. One thing like that, and it changes everything. Look how it changed you."

She marshaled her strength. She had to. Calmness. *Put it away.*

Kelly-bell. My baby girl.

"I like my life. I like who I am. It's a trade-off. That's how it works." She paused, feeling the hard consonants in her words. "I'll see you soon, okay?"

His bony shoulders turned in and he looked at the floor and nodded. "Yeah, okay."

She opened the door and stopped. When she turned around he was still standing there. Suddenly she collapsed into his arms, smelling the beer and thin sweat on him, traces of sawdust. She put her face against his neck and held on. He pulled her tight against him.

His breath pushed on her hair. "I'm sorry, Kel."

She could hardly speak. "It's okay. It wasn't your fault."

She felt a kind of pressure release inside of her. After years of dreading this, avoiding these emotions at all costs, now it was here, and she held on for as long as she could until the old self-defenses kicked in and she let go of Rick and stepped away, looking down, wiping her face.

She gave him a quick glance and saw he was about to speak, but she turned and walked to her car and got in.

Somewhere a dog was barking. She'd never asked Rick what kind of dog he had, or where it was.

A vehicle was coming down the street. She watched it pass — it was Uschi. She was looking out. Kelly saw the heads of two little kids in the back. Her niece and nephew.

Uschi turned into the driveway as Kelly keyed the Mazda's ignition. She took off down the street without looking back. That was enough healing for one goddamn night.

Had to keep moving forward.

She drew hard breaths through her nose.

In this life you have to move forward. It's the only way.

And she cried out and struck the steering wheel with the palm of her hand.

Kelly-bell.

* * *

She didn't even know how long she'd been sitting outside of her mother's house, watching the place until the lights went out, when her phone rang.

"Someone just tried to call Ted Archer," Blanchett said.

"Who?"

"Wasn't blocked. Phone is registered to a Jason Sandaker."

She searched her memory, sure she'd seen the name somewhere but unable to specifically place it.

"He works at Xylem Technologies," Blanchett said.

With Blake Haig, Kelly thought, starting the car. To Blanchett, she said, "Send me everything you've got on him."

CHAPTER NINE

Xylem was housed in a two-story building walled in mirrored glass reflecting the parking lot street lamps and dark trees. Kelly parked the Mazda and phoned Orzo while she waited.

"Agent Roth." He sounded dozy. "What can I do for you?"

"A co-worker of Blake Haig's called Ted Archer's phone just a little while ago — Jason Sandaker."

She heard Orzo moving around, perhaps the creak of bed springs. He sounded more alert when he spoke again. "No shit . . . are you — is your guy able to triangulate a location?"

"He's working on it. I'm at Xylem now, hoping he's just about to get off shift. I'd like a little backup."

"Absolutely. I'll put the word out right now. Sit tight. Sandaker? I don't think he ever came up."

"He has now."

The next call was incoming, from Blanchett. "I got him," Blanchett said. "He's at a diner in Solvay. I'll send you the address."

She switched back to Orzo and asked him to relay the new information to the patrol officers responding and then she got moving.

Ten minutes later, she arrived at the all-night diner and parked outside. She couldn't see Sandaker through the windows, but knew he was there — Blanchett had provided a license plate and the car was in the lot, a green Toyota Camry, rust around the wheel wells. Blanchett had also sent everything else and she scrolled through it on her phone. Sandaker's record wasn't earth-shattering; a few minor blemishes, traffic violations and one misdemeanor for disorderly conduct, but that was it. His picture reminded her of Rick. Narrower through the shoulders, slighter all together, but he had that Central New York thing — a youth of pool halls and street corners, nights driving up and down the strip, drinking beers at the lake.

She watched the diner. What was this co-worker of Blake Haig's doing calling Ted Archer? The thought was chilling: if Sandaker was the guy, if he'd been the one to call Ted Archer before his suicide, then he was either the killer, or he'd been messing with Ted Archer in some sick game.

Orzo's patrol officers weren't there yet so she waited. When an Auburn cruiser finally pulled in, she got out and went over.

"Hi, thanks for coming. You mind just sitting here? Keeping an eye? I just want to get a look at him, see who he's with if anyone, then we'll take it from there."

"Sure." The officer, young and blonde and pretty, picked up her radio and updated her status for dispatch. The one beside her, male, looking about twenty years old, just stared out.

Kelly approached the diner. The main floor was elevated and she couldn't see in the windows so she went inside. A waitress told her to just sit anywhere and Kelly winced at the attention, then spotted a table near the back.

Sandaker was sitting there, but he wasn't alone. Her heart raced as she registered the familiar faces of Blake Haig, plus Russell and Matthew Harbaugh — Danica Payton's brothers. They were all together.

She looked for a second longer, just to make sure, then hurried out the doors.

"Blake Haig," she said to Orzo once she was back in the Mazda. "He's meeting with the brothers of another victim, and his co-worker just called the *husband* of one of the victim's."

"So they don't know Archer is dead."

"Could be."

"What do you think they're doing?"

She could go in and ask. It could be that simple. Take Orzo's cops and walk up to the table and say hi, one of you just called a dead man's phone. Care to explain?

That wasn't the smart move. Whatever they were hiding, they weren't going to come out and admit it just because she asked. She'd have to get Auburn to take them in and hold them, and they'd clam up and ask for lawyers. Better to approach them individually — Sandaker seemed the best bet and had been the one who called Archer's phone.

"Tell me about this guy," Orzo said.

"Lives at 415 Fawn Circle. Thirty-three years old, no wants or warrants. Agent Blanchett hit everything, including employment history. He's been with Xylem for three years. Prior to that he was up in Plattsburgh, New York, working for Georgia-Pacific."

"What's that? I heard of that."

"Lumber. Gypsum products. They make plywood and oriented strand board. He drove a forklift, loaded and unloaded trucks, was there for six years. Now works for Xylem and he's at Bonny's Diner with Blake Haig and Danica Payton's brothers. Did the brothers work up at Georgia-Pacific, too?"

"You'd have to check with Broward but the Harbaughs have never left the area that I know of," Orzo said. "Well, one of them did college at St. Bonaventure. Lasted one year. Russell works for a mechanic in Liverpool. Matthew — he's got a job at a gun shop down in the city."

"A gun shop."

"Yup."

"All right. I'm waiting for Sandaker to break off from them and we'll have a little chat."

"Keep me posted. And keep my guys with you."

She waited outside for a half an hour before the four men came out together and briefly huddled for conversation. Danica Payton's brothers stuck together while Blake Haig and his Xylem co-worker Jason Sandaker went their separate ways. None of them noticed the Auburn police car parked back in the shadows, or her. She followed Sandaker's beat-up Toyota out of the lot.

The vehicle turned onto an entry ramp and headed east on 90, a major interstate.

She glanced at the Auburn PD vehicle, cruising along behind her, no lights. Time to make a hard decision — taking a run at Sandaker with two Auburn cops was going to scare this guy into next week. If anything was going to jump off, seeing uniformed cops would likely trigger it. Was she ready for that? Did she think this was the Park Killer, driving around in his shitty old Toyota, some guy who operated a forklift for a living? The man she was after seemed craftier than that. Or, first appearances were misleading and something else was going on, something Sandaker might hide with local PD breathing down his neck. That meant bringing him in and a long night.

She called Pete Blanchett who was back at the hotel and gave him an update. He was already tracking her phone and knew where she was.

"Can you do me a favor and call Orzo? Ask him to get his PD to back off. Tell him to have them keep out of sight when I get to Fawn Circle, put them a block away."

"You sure?"

"I want Sandaker to be candid, if possible."

Sandaker took an exit ramp and she followed him through the residential streets and watched as the Auburn police car finally faded back. When Sandaker turned into the driveway of a modest little house, they were out of sight. She pulled in behind him and he got out of the vehicle, stared into her headlights, looking curious but unalarmed. Kelly rolled down the window and prepared to identify herself but Sandaker suddenly ducked back into his vehicle.

She scrambled for her piece as she opened the door. *Shit.* Using the door as a shield, she took aim. "FBI! Let me see your hands!"

Sandaker slowly reappeared. He lifted his hands over his head and scowled in the bright wash of headlights. At the same time someone turned on a light in the dark house.

Kelly eased out from behind the door and approached Sandaker, her grip steady. "Keep your hands up like that and take a step away from the vehicle."

The front door to the house opened and a woman leaned out, looking sleepy. "Jase? What's going on?"

"Stay right there, ma'am. FBI. Don't move."

"It's all right, honey," Sandaker said. "Just a minute."

Kelly took a cautious step closer. "What were you reaching for?"

He gulped. "I've got some weed with me."

"Marijuana?"

"I'm sorry, it was just . . . I just thought you were someone else."

"Who?"

He didn't answer. His wife stayed in the door, wearing a bathrobe. She looked cold, and about a day away from going into labor. "Go ahead and go back inside, ma'am. I just need to talk to your husband. Everything is all right."

The wife didn't move until Sandaker gave her a look and a nod. Then she slowly closed the door and moved to the window to watch.

"I don't care about your marijuana," Kelly said. She got close enough that she could see into Sandaker's vehicle. She didn't see any baggie of weed, but she didn't see any gun either. "That's all you were going for?"

"Yes ma'am."

"Get it for me. Let me see. Move very slowly. I see a gun and this is going to get scary, you understand?"

"I understand. Yes." But he didn't move for a moment. Finally he lowered his hands and got back into the car, leaned over and popped the glovebox. Kelly's heart was pounding so hard it was tough to hear anything but she relaxed a little when he pulled out a rolled-up plastic bag with some dark chunks inside of it. Looking slightly embarrassed, he passed it into his left hand and raised it up for her to see.

"Fine. Put it back. What were you going to do with it?"

"Ah . . . smoke it."

"I mean when you were going for it just now."

"I don't know. Chuck it into the street." He closed the marijuana back in the glovebox.

"Now back out. Go nice and slow, keep your hands out in front of you."

"What did I do?" He struggled to get to his feet without the use of his hands but finally pushed himself standing.

"Step away from the car."

He did. He glanced back at the house where his wife was still a shape in the window.

"What were you doing tonight?"

"Tonight? Working. I work at Xylem. It's over in—"

"Afterward. You met with some people at Bonny's Diner."

He swallowed again, but his eyes acquired a defensive look. "You were *watching* me?"

"You met with Blake Haig and two other men. Where do you know the two other men from?"

"They're friends of Blake's. His wife was killed. And their sister was killed."

"So what were you doing with them?"

"Blake . . . he, ah, he just asked me to come along."

"Why? Why'd he want you there?"

"I don't know." The guy was a terrible liar. "I mean . . . I don't know if I should . . ."

Kelly lowered her weapon and holstered it, deciding the threat had passed. "You have kids, Mr. Sandaker?"

"No. Well — about to."

"We could take this somewhere private. Get some more police involved, like the ones waiting over there just past those houses."

Sandaker looked in that direction as if he could spot them.

"Or you could just talk to me, then go inside, back to your wife. She seems pretty worried."

He gave the house another glance and raised his shoulders, let them drop. "Ah, man. All I know is that they think the detective on their sister's case, um . . ."

"Detective Faber."

"Yeah. The one who got fired or whatever. They think he did a shitty job — sorry, crappy job — and that they let her husband go up to his place in the Adirondacks, and they're not too happy about it."

"What's that mean — they're not too happy about it?"

"They just, you know, they think that the cops aren't really doing a good enough job, I guess."

"So they're running their own investigation."

"It's the brothers. They're like . . . they're passionate guys."

"But when did they start talking to Blake Haig? And why are you involved?"

"Blake, he, um — he went to the funeral. For Danica Payton. And he started talking to the brothers. I'm there because, I dunno . . . Blake and I go back a ways. We started at Xylem together. I think he just likes having me around because these guys are . . . they're a little unpredictable."

"He's afraid of them?"

"I mean, maybe. They're intense. Blake's kind of soft-spoken. I'm not saying he's weak or anything. His dad worked for Xylem until he died. His mother, you know, she's up in Utica at one of those places. Has dementia."

"How many times has Blake met with the Harbaugh brothers?"

"One other time. Tonight was the first night they asked me to come."

"And what was discussed?"

Sandaker looked like he swallowed a bug. He stared at the ground and kicked at some pebbles. "I can't, I mean . . . that's like ratting or something. You want to know what they think, you should talk to them."

She felt a flash of anger. She'd gotten into this work to prevent bad things from happening and on this case, it felt like she kept bumping into the same obstacles — pride, territoriality, a distorted sense of honor. "All right, I can understand. But can you tell me — aside from considering Detective Faber incompetent and wishing Roger Payton was around — what? Do they think Payton did it?"

"They think he knows stuff he's not talking about. That's all I know. Okay? With these guys it's a lot of tough talk, a lot of going in circles, if you asked me. I went along because Blake is a friend. But I'm going to tell him tomorrow I got my own stuff to—"

"Do me a favor and keep this between us for now."

He blinked. "Keep it . . . ? Yeah all right." He just stood there, holding his left shoulder with his right arm, shivering a little. "Can I go now? I won't say anything. I'm done — I won't even meet with them again. I won't call, I won't do anything."

And there it was. "Call? What do you mean, you won't call?"

He got that look again, regretting that he'd just said too much, should have quit while he was ahead. "Russell didn't have his phone. So they used mine. To call the other guy, the one who just had his wife and kid killed."

"Why'd they want to call him? Mr. Sandaker? Why call him? Invite him into their investigation? Or something else?"

"He, ah, he didn't answer."

"That's not what I asked."

"I don't know." He glanced at his car. "Well, maybe they wanted to see how his case was going. If anything had . . . changed or anything."

"You mean if someone else had gotten in touch with him?"

"They didn't say anything about that. They just wanted to talk to him. They don't tell me much."

"You sat there with them for a *half an hour* . . ."

"They think it's the mall," he blurted. "Like that pedophile guy who followed the woman and her daughter home from Great Northern? Russell and Matt, they think it's like that, and that's where this guy picks his victims."

Kelly's nerves were humming. "Why do they think that?"

"I don't know. I really don't. Honestly, ma'am, I didn't want to be there."

She decided she'd gotten enough for now, and started back for her car. "Don't go anywhere, Mr. Sandaker — to be continued."

"My wife is going to pop any day now," he said. "I'm not going nowhere."

CHAPTER TEN

Friday, November 30

She spent the morning in Broward's office looking through Danica Payton's bank statements. Starkey and Giovanetti had invited her to make her base in the US attorney's office in Syracuse, but that was too far away and too sterile. She wanted to be *in it*. And she liked Broward's little set up; quiet with just her and one patrol officer working the main desk, the heat whirring softly through the air ducts.

Danica Payton's statements showed twelve months of spending on her debit card and credit cards. Kelly spread them all out on the desk.

Broward came in. Snow dusted his police parka. "So you had quite a night. I just talked to Orzo."

She gave him the whole story, including what Sandaker had said about the mall theory.

Broward seemed to shrink. "Yeah, those Harbaugh guys . . . I'll get them to come in. Where do you want to do it?"

"Ask them to come down to your office. Tell them you want them to meet the FBI agent working their sister's death, just keep it light."

Broward nodded and looked away. He probably felt inadequate — there'd been a detective in his department who had botched the case, and the victim's brothers didn't think local law enforcement could catch her killer.

"Your guy Wagner called me this morning, too," Broward said.

"I told him to."

"Okay. So, you know that the rifling tests came back negative for Archer's gun on all victims. It wasn't him. Severin's not going to be happy."

She'd known it wasn't Archer but leaned against the desk and thought about it. "Severin is already unhappy."

"I hear you. He can be . . . you know, like he was yesterday. But he's all right."

"You think everybody is 'all right.'"

Broward pointed at his wavy hair. "Tinfoil hat, a little bit — Severin thinks everything is a conspiracy. But this sews it up, I guess. Least as far as Ted Archer. He didn't shoot anybody besides himself."

Maybe a little crude, even for Broward, but at least he was on the same page as her. It was locked now: based on the tests of Ted Archer's Winchester 94, the projectiles recovered from his wife and the one embedded in a nearby tree hadn't been fired from his gun. The Danica Payton and Tammy Haig crimes didn't match Archer's weapon either. And so he wasn't a killer, hadn't taken his life in a fit of guilt.

Then why?

Overwhelmed by grief? Maybe.

Because Detective Severin's skepticism had been the final straw for a man already hanging by a thread? Or because the killer had gotten into Archer's head, pushing him toward suicide? *See how I take a man's family, watch how he self-destructs.* She couldn't see Jason Sandaker for that, not the way he was last night with his mouth hanging open and his baggie of weed in his hand. No way. The killer — the caller — was someone else.

He says he can end my pain. It's in my mind . . .
Keeps talking about the nature of suffering . . .

Three men left behind after losing their families. One dead now. But between the negative gun match for Archer and her first-hand experience with Jason "aw-shucks" Sandaker, they were still in the dark.

Meanwhile, the Harbaugh brothers were operating their own little investigation. They thought their sister's husband, Roger Payton, had been overlooked as a suspect.

Broward looked around at all the Danica Payton paperwork. "How we doing?"

"Think I need to go to her house."

"Okay. We can do that. Hang on." He left and came back a minute later with a small manila envelope and shook out a set of keys.

"You have keys?"

"Yeah, Roger gave us a spare before he went up into the Adirondacks. I said, you know, we might need to look around from time to time. He was fine with that."

* * *

She followed Broward to the Payton's home in Liverpool.

"Danica's family originally owned this place," Broward said. "You can sort of see the original structure — see that right there? Then Danica's father added on this front addition and over here — walk with me — the deck around the back here, and this whole section."

The back yard was unkempt, the grass long and covered with autumn leaves. Broward pushed the door open to a foyer with hanging jackets and boots, a washer and dryer, everything still and cold. She noticed dog hair on the carpet.

"They have pets?" she asked.

"They had a dog. Nice Golden Retriever. It went to one of her brothers — I think Matt took it in. I mean, it was her dog from before she and Roger got married. I think he liked the dog, but it's getting old, and I think he just . . . I don't know. It went to the brother."

They passed through a large kitchen with an impressive cast iron stove. The house had a musty smell and some of the floors were uneven, yet there were signs of money, like the stove. Some modern art hung from the living room walls.

Kelly mused over a series of framed black-and-white photos showing Danica with Roger. Paris, she recognized. Then some place tropical, maybe Belize. One in Times Square.

"So you wanted to look for receipts," Broward said. He pushed aside a stack of boxes and opened a door to a back room. After he clicked on the light and waved a hand at the cramped space she saw more boxes, piles of paperwork, tons of photos tacked to the walls, more travel mementos.

"Roger likes old signage," Broward said, pointing to a corner. "You've seen it — The Post is full of 'em. Old gas station signs, soda pop — I think there's one in here for *Foot Rest Hosiery* . . . yeah, look at this. Little girl on a swing. Oh and this is *Golden Shred Marmalade*. Classic. He loves this antique stuff. Here's one — this is my favorite: 'Suits, Cleaned and Pressed — fifty cents.' The good old days, I guess."

She was looking at one for *Muratti's Young Ladies' Cigarettes* and feeling a little uncomfortable. Roger Payton had given Broward a key, but being in someone else's home when they weren't there felt slightly wrong, especially as the woman who'd lived here was dead.

Kelly opened the top right drawer of the roll top desk. Pens and pencils, a pack of cigarettes, hair ties, a cigar-cutter. The larger bottom drawer contained files. "They both used this office?"

"I believe so."

"Can you check that file cabinet for me?"

They spent close to an hour looking at every receipt they could find. The unheated house got to her. Something about being cold indoors was even more bone-chilling and a couple of times she saw a wisp of her own breath. "This isn't going to work. I might have to subpoena for Roger's bank statements, credit cards."

"Oof. Yeah. Well that's going to take a little time. It might help if you told me exactly what you were looking for. We could get some more hands on deck. What about—"

She held up a crumpled receipt and turned it toward the light.

Broward came closer. "What you got?"

"DSW. Women's running shoes. Purchased on Sunday, May 20, this year." She looked up at him. "Roger bought his wife some new shoes. Not that we need to, but I bet if we took the sneakers in evidence over to DSW, they would be the ones on this receipt."

He just stared, and then the corner of his mouth curled up into a goofy smile. "I see where you're going now."

"What time is it?"

Broward checked his watch. "Not quite ten."

She took her phone out and went through her contacts. She found the one for Blake Haig and dialed. Broward kept looking at her with that bemused expression.

"Mr. Haig?" she said.

"Yeah?"

"Not a telemarketer, I promise. Agent Kelly Roth. We recently spoke at your house."

"Right, yeah, I know who you are. You want me to come in? I heard what happened and I'm — well I'm going to be working a double tonight into tomorrow morning, but maybe after I—"

"I appreciate that. I appreciate your openness. We would like you to come in and talk with us, yes, but right now I need to ask you one question."

"Sure."

"Do you keep all your receipts? Or would you have kept any of Tammy's?"

"Uh, I haven't really hung on to any of Tammy's things. You know, like I said . . ."

"Maybe you could check for me. Even look at your bank or credit card statements, anytime around eight months ago to about a year ago. I'd really appreciate it."

Silence on Haig's end.

"Mr. Haig? You there?"

"Is there a lead or something?"

"I'm just putting my timeline together. Boring cop stuff, but important. I'll reach out to you soon." She flicked a look at Broward who was looking on, rapt with attention.

"Because I think someone was following us at the mall once," Haig said.

She stiffened. "Did you speak to Detective Orzo about that?"

"Yeah. Absolutely I did."

"And what did Detective Orzo say?"

"I don't think he took it very seriously."

Broward gave her a quizzical look as she determined her next move. "All right. Well I'm going to look into it. And you'll be around, right, Mr. Haig? So we can talk this all through in person."

"I'll be around, yeah."

"Thanks."

She ended the call.

"What did he say?" Broward asked.

She showed him the receipt. "When I was at the Archer's house yesterday morning, I saw a receipt for Dick's Sporting Goods. Looked like football stuff Ted Archer had bought for his son. Blake Haig says he and his wife went to the movies at the Regal. These are all places in the Destiny mall. And Haig just told me he mentioned someone following him and his wife there."

"He reported it? I didn't see it anywhere."

"I didn't either. He might've said it to Orzo at any point, Orzo dismissed it — it never went in the official report."

Broward took a moment. He put his hands on his hips, the palm of his right hand resting on the grip of his gun.

She waved the receipt. "We know Roger was there because it was on his personal credit card. He's buying women's shoes? Then she's with him. They went together. Blake Haig and his wife were there together, too. And I bet if we look into it, Megan Archer went with her husband and son to Dick's Sporting Goods."

He looked doubtful. "I mean, I go to Destiny. Probably every person in Liverpool has been to Destiny. Auburn, Constantia. Everybody goes . . . just maybe not Severin."

"We've found no link between the victims, but if we include the meeting of Blake Haig and the Harbaugh brothers, even after the fact, there is. And they think there's a connection to the mall. Our killer has got a place where he nests, where he watches and decides."

"Only one of these guys is going to talk to me without an arrest," Broward said. "And that's maybe Russell. My ex-wife took her car to his shop for a few years."

"Let's go talk to him."

* * *

Russell Harbaugh was standing beneath a vehicle in the garage. He was poking at something in the undercarriage of the car. He glanced over as Kelly and Broward approached, finished what he was doing, then pulled a red rag from his pocket and wiped his hands.

"Chief Broward. How ya doing?" he said.

"I'm okay, Russell. This is Agent Kelly Roth of the FBI."

"Yeah, I saw her on TV. How's it going? Get my sister's killer yet?"

"That's what we're here to talk about," Broward said.

Russell sniffed, then finally gave Kelly his attention. "Yeah?"

"I know you've been meeting with your brother and Blake Haig and Jason Sandaker."

"It's a free country. Well, what's left of it."

"I don't have any problem who you associate with, Mr. Harbaugh. I understand — Danica was your sister and you want to know what happened to her, find the person responsible. So do I."

"Does that get you a promotion or something?"

"I grew up here. I don't like to see my community afraid like this. Some sick son of a bitch running around out there doing this to women and children. I want to put him away."

She had Russell's full attention now. He wiped his hands on the rag again. "Good. That's good, Agent, uh . . ."

"Roth."

He gave her a direct look, his icy blue eyes probing. "Rick Roth — that your brother? Played basketball?"

She nodded. "Yes."

"I remember Rick Roth. We played against Baldwinsville a lot. I'd get stuck covering him. The guy was all arms and legs." His eyes flitted to Broward. "So what do you need from me? First you get FBI, now you want to know what I know."

Broward opened his mouth but Kelly could sense a pissing contest in the offing so she beat him to a response. "That's fair to say. A lot of the time, civilians know more than we do. I'd like to hear what you think happened to your sister."

Russell looked over her shoulder. She turned around. A guy in blue coveralls was leaning back in his chair in a small office that attached to the garage. He was eating a sandwich and watching them. When Kelly met his gaze, he dropped back to all four chair legs, and went out of sight.

"It's just about my lunch break," Russell said.

"What do you usually eat?" Kelly asked. "I'm buying."

He grinned for the first time, revealing straight white teeth. Danica had been a star athlete, beautiful, and her older brothers were handsome and in excellent physical shape. Russell seemed smart, too, the tough guy a bit of an act. He gave Broward another quick look, measuring him, then said to Kelly, "That's all right. We can talk right here."

"Fine. I'll come right to the point. What makes you think that the Destiny mall is part of this?"

Russell walked out from beneath the suspended automobile. He took a wrench from his back pocket and dropped it into an open toolbox where it landed with a clatter. He tossed the rag in after the wrench. "Instinct," he said.

"Instinct?"

"The sicko who used the Great Northern Mall to pick out the little girl and her mother — he hung out there and he followed them. They were from Liverpool, but you probably know that."

"David Renz."

"Yeah, that's him. So, different mall, same idea."

"And that's it? What else?"

"Roger and Dani went there a lot together — to Destiny. When I talked to Blake Haig at Dani's funeral, he said they did too. And then he said he thought someone was following them, him and Tammy, the last time they were there together."

"So who came up with it first? You and your brother, or Blake Haig?"

"I don't know. It just kind of came out."

She thought about that — a case of an idea circulating and no one quite sure who'd had it first.

It needed to hold up if she was going to get Genarro behind it and really get moving.

"Did you ever call Ted Archer? Ask him about it?"

"I did, actually. I called him last night."

"From your own phone?"

He narrowed his intense blue eyes. "From someone else's, actually. My phone was dead."

"From whose phone?"

He sucked at his teeth. "Jason Sandaker. My phone was out of battery. But Archer didn't answer."

It matched up, unless they'd already spoken to each other to get their stories straight. Which was why, despite concerns they were going to resist telling the truth, you still got everybody rounded up and put in separate holding rooms so they couldn't collude on a cover story.

You might have screwed up, Kelly.

"So," she said, looking up into Russell's face, "just that? Just the idea that your sister and her husband and Blake Haig and his wife had visited Destiny? And the David Renz case. That got you thinking in a certain direction."

Russell didn't answer, just breathed with a mean energy. On second thought, the tough guy thing wasn't just an act — he looked like he could take a man apart if he had to, piece by piece, same as a car. Broward was a big guy, too, but the chief seemed diminutive by comparison, standing there and biting his tongue.

"Yeah," Russell said. "That got me thinking in a certain *direction*."

She lowered her voice. "Come on, Russell. I know you're holding out. Something else happened. I think the person who killed your sister has more on his mind than just murder. There's more to it." She hunted his face for any giveaway until he turned his head away. "Blake Haig told you something else. Didn't he?"

He started to speak, then snorted. "I think, ah, I think that's it from me, Agent Roth."

She gave Broward a look. "Will you excuse us for a second, Chief Broward?"

It took a moment, but then he seemed to understand. He gave a slight nod and went out into the sunlight.

"Look," she said to Russell. "I get it. Small town department, you feel like Detective Faber and Chief Broward dropped the ball."

Russell turned toward her. "All right, yeah, we came down pretty hard on Roger. Maybe we were wrong, I don't know, but that was before. When we talked to Blake at the funeral, all this came up. So we go down to Destiny and look around and sometimes we take some pictures and meet with him and show him. You want to arrest us for trying to figure out what happened to my sister? Or Blake's wife? Go ahead."

"What's the description?"

"Blake says an older white guy wearing an Orangemen hat. He noticed him in the food court when they were eating, guy just sitting by himself, looking over every once in a while. Then they went to the movies and the same guy was there waiting in line to buy tickets. He says he looked around for him in the theater but he wasn't there. That's it. He didn't say anything to the cops about it when his wife was first killed. But when we got together with him and we were talking about the two killings being alike, Matt started talking about the Great Northern Mall and that fucking pedophile David Renz and that's what Blake told us."

"Did Blake Haig and Roger Payton talk to each other at the funeral?"

"They didn't talk. Blake didn't want to make a big thing out of it. He wanted to pay his respects, keep a low profile because the media were around. But Matt and I started talking to him, we went out for drinks afterward, that's how the whole thing got going."

"And that's all he's told you. He hasn't said anything else."

"No."

"You're sure?"

Russell stepped close enough for her to smell sweat and oil.

She forced herself to stay poised as she spoke. "I need to know if the perpetrator contacted Blake Haig. Because he contacted Ted Archer. And that's why I showed up at the diner last night, because Ted Archer killed himself, and we have his phone. If someone called Blake — if this guy from the mall called him, I need to know."

Russell picked up the wrench and the rag.

"Mr. Harbaugh, are you not telling me because the killer told Blake if he contacted the police, he'd never give himself up, he'd never be found? That wouldn't be it, would it?"

"Have a nice day, ma'am. Tell your brother Rick I said hi." He reached up into the undercarriage and started working.

"You're never going to get this guy on your own. And, yeah, you'll all end up in jail for interfering with a federal investigation."

He cranked the wrench and pulled a car part loose and dropped it to the ground with a clang. "Do what you gotta do."

Kelly released a breath and turned away, toward the bright square of sunshine framed by the garage door.

* * *

She was ravenous. Maybe it was all the stress and adrenaline.

Broward slurped his noodles and peered into his bowl. "What is this again? Tom something?"

"Tom Kha Kai."

"It's good." He took another bite and washed it down with a drink of his soda. "I knew I'd get you to come out to dinner with me eventually."

"Humans require nourishment, Chief Broward. Sing unto the Lord a new song."

Broward wiped his mouth with a napkin and sat back. "All right, so talk to me."

"We need to get Blake Haig to sign a statement that he was followed at Destiny mall."

"Agreed. If he called Archer — or the Sandaker guy did — then they didn't know Archer completed a suicide. That's one thing. God, these freaking guys. What else did Russell say?"

She told him and Broward said, "So they're running around taking pictures of people at the mall. But Russell wouldn't admit if the unsub is communicating with Haig?"

"No. But we need to be watching them. They think they're going to get him on their own."

"I only have a few guys, and Haig is in Orzo's jurisdiction. I'll call Orzo, see if we can get some more people out there to keep an eye on them. Jesus — bunch of cowboys."

It was different counties, too, and Major Crimes didn't really do surveillance, anyway. She needed either state police or her own reinforcements.

They ate in silence, thinking it all through.

She watched him for a moment. "I'm sorry if when I asked you to leave . . ."

He lifted his eyes to her and waved a hand in the air. "I get it — good cop, bad cop. You don't have to worry about that with me."

"Don't have to worry about what?"

"Ego."

She found that hard to believe but didn't say anything. Finally Broward regarded her again and surprised her by sticking his hand out, as if to shake. "Agent Roth. Kelly. I'm Robert. I'm a divorced forty-year-old man with two daughters who likes learning about birds and watches YouTube videos on fly fishing. My most prized possession is my '72 Harley Soft Tail. Or my signed U2 album. Your turn."

She blinked at him for a moment, her mind seizing on a detail. "U2?"

"That's right."

"You have a signed album . . ."

"That's correct. They came to Saratoga when I was . . ." He looked up at the ceiling. "Fifteen. The Zooropa tour. I thought they were the shit. That's my deal."

Finally she gave his hand a quick shake and returned to her food.

"You?" Broward asked. "Bet you were a big Tori Amos fan."

"Please."

"You remember that video where she's naked or something playing the piano? She's throwing her hair back, bouncing her legs." He took another sip of his soda.

"I listened to the . . . are we really doing this? Are we talking about what music we listened to?"

He kept his eyes on her. "Well, we could talk about what happened to you."

When she felt the humor draining and didn't answer, Broward went on. "That reporter, Oxley, called the station and asked me for a comment."

Her stomach clenched, appetite gone. She set down her cutlery and lowered her head, asking herself why the men in her life seemed to feel the need to keep digging around in her past.

Broward wiped his mouth again. "You grew up here, I know that. And the reporter wanted to know if I thought 'the incident' was going to affect your handling of the case."

"Uh-huh. So, getting something to eat was a pretext for an interrogation."

"No, not at all."

She felt vulnerable. "You want someone else to consult, I can give you the number for my supervisor."

"Kelly, no. I'm just . . . getting to know you."

"My personal life is irrelevant."

He raised his eyebrows. "Is it? You being here has nothing to do with local knowledge? Your supervisor didn't see that as a benefit?"

"Okay — I went to West Genesee High School. My mother lives in Baldwinsville. You're right. It's easier to get around — no GPS required. Otherwise it hasn't had any bearing on the work."

He seemed to sift through a couple of emotions before he nodded and said, "Okay. I guess I can buy that." Then he shook his head and lowered his gaze. "Too bad though."

"Sorry?"

"I thought maybe you were top of your class, or something." He put on a dreamy smile.

"Nope. I'm just a local. And if we want to talk about things affecting the handling of a case, maybe we can talk about the waitress at The Post."

Broward leaned back. "What are you talking about?"

"I just hope you started up with her before Danica Payton was murdered and ended it the second that happened. Otherwise you're sleeping with a witness."

"I, ah . . . I, ah . . ."

"What's the matter? Flirting with the FBI agent took a turn?"

"Hey, come on . . . don't be like that. It was before. Just a thing. I cut it off as soon as the . . . as soon as Danica Payton happened."

"You sure? Because you told me a waitress at The Post picked up Danica Payton's phone off the bar. That you eliminated her through fingerprints. Was that the waitress? Courtney? And maybe it was one of those real estate agents of yours who called Oxley, or maybe it was her."

"I cut it off. As soon as the case landed in my lap. I don't know why you have to come down on me like this. Courtney wouldn't do that. She wouldn't call the newspaper on you."

"What do you want from me, Robert? You want to ask me about myself? Do I seem like I need a friend?"

His expression hardened. "That's kind of harsh of you, don't you think? I was just—"

She got up from the table, feeling embarrassed and angry. The work wasn't supposed to have anything to do with her, personally. Feeling sorry for herself, she regretted saying yes to Genarro. But had there been a choice? Genarro had thought he was throwing her a soft ball, a case on familiar turf. But then Ted Archer had killed himself, and Blake Haig had acted like someone brainwashed in a cult, and the two brothers of a victim were playing private investigators. Maybe it was a major mistake not bringing in Sandaker and the rest when she'd had a chance.

This was all new. And meanwhile the killer was messing with the families of his victims and she didn't know why, what purpose it served.

Maybe there was no purpose.

"Hey," Broward said. "Where are you — come on — Kelly . . ."

She'd gone over to the waitress with her wallet. "Can I get the bill?"

The waitress nodded and smiled warily and hurried away. Broward got up and put on his jacket.

He matched her quick pace as she crossed the street to the hotel. "Look, I don't mean to overstep or anything. Hey, Kelly . . ."

She stopped and turned around. "I'm sorry about that in there. I went too far and I'm sorry."

"No, it's all right — I get it. We got a lot going on. I get too personal; it's a problem."

"I don't want to offend you. I appreciate your effort to be friendly, but I'm here to do a job and I've got a million people to call and things to do if I'm going to get surveillance up on the biggest mall in the state."

An icy wind skirted the corner of the tall gray block of hospital, carrying a dance of snowflakes. She stopped and stared into the white, twirling motes, brought back to the day it happened. Lying on her back in the alleyway, looking up at the sky after Danner finally left her, it had begun to snow. Just like this.

Her breath slipped out in thin plumes. Broward watched her.

"You find out something happened to me, and then what? That defines me?" she said.

"No. It doesn't have to."

"That's all anyone has time for. The FBI brains trust calls it a fundamental attribution error — one event, one moment, and you're branded for life." She buried her hands in her pockets and looked at him as he stood blinking, his nose red from the cold.

"I don't . . ." Broward said. "A fundamental what?"

"I was assaulted. The summer before I went to college."

He was quiet for a moment, looking at her, then glancing away. "Where'd it happen?"

"A club called The Avenue, downtown."

"Yeah, I know it."

"I left for the night to catch a cab and they caught up to me. One guy and a bunch of his friends." She took a breath, looked into his eyes. "Okay?"

"Okay."

She waited for him to ask if she'd pressed charges. That was usually the next question. Followed by her attempt to explain how twisted and confused the feelings were following the attack, the cloud that descended over her and lasted for months, even years afterward. The strange, senseless fog of guilt she'd tried to escape, tried so hard that she would take long and fast drives, as if she could outrun it, until she finally wrapped her car around a tree at age twenty.

The scar across her chest, two on her arms, were from crawling over broken glass as she freed herself.

Broward asked, "Who were they?"

"They were guys my brother grew up with. Our father died before that and I was going out too much and Rick had left home at that point. He blames himself, thinks he should have stayed around our home, helped my mother, me and my sister. He thinks if he was around it never would have happened. It's not his fault though. For one thing, my mother didn't make it easy. She doesn't like to be helped."

Kelly searched Broward's face, waiting for him to say that the apple didn't fall far from the tree. But Broward just stood there, his silence inviting her to finish.

"These guys happened to be in the club when I was in there. One of them thought it was okay to hit on me and I turned him down. They followed me out, followed me around the corner. The principal was Craig Danner. I let him back me into an alley, thinking I could talk my way out of it. The others with him stood around providing cover. He called me a cock-tease, said I wore things to get him excited when he used to come over to my house to see my brother. When I tried to get away, he grabbed me, took me down to the ground, pinned me there. I couldn't get up . . ."

It had been years since she'd let the memories fully surface and she could feel them, like living things, twisting within her, trying to break free. "Some people saw something happening and started yelling and came over. Danner and the guys took off before any of them could be visually identified. I went to the police, they picked up Danner the next day. I had pictures of the bruises, I had my story. Danner said he'd never been to the club, never saw me, but that I had a thing for him and made the whole thing up because he'd turned me down because of my age — too young for him. It was a lie, but he maintained that he never did anything, never knocked me down and got on top of me and started unbuckling my pants, jammed his hand down there while he spat in my face."

She looked up at Broward and his face was turned into the wind. Then their eyes met and he said, "I'm sorry."

The wind tugged at her clothes some more, and the fine snowflakes moved sideways through the air until an updraft sucked them higher, toward the buildings shouldering together around them.

"We anticipated the media might try to make something out of me being on the case."

"I won't say anything to them."

"It's fine. Say whatever you want to, Robert."

He shook his head. "Nah. To hell with that. And, by the way, of course I think it's a good idea, you being here. So don't go thinking I want to call your supervisor." He sniffed and shrugged himself deeper into his jacket. "That's how I see it anyway."

Not knowing what else to say she said, "Okay then."

"What happened to Danner?"

"He took a deal. Entered an Alford plea — said he wanted to spare everyone drawing it out, he would take one for the team."

"An Alford plea — guilty but not guilty."

"He got probation so he could continue with school." She studied Broward's eyes some more and said, "But he never admitted it. Ever."

Broward rubbed a hand over his face. "I'm just used to getting to know the people I'm working with, that's all."

"I know."

"I want this guy. That's all that matters to me. And maybe what I said about ego, maybe this thing has got me a little fucked up. I got these Harbaugh guys and half the town thinking I can't find my own ass in the dark. I want to find this psycho and nail him to the wall."

She let it all settle, finding it easier to look at him now. And maybe this was for the best — better that things were out and they could focus on the work. "Good," she said. "Now let me get up to my room and get set to go talk to Blake Haig again. I'll see you in a little—"

"It's interesting though." He fixed her with a curious look. "You had this happen to you, and there you were today standing up to Severin, saying that our guy is trying to make victims of the men. Trying to hurt them."

"What does that have to do with anything?"

He stuck a finger in the air. "And that question is why you're the right person for the job."

She searched for a response and was saved when Broward frowned and plucked his phone from his belt. "Uh, Chief Broward here . . ."

He turned away. Kelly thought about slipping away, but then Broward's voice dropped. "Oh no . . . Okay . . ." His expression grim, he continued to listen another few seconds and then said, "Thank you. I'm with Agent Roth. We're on our way." He rang off and stuck the phone away and locked on her with his gray eyes, a nerve twitching in his jaw. "There's been another one. Same MO. Back of the head, one clean shot. She was in Camillus Park."

Kelly's stomach formed into a hard knot. "Oh God."

"Yeah. We gotta go."

"Who found her?"

"Another woman called 911 from her cell phone at 10:15 this morning. The victim isn't dead yet. They rushed her to Amherst but it's not looking good."

CHAPTER ELEVEN

Kelly's shoulder mashed against the door as Broward took the corner at speed. She kept the phone to her right ear, stuck a finger in her left and tried to hear the detective from Camillus. "The victim is confirmed as Jessica Carter-Spence," the detective said.

"She was alone?"

"Alone. Has two kids but they're at school and daycare."

Broward said, "Tell them we're about five minutes out." He hit the gas as a streetlight turned to yellow and flew through the intersection. His police lights were flashing. "Get out of the way! Get out of the way!" The road was busy. He made the next left toward Camillus, tires squealing with the tight turn.

Camillus Park was in a residential area, the playground bright with primary colors, but a child's slide and swing set took on an ominous look surrounded by law enforcement vehicles and strobing lights. A Camillus patrol officer lifted the crime scene tape and Broward rolled through.

A female detective waved them over when they got out of the car. She handed Kelly a plastic evidence bag containing a single brass casing. Kelly saw 30-30 WIN stamped around the primer. She handed it back.

"The Spence family live just over on Shaker Heights Road, a cul-de-sac," the Camillus detective told them. "The husband said she walks this route in the afternoon to pick up her youngest from daycare. Does it most days. Cuts up through Fox Drive and over to North Way, then back down, goes home, awaits the bus bringing the older one home. That's her routine."

"Where's the husband now?"

"With the victim at Amherst Hospital. There was talk about airlifting her to Albany, but they didn't. She was DOA."

"Do the children know yet?"

"No. They don't know anything yet."

"And we have eyes on them?"

"There's a patrol officer sitting outside of the school. We don't have one deployed to the daycare yet — there's only five officers on shift and we—"

"Where is it? Where's the daycare?"

"It's just around the corner, on North Way."

Kelly was already running to Broward's car. He chased after her.

"Gimme your keys," she told him.

He tossed them to her without arguing. Kelly pulled the door shut and keyed the ignition and was rolling forward before Broward had his door closed all the way. She saw him stretch his seatbelt across his chest as she took the corner out of the parking lot and hit the gas, thinking about a killer bent on destroying families. Maybe Colton Archer had been collateral, maybe not.

She drove fast but carefully. "Which way?"

Broward swung the terminal in his car to face him, tapped at the keys. "Take a right up here. It's a quarter mile."

She pulsed the gas and drove as fast as she dared along the narrow residential street until Broward said,

"There," pointing to a small brown house where a Camillus patrol car was just arriving. Broward flipped on his deck lights and they flashed red and blue as Kelly stopped the vehicle in the street and got out, started running for the house.

The patrol officer saw her coming. "Hey! Hey!"

Broward moved for him with his badge out. Kelly took the concrete steps up from the street and onto the lawn. Sprinting up the walkway she reached the front door and found it unlocked, swung it open and could already hear children singing as she moved into the warm home. She had her ID out and held it up as a woman stood up in the back room, looking alarmed. Half a dozen preschool kids sat in a circle singing, "Take Me Out to the Ball Game."

Kelly met with the woman in the kitchen between the back playroom and the short hallway. "I'm with the FBI." She took a quick breath. "Is everybody okay here?"

"What's going on?"

"There's been an incident."

"I heard sirens." The middle-aged woman had dirty blonde hair in a French braid, large brown eyes. "Twenty minutes, a half hour ago."

Kelly put away her ID, still getting her wind back. "All the children are present? Is there a child here named Spence?"

"Of course. He's right here." She made a gesture towards the children in the room behind her. They were losing the song and breaking apart into laughter and chattering. The woman pointed to a little boy with ginger hair, dressed in denim overalls. He rolled on the floor and kicked his legs in the air.

"Ma'am, I just need to have a look around the house. Okay?"

"What is it?"

"An officer from Camillus is on his way in. He'll explain. I just need to make sure everything is safe, all right?"

Broward and the Camillus patrol officer came in through the front door. Kelly went to greet them and they agreed on a strategy to secure the premises. She'd circle the house, Broward would check the rooms while the Camillus officer kept his eyes on the children and spoke with the care provider.

She went outside. The way the house sat up on a rise, the park was visible in the distance as a cluster of leafless maples and still-green pines, the colorful jungle gym, the cop lights shuddering. She drew her gun and started around the house. Behind it was a small yard with a sandbox, a plastic playhouse. A cedar hedgerow marked the back of the yard, a two-stall garage attached to the house on the other side. She found an exterior door unlocked, held her breath and jerked it open, then put both hands on the weapon and cleared the space — just a purplish Honda CRV and scents of grease and oil, no one hiding anywhere.

By the time she got back to the front of the house, Broward was coming out the door. "Everything's good inside."

She could feel the pulse still working fearfully in her throat but she holstered her weapon and nodded.

* * *

Broward didn't say anything on the short drive back, just kept his hands on the wheel. She knew what he was thinking — why react so strongly when the killer had never attacked family members in more than one spot? She didn't have an answer — it had been a gut thing.

He parked near where they had initially arrived, held the crime scene tape above their heads and Kelly passed through. Cops and techs in white coveralls moved through the trees behind the playground, some heads turned as people looked at her. More residences were visible on the far side of the park, through the sparse woods.

Kelly found the Camillus detective by the marked spot where the victim's body had lain.

"I'm sorry," the detective said. "I should have sent patrol immediately." She was in her early fifties, short hair in a fashionable choppy cut, tinged silver. Bright, hazel eyes. She put out her hand. "Janet Capervay."

"Kelly Roth. I think you did fine."

"Everything okay up there?" Capervay tipped her head in the rough direction of the daycare.

"We think it's secure."

Capervay gave a nod and said, "The witness had her own kids with her and she was a basket case. I have her statement. She came in headed toward the jungle gym, thought she saw something back here — you can see the path where the victim cuts over to the other road on her walk." She gave a mournful shake of her head. "The witness said the victim was still breathing. That's what she told 911 when they asked her. She was shivering all over when I got here, looked like she was going to either need an ambulance or she was going to pass out so I had patrol take her home."

"I understand."

Capervay's gaze drifted to the people combing through the back woods of the park. "The projectile went through the skull. They're out there looking for it. And they're going along Winding Way back there and checking if anyone has a bullet in their living room. We got our hands full."

Kelly glanced at the civilians, still growing in number at the edge of the crime scene tape. "Anybody see anything? What are those people saying? Any cameras on the park?"

"No cameras on the park — in fact, the town just had a meeting two nights ago about getting them installed." Capervay pulled out a notebook and flipped a page.

"We've got one eyewitness says he saw a blue Ford Taurus, other says she saw a white Jeep Cherokee. Nothing on video. Two different people heard the shot, one thought it was a vehicle backfire. She got here about a minute after, found the body. This park here gets busy in the later afternoon, kids out of school. During the day, a few people here and there, like the witness with her two preschool kids. Fewer people though now that these park killings have been happening. According to the ER at Amherst, the victim succumbed en route and attempts to revive her were unsuccessful. Medical examiner is talking to the hospital now as they present it over the phone — I'm headed over there."

"I'd like to go with you," Kelly said.

Broward touched her arm. "Can we have a word?"

"What are you thinking?" Broward asked. "I mean, this is our guy."

"I think so."

"What's the matter?"

"It's different. It's messy. Two kids? One at school and one at daycare and he leaves them out of it — why? Even if it's a quiet time of day here, this isn't Island Park at nine p.m., or Three Mile Bay where no one notices for three hours. Multiple witnesses, right in the middle of a neighborhood."

"Two weeks since the Archers," Broward said. "They're getting closer together. He's getting bolder, a more populated area."

"He might be." She was on edge. The victim had been breathing. She'd lain there bleeding out for fifteen minutes while one of her kids sung kiddie songs at the daycare less than a mile away.

"He's changing things?" Broward asked.

"It's like he rushed. Doesn't it feel like that to you? He's getting something done, checking it off a list. If he's shooting from back over there, the parking lot near where the people are standing, that's his farthest distance yet. And it almost doesn't work — she nearly survives."

"He's got a time constraint, maybe. He only has just so long to get this one done . . ."

"What's the husband's name?"

"Brandon Spence."

"I'm going to talk to him."

* * *

She showed her ID for the front desk at Amherst. A local cop led her and Capervay down the hall towards the ER.

Brandon Spence sat in the waiting area, his head in his hands. There were family around him. Kelly hung back as Capervay waded into their heavy grief.

Capervay spoke to them for a few minutes.

"They've sent someone to pick up the children — Brandon's sister," Capervay told Kelly. "We need to give them a little space."

"I have reason to believe these murders are connected to the same perpetrator, the same gun and execution-style killing, and that the perp has communicated with at least one of the victim's husbands after the shooting, maybe more than one."

Capervay stared at her. "Jesus."

Brandon Spence looked utterly lost, shattered, stranded in a world that had become suddenly alien. But unlike the others, Spence still had children to care for. As if the killer was experimenting, trying different combinations, a malevolent angel toying with lives.

But this one could also be different for another reason. Rushed and incomplete because of a changing agenda. She'd seen it before with Billy Bath, dumping his victims in the creeks and rivers — in the beginning he'd make sure they disappeared under the water, by the end he was leaving them in just a few inches of water. Bath's killings had also gotten closer together. The Park Killer

150

was speeding up — someone else was next, possibly only days away.

"Tell you what," Capervay said quietly. "We found the casing, we're going door to door in the neighborhood. One witness saw the Jeep two or three minutes before another witness heard the shot, the Ford Taurus was seen a little closer to the shot. We're running it all down. Let me see where we get. I'll keep a close eye on him and if anyone calls him, you'll be the first to know."

They stood in the hallway with the waiting room in view.

"It can't wait." Kelly crossed to the waiting room before Capervay could stop her. "Mr. Spence? I'm Kelly Roth and I'm a behavioral analyst with the FBI."

He was staring into space, knee bouncing with nervous energy. After a moment he looked around at her. "Okay."

"I'm so sorry for your loss."

An eagerness, a hunger, crossed his features. "They won't let me see her yet. Can you let me see her?"

The family and friends watched her. Spence wanted to see his dead wife but local PD or hospital staff was keeping him out.

"I'll walk you in myself," Kelly said. "But I have some quick questions for you first. Is that all right?"

He got to his feet with some effort. "I need to see her. Please."

Kelly looked around, saw a nurse watching, and called over. "Where is Jessica Carter-Spence?"

"Ma'am . . ." Her eyes flicked to Brandon Spence and back to Kelly. "We have yet to present the official death notice. The medical examiner is still—"

"Where?"

The nurse looked at Kelly, swallowed. "In the treatment room she arrived to. Right there, number 8."

Kelly walked him down the hall, Capervay on their heels. The door was closed and Kelly stopped in front of it, then turned to Spence, put a hand on his back. "She's going to have the IV in her, tubes, anything they did in treatment will probably be as it was, but they'll have covered her in a sheet. You can't touch her, okay?"

The veins stood out on his neck as he swallowed hard. "Okay."

She opened the door before she could talk herself out of it. "Agent Roth, FBI," she announced, and the emergency nurse stepped aside. Brandon Spence reached for his wife.

Jessica Carter-Spence was covered in a white sheet. Her husband looked her over, trembling. He took the top edge of the sheet and started to draw it down and Kelly moved closer and put a gentle hand on him, stopping him just before his skin contacted hers. They'd bandaged her head and her eyes were closed, her skin already graying, lips blue.

"Oh God, oh baby . . ." Spence dropped to his knees beside the bed with his hands over the sheet on her chest and cried.

"Your wife was taking her walk," Kelly said quietly, "before she picked up your son from daycare. Was there ever a time she was with the kids alone? Did she take them to the playground after school some days?"

He stared at his wife's face. "Sometimes, yeah."

"Was she alone with them a lot?"

"Alone with them?"

"Just your wife, just Jessica and the kids. Was there a time each day she was alone with them, in the park, or somewhere that was isolated, quiet?"

"No. Not really. Just the playground."

"Mr. Spence? Have you received any texts or calls from someone claiming to have done this?"

He looked up at her. "What?"

"Has anyone contacted you saying they shot your wife?"

Spence just stared at Kelly. Then, as if a switch had been thrown somewhere inside his mind he stood up and glanced at his wife again and strode out of the room. Kelly ignored Capervay's glare as she walked past her and followed Spence back into the waiting area.

"Sherry? You got my phone?" he said.

Sherry snapped out of her own little trance and looked around, then dug through her purse. "Um, I think you left it on the . . . here it is." She held it up and Spence grabbed it from her hand and studied the screen, thumbed through his call log.

"No — no one called me." His transformation was stunning. Grief-stricken and lost one moment, full of purpose and direction the next. He gave her a direct look. "What's going on? Is someone . . . ?"

"We'll look at your phone, just to be sure," Kelly said. "I have another question. Have you ever been to the Destiny mall?"

He blinked a few times, like he was having trouble seeing, then swam back into the present. "Sure. Destiny. Yeah. Uh . . ."

"Can you remember the last time you were there?"

"I don't know."

"Please think. I know this is hard."

"I think it was about a month ago. Yeah. It was in October. There were Halloween decorations."

"Do you remember which stores you went to?"

He squinted as if he had a headache, like the sudden promise of finding out who'd killed his wife was already ebbing away. "We went to, ah . . . we took the kids . . ."

Capervay approached them. "Okay," Capervay said softly. She touched Kelly's shoulder. "Let's—"

"We went to a few places. Old Navy, CVS." He looked at the floor and nodded. "And then we ate in the food court. We talked about seeing a movie."

"Did you see a movie?"

"No. We got a mask for Charlie in CVS . . . you know a Halloween mask, Casper the Friendly Ghost. We just ended up coming home. The four of us snuggled up in the bed . . ." He suddenly lurched forward and grabbed her. His breath was sour, his eyes bloodshot. "What happened to her? What happened to my wife?"

* * *

Kelly slipped into the stairwell for privacy, called Genarro and described the situation. "We need to kick this up to a whole other gear, make it officially a multi-agency task force — and I need people, more than Blanchett — I need field agents ready to move."

"Kelly . . ."

"What?"

"You're a good researcher . . ."

She closed her eyes and bit her lower lip. She took a breath and settled. "This isn't about emotion. I just need support. There're too many people, too much to do — I'm just inching forward. And I've got solid reason to believe the unsub is using a mall as his hunting ground. We need to—"

"What's pointing at it?"

"I've got victim receipts of purchase from stores in the Destiny mall, plus admissions from the husbands that they were there, dating a month to four months prior to the murders—"

She felt the doubt in his silence.

"It's more than coincidence," she said. "I've got Archer and Payton. Brandon Spence says he was there a month ago. Blake Haig says he was followed. And there's more going on with Haig. He's been meeting with Danica Payton's brothers and they've been running their own surveillance on the mall."

"What about Archer for it — the gun?"

"I haven't had a chance to tell you — rifling came back negative. It's not Archer."

"So what are you asking?"

She swallowed. "We need to watch the mall. This is where he's picking his victims."

"Kelly we can't put up this kind of surveillance based on shopping receipts and what some sawed-off angry brothers think. Or what a bereaved husband thinks."

"The victims are carefully selected and he needs high volume and enough time."

"Why not anywhere else? A restaurant. Facebook."

"A restaurant, and he'd have to be eating there every night of the week and would draw attention. Facebook might help him a little but doesn't tell him enough about routine, doesn't show him the real people in the flesh, interacting, living their lives. And they're all going to Destiny, not Great Northern or someplace else. I checked. For fuck's sake, Jack! She was left dying in a fucking family park. Lying there, bleeding out, until someone found her. I was just in the room with her husband and he practically . . ."

Kelly collapsed against the wall and covered her mouth to keep from saying anymore.

Genarro was right. This was too much for her; she couldn't handle it. She sat at her desk, entering the minds of serial killers from a safe distance, sipping her coffee. He was out there right now killing women and children and she wanted to gut him like a fish. Take a knife and unseam him from his chest to his balls and let him spill out over the floor.

Still breathing.

Genarro was silent. "Anyone who says there isn't emotion on a case like this is lying. I know you can handle it and put it where it needs to be put. But I've actually got someone ready to go. First we had the thing with you being recognized in the press and I started looking—"

"I've established a rapport with certain people. There are witnesses for this last scene. I'm getting somewhere that—"

"Dixon has your most recent summary and psych profile. And you just said you were inching along."

"You're talking about Mark Dixon?"

"As soon as we had the thing with the phone and you thought this guy might reach out, I pulled him in, debriefed him. Dixon is set to deploy and can take the reins."

Lying there, left behind.

"Roth, you there?"

She snapped to attention. "Yeah."

"Listen to me. Listen up. Okay?"

"Okay."

"If you want to get a net around the Destiny mall . . . okay. I'll make it work. It's going to hurt and I'm going to get shouted down but I'm going to trust you. The deal is, though, you play nice. Dixon comes in, let him take over the operational aspects. Let him work the tip-line, work the surveillance, monitor the public spaces. This isn't a demotion. This frees you up to do what you do best — figure this guy out while Dixon works alongside you."

"Thank you, sir. Jack, thank you . . ."

She went back to her hotel. She'd been called in to consult, to help investigate, but there'd been another murder on her watch. It was more than she could handle, but she wasn't going to give up now. She was in this thing until the bitter end — she wouldn't stop until she caught him.

* * *

He watched the new family get into the minivan. The little boy squawked about something and the killer raised the binoculars for a better look. The toddler was upset that he didn't get to open his own door, apparently. The mother opened up and now the kid wanted to climb in by himself.

The fully-loaded grocery cart started to roll away. The older child, in an army-style jacket and a puffy hat, grabbed for it. No dice. She chased it and retrieved it, skidding on her feet. Finished with the toddler, the mother caught up, stopped the rig and the second child from getting ploughed by the pickup truck coming through the lot.

What an ordeal. Jesus, really, what a thing — a sweet little family, death or dismemberment lurking around every corner.

When they finally got rolling, he put away the binoculars and followed them out of the grocery store parking lot and onto the main road. Traffic was thick but a little better now that Thanksgiving was over. It would be crowded again when everyone piled on for Christmas.

A chaotic time of year. He knew people got depressed — from Halloween to turkey day to the big fat guy in the red suit, it was a constant build-up. While the body actually wanted to slow down in winter and conserve calories there was no such luck for modern humans, who gorged themselves with food and sweets and ran around in a consumer-crazed, overscheduled madness. It was a tough time of year, too, for cops to keep their eyes on the ball with so much going on amid family pressures and expectations.

But this family looked happy. He'd always been able to read people and he knew it when he saw it. Some folks stood out, like birds with bright plumage compared to dull pigeons.

When they pulled off into their neighborhood he followed for a while along the oak-lined streets. Long before he'd moved here, when the area was first developed, the trees had just been saplings. In another twenty or so years, they'd be mature. Things were constantly growing and changing; everything was on its way somewhere else with no continuity besides people's applied illusions. A tree which had been a seed would one day be lumber or dirt.

PART TWO

You are a network of electrical impulses.
An organic machine adapting to an environment.

CHAPTER TWELVE

Sunday, December 2

Mark Dixon rotated back from Iraq three years post-9/11. Dixon and a fresh crop of FBI recruits focused on homeland security and ran numerous ops involving the surveillance of airports and government buildings. He was seasoned. He was also tall, dark-skinned, and quietly intense.

By the end of Saturday there were half a dozen more FBI agents staying at the hotel. Eight, including Kelly and Blanchett. They'd established an operations center at a sheet metal company in Somerville, a huge Quonset hut the size of an airplane hangar with phone and internet connectivity, emptied the space out, brought in chairs and desks and phones, whiteboards and monitors. They'd opened the new, joint tip-line and gone over the call logs from the various departments. By midnight everyone went back to the hotel for four hours of sleep.

At 3 a.m., Kelly was still awake. She got up and dressed and went out into the hallway and knocked on Dixon's door.

He opened up wearing sweatpants and no shirt, hair messy, gun in hand. A .38 caliber pistol, a two-inch-barreled weapon typically used by criminal investigators and counterintelligence personnel. It was double-action — point and shoot — and it matched his personality.

"What is it? Everything okay?" He blinked a few times, stuck his head out into the hallway and looked around. "Come on in."

The hospital lights across the street gave the room an amber glow. It smelled like aftershave and leftover dinner. Kelly sat down in one of the chairs while Dixon perched on the corner of his unmade bed, set his gun on the end table and studied her. "What's on your mind?"

"I want to know what's on yours."

"We got a hundred phone calls in the first hour. Rounded up the mail — there was one plastic baggie with a glove in it someone found in a park, with a note saying we need to check it for fingerprints."

"I saw that."

"We've looked at two hundred pictures: every guy sitting alone in a car at a store. Local cops are looking twice at every white Jeep Cherokee and blue Ford Taurus. And we're going to start checking gun ranges. Local PD ran down a few but did less than stick their head in the door and look around. There's the Syracuse Pistol Club in Liverpool, the Fayetteville Manlius Rod & Gun in Manlius, The Dewitt Fish & Game Club in Jamesville. More in Bridgeport, Jordan, and Pompey." He rubbed a hand against the short hair of the back of his neck and continued, "There's a sportsmen's club in Camillus, where Jessica Carter-Spence was killed, but that's pistols only. The place in Dewitt is for skeet shooting. But there's dozens of places for rifles, including a National Shooting Preserve in Vernon. It's gonna take twenty people working around the clock for weeks to obtain subpoenas and check all the memberships and video. And in a few hours we put up surveillance on the mall, which is an even bigger undertaking."

She stayed silent.

"Can I ask why you're in my room at three a.m.?"

"Things were busy today. We never really got a chance to talk."

He studied her with wide-set, light brown eyes. "Briefing is seven a.m."

"That's not what I mean."

He sighed and sat back, spreading his hands behind him on the rumpled covers. "How do I feel about it, right? That's what you want to know. Okay, I'll level with you. I think that this much manpower, this much surveillance, all based on your psych profile? It's not where I would go with this, but orders come down and I do what I'm told to do."

"It's not based on my profile, it's based on evidence in custody and witness statements. Blake Haig wrote everything out for Orzo, signed it."

He looked at her for a moment. "I think Genarro trusts your instincts, and that's fine."

She decided that was good enough. "We need to watch Russell and Matthew Harbaugh."

"I read the report, and we will." His gaze continued to drill. "What are you really here for, Kelly?"

She took a breath. So much had been going through her mind the past few days, much of which she was fine to keep to herself, some she wished to share with a confidant. The local PD was not the group to spitball with, but Dixon, even if he served a vastly different function than her, was of the BU cloth. He was her people. "I was thinking about Charles Whitman."

"Okay. Whitman."

"During training his was one of the first profiles we looked at."

"Kelly, you know, profiles are not in my wheelhouse."

"But you remember Whitman."

"Yeah sure. Texas Tower Sniper."

"Before he killed his wife and his mother and climbed the tower at the Austin campus he wrote about having strange thoughts — he didn't understand where his anger was coming from."

Dixon just looked at her.

"He kept a journal. He wrote that if anything happened to him, he wanted an autopsy. And after the police took him down, the medical examiner cut him open and found the brain tumor pressing against his amygdala, the region of the brain that regulates aggression."

Still Dixon didn't respond.

"The Harbaughs talked about David Renz. He was on house arrest for child pornography and he tricked his ankle bracelet, went to the Great Northern Mall, found a girl and her mother and followed them. When they caught him, people said, this is a monster. He even looks like a monster — he's got that facial deformity. He was bullied as a child, he went through all these horribly painful surgeries. He had one of the worst kinds of childhood you can imagine."

"Kelly, I'm trying to follow . . ."

"There are physical correlates in the brain to psychopathology — chemical imbalances, tumors — there are neuronal knots of past trauma and abuse. Killers aren't born, they're made."

"So you want to know what made this guy."

"We thought, maybe he lost his family, but that doesn't really track. So, something else. He's got something degenerative, something in his brain. But I can't see it. I can't feel it. What it feels like is . . ."

She had it on the tip of her tongue and it slipped away.

Dixon sat up straight and smoothed his hand over the blanket. "How I see it? These guys are like bad weather. I don't care what caused it, I'm going to protect myself from it. I'm gonna build levees and reinforce the walls and next time maybe I don't get hit as hard."

The words came to her. "You find a pattern, you see something in the MO, and maybe that helps you catch him. This guy . . . I mentioned something during my presentation to PD, about lack of love. It didn't really go over. Everything I've seen, everything I've been taught — these things always come out of trauma. But today, it's a different world than Whitman's, even Billy Bath's. Loneliness is loneliness, trauma is trauma, but there's more room for isolation now. Or, it's different. The social isolation. Didn't someone say that a city was the best place to be alone? More people, more loneliness. He gets them when they're isolated because he feels isolated. He reaches out to a captive audience because he's unheard, he's unnoticed."

"He's just a man, Kelly."

After she was quiet for a few seconds she said, "We can't stop this."

"We'll find him."

"Maybe we can find *him*, maybe we can find our guy . . . but we can't stop this."

Dixon looked at her then turned his face to the window and looked out at the low sprawl of the city, the orange lights and the slice of highway, red taillights crawling. He didn't seem to know what she meant, and maybe she didn't either. But she felt it.

He kept his back to her. "Everybody gets like that. You're just thinking about it too much. Focus on what you can, what's solid."

She stood up, feeling more dread and loneliness than expected after talking to Dixon. Genarro thought she was losing objectivity, taking it too personal, probably Dixon did, too. And how was she supposed to not do that? It was supposed to be her considerable education and superior pattern-recognition saving the day. But it wasn't hubris, it was fear.

It scared her a little, the idea of some cold, academic killer — a killer who eluded categorization. Who had no motive other than some kind of darkness of the soul. But that was backwards, wasn't it? Ideas about evil and demonic possession preceded modern psychology and neuroscience. Maybe her doubts, the sense of helplessness, was a taste of what happened to every other cop eventually; a turning toward gut instinct when every rule you knew had been broken.

"There are the questions you ask," she said to herself as much as to Dixon, "did he go to public school or was he more likely home-schooled? Is he affiliated with any religious or political or racial movements? Has he been in the military? Did he have many friends growing up? But on this thing I just . . . I don't know if it matters. And maybe we're missing something that . . ." She turned toward the windows but the precise thoughts evaded her again, like trying to recapture a dream.

Dixon rose and she saw his reflection in the glass as he stood behind her. "Get some rest, Kelly. We're back at it in three and a half hours."

* * *

Local PD had been excluded from Dixon's morning briefing, it was FBI only. The men and women present held a ready look in their eyes, something she'd become accustomed to in Stafford, something she felt was missing when she'd given her own presentation to the local cops. Now it was the other way around — these people were strangers while Broward and Orzo and the rest were becoming familiar.

"Destiny mall is run by the Apex Group," Dixon said as another agent passed out printed information. "The owner and his family have been around a long time. They own a ton of property in the Syracuse area, Buffalo, New York City. The core idea behind Destiny is that it's a destination, a regional mall where people come from all over and stay a long time. There's even a hotel on the property."

Kelly read from the documents she was handed as Dixon continued. "Apex used to have its own employees for security, but as the mall increased in size and traffic they outsourced to a private security firm. There's not a lot of crime, but sometimes you get groups of kids, they tend to come up from the south side and there's been some fighting between them. As a result, children under the age of sixteen are supposed to be accompanied by an adult at all times. Apex also employs off-duty Syracuse police officers, typically on weekends. They're armed and in uniform. They've been apprised that we're a presence, and they're there if we need them."

He pointed to a bank of monitors that were currently blank. "We're working with the security firm on getting into the cameras — there are three hundred and fifty between the concourses, stores, skyway, parking garages and outer parking lots — but otherwise we're on our own.

"We'll do regular sweeps of the parking lots for a white Jeep Cherokee and blue Ford Taurus. Everybody — you have your procedure if you spot one of these vehicles. I'll let Agent Roth finish up."

She took the front. "First — and this goes without saying — we don't want a single living, breathing soul to know that we have eyes on this venue. As far as local law enforcement, only the original players have an idea we're watching it, but even they're not aware of the scale and scope. We don't want or need them to be." She gazed over the half dozen agents at the same time she pictured Joel McKenna sitting along Onondaga Lake watching the ducks. "I believe that this mall is the killer's hunting ground. He observes, selects candidates, and follows them on from there. We're looking for a male, Caucasian, in his thirties or forties. Chances are he's aware of the cameras and he could be in a baseball cap. When we factor it all in — his choice of weapon, the range he shoots from — he's not a big man. He's not overpowering his victims. He likes to keep a distance."

A male agent raised his hand. "Why do we think he's going to be there at all? I mean, now? There's been big gaps between the murders . . ."

"They're getting closer together. I think he's got multiple projects going on at once." She read the room. "And I've chosen that word because I believe it's how he sees them — as projects. He's got to go through multiple candidates before he finds just the right one; it takes time. But that's okay because he likes to keep busy. Keep moving. Like he's running out the clock, or running from something . . ."

Another agent piped up. "Let's say he tags someone he likes — a potential family — and he follows them out of the mall. There's — I don't know, five, ten acres of parking lot out there — how's he going to chase one home? He'd have to be parked in proximity, otherwise he's gonna lose them."

"That's a good question. He's not. My guess is he's getting the license plate, going online to get the owner's name and address on the reg."

Dixon cut in. "You have to pay for those license plate reports with a debit or credit card — SearchQuarry dot com or any one of those sites. So that's another way we'll come at this — go into the sites and get the user info. We can have that on hand to cross-reference any POIs."

She looked at Dixon. "Are we going to be able to isolate certain cameras, prioritize them? We should focus on certain areas, places that are family-oriented, places for kids to play."

"We're going to bring that up when we meet with Gonzalez." He got to his feet again and told the group: "That's head of security, he's meeting us there later today."

"I'd like to take point on that," Kelly said.

Dixon showed reserve. "Agent Roth I think you'll serve best remaining here, you can overview the—"

"Sir, we're at the end of one of the busiest shopping weekends of the year, the weather is lousy — tens of thousands of people will be moving through this place today — I'd like to have eyes-on. It's been years since I've spent any time there and going through it will help refresh me."

"All right," Dixon said finally. "Agent Webber goes with you."

* * *

Webber caught up to her outside the Quonset hut. "So you know this place?"

"We're burning time. We need to get there and get our eyes open." A wet snow was piling up. She opened the driver's side door and a gust of wind cranked it back on the hinges.

"I'll ride with you?"

When they arrived at the mall — like a small city unto itself — they had to park at a faraway lot and take the skyway over which fed into the second level. A giant video screen hung in the clerestory space straight ahead, slowly swiveling while it advertised winter apparel. She hadn't been here for almost a decade, and it had always been a busy place, but this was like Grand Central Station ten minutes before the workday started, even with some people probably still at church. The mall was massive, over two million square feet, four levels. It took a person about fifteen minutes to walk from one end to the other and to cover the whole thing amounted to three miles walking distance.

Webber stood beside her, taking it all in with a cop's calm readiness. His voice was almost drowned out by the din. "What now?"

Cameras in the ceiling were hidden in dark glass dome enclosures. She scanned faces, noted nearby stores — Kids R Us and Old Navy — and approached a kiosk that displayed a simple schematic of the four floors, including the new third-floor wing constructed a few years before. A

167

fifth floor, where security nested, wasn't included on the public map.

"The Spence family purchased their son a Halloween mask from the CVS," she said to Webber, "they also mentioned the food court. Haig said he'd been followed after leaving the food court. Let's start there."

"We're not going to security? Gonzalez is supposed to meet us."

"We're early. I want to get a look at a few things myself first. You want to go ahead and wait for Gonzalez, be my guest."

He ran a hand over his ginger-colored crew cut. "I'll stick with you."

The food court was second-level, other end, and he hustled to keep her pace. "You know — I admire you. You're here, on your own for days, and then there are agents everywhere."

They went around some more people, a slow-moving pair of mothers or nannies pushing huge strollers.

"More agents mean we're getting somewhere," she said.

Something made a loud pop. Webber tensed and Kelly saw his hand move inside his jacket and then saw the people laughing with a deflated balloon on the floor between them, a bunch of other balloons still aloft.

Webber's hand eased away from the grip of his hidden sidearm. "I hate all this commotion. How do people stand it?"

They reached the food court, at least a thousand people sitting at tables or lining up for fast food. A good place to sit and observe people, but chaotic. She imagined the killer desiring something a bit more controlled, like waiting for the ducks to drift into the cove. They took the escalator to the next level, walking around people as the automatic stairway ascended, and had a look at the Regal Cinema section.

This time of day was slim pickings. It was too time-constrained. How long could a lone man sit watching before he drew attention? If he wanted to blend in, it wasn't the best scenario.

Kelly moved on. "Second and third levels extend into the new addition — there's a ropes course there."

The mall had seen 30,000,000 visitors the previous year, averaging 80,000 a day. There were 6,000,000 people living in the primary trade area — an area that included Liverpool, Auburn and the other cities — almost the population of New York City. Dixon said they'd sweep the parking lots, but there were 9,500 free parking spaces and 2,000 enclosed parking spaces. An agent had guessed ten acres — the mall sat on twenty-five.

Family-friendly shops needed to be flagged, such as the CVS, with extra emphasis on shops with benches in proximity. Some of those benches were observed by cameras. For the ones that weren't in view, they'd have to post a spotter.

The impressive ropes course at the far end of the level was festooned throughout a section of the addition — the largest suspended indoor ropes course in the world. Children and their parents navigated shaky bridges and climbed jittery ladders while hooked to safety cables. Kelly leaned against the railing and watched a father help his young daughter move along a ropy catwalk above. Surrounding the course were several benches, plus a section of leather chairs on the far side of the web-like climbing ropes and bridges.

He's isolated, lonely. He people-watches in the most inconspicuous way. Sits with a shopping bag, sips a drink as he studies the people coming and going. It's the benches.

There're benches in Onondaga Park.

He wants to be heard . . .

The breadth of it hit her again — how many benches were there throughout the mall? One hundred? More? How long did she have to produce tangible results before they pulled the plug? A couple of weeks? Less? The killer could be targeting people from here. Or at the CVS. Or the Apple store. The Best Buy. He could be sitting outside a vintage clothing store or a jewelry shop or one with scented candles as likely as anywhere else.

Her phone vibrated against her hip. Blanchett.

"This is Agent Roth."

"Roth," Blanchett said, "another text just came through on Archer's phone."

She walked away from the ropes course and someone nearly collided with her, then went around with apologies. "Is it Sandaker?"

"Nope. This one was ID-blocked but I cracked that and got a number. Don't have the caller yet but I'm going to link to you, standby."

CHAPTER THIRTEEN

She stared at the text while people moved past her, parting like water around a rock.

Ted are you there?

Ted Archer had been blunt and used common texting abbreviations — Kelly decided to respond as if she was Ted. It seemed like the guy didn't know that Ted had killed himself.

She hesitated, nerves jangling, then typed: *Is this U?*

Yes it's me. Are you ready to keep going?

I'm ready.

Ten seconds passed. Slowly. Webber drew closer, looking excited. Blanchett was tracking down the number and working to pinpoint the signal as it pinged off of area towers, leaving her to deal with the caller.

The phone shook. *Where are U?*

She thought about it some more — the suicide had been successfully kept out of the papers and off the airwaves so far but Severin could've told anybody, the neighbors might have talked, family members could've come by the house. Severin's people were watching it but not around the clock — they didn't have the personnel.

The caller might know and be playing a new game. With her.

She typed anyway, *I'm home.*

She turned to Webber. "It's him. You drive."

They started running through the crowd, and the phone vibrated again.

Good. Have you given any thought to what we talked about?

She thought of Archer's notes — the nature of suffering, the nature of the mind.

Was he asking about suicide? A way to end the suffering? She played it safe: *I've thought about it.*

"Get on with Agent Blanchett," she said to Webber. "Tell me what he's seeing."

Webber jogged beside her as he went through the contacts on his phone and found the right number.

The cold hit her in the parking lot.

"He's getting it," Webber said with the phone to his ear.

They jumped in Kelly's Mazda. Webber started the engine.

There was a new text. *Good. You kill me, you will still suffer.*

A moment, then a follow-up message: *Or you choose to let them go, erase them from your mind.*

She felt a trill of hope. It sounded more and more like he meant suicide, which meant he didn't know Archer's fate. She had to keep it vague, keep it rolling, but another text popped up as Webber hooked out of the parking area and got moving toward the highway: *I have some things you need to look at. I'll send the links in a minute. They'll help get you started.*

Again she tried to think like Archer, a man alone in a house, stuffing pillows into the bed where his wife once slept, not knowing the face of the man who'd taken everything from him, or why. She wrote: *Will U still tell me who you are?*

The phone wiggled in her hands. *Yes. If you want.*

Her fingers flew. *I want that.*

He responded with a link to a YouTube video. Followed by another.

Driving them up onto the onramp of the highway and still on the phone Webber said, "We have a location."

"Tell Blanchett he sent me links. Two links."

Webber relayed it and reported Blanchett's response. "Don't open them. Could be viruses, he says." Webber was silent a moment, listening. "The cell signal originates in Fleming."

She knew it — a small town just five miles south of Auburn.

The phone vibrated again. *Now you know me.*

Webber drove fast to Fleming. She took over talking to Blanchett. "The cellular is registered to Adam Grumett, from Fleming. Is that someone we know?" he asked.

Grumett . . . familiar, from somewhere in Orzo's report. Or even talking to him for the first time at Island Park. "Tammy Haig's psychology teacher? The class she was taking?"

"Right now we've got the signal source about half a mile away from Grumett's address on Dublin Road . . . what's Bogart Wesley?"

"I don't know."

"Dixon is on the way and Cayuga County is just getting there now."

"To Grumett's address or to Bogart Wesley?"

"Bogart Wesley. I've sent it to your phone."

She studied the map and gave Webber further directions until he started to slow down and pointed. "Okay, there it is — it's a church."

The building was red brick with a steep-pitched roof attached to a belfry. Webber hit the brakes behind two Cayuga County cruisers parked in the road. They exited the vehicle with weapons drawn. They hunched down, keeping cover. Dixon arrived and got out and ran toward them.

"You call it," she said to him. They could wait for more back up, get a whole team of FBI agents in black flak jackets and high-powered rifles, or they could take it down now, with local PD assisting.

"Let's just everybody take a breath," Dixon said. "I don't see any movement." They watched the church, which sat on the corner of route 34 and Breaker Way. There was a small building beside it, probably a rectory. Across Breaker was a cornfield. The land was flat, the trees brown and scrubbed, a few red leaves pushed along the road by a gentle breeze. The phone call had come in twenty minutes ago, maybe twenty-five.

Now you know me.

The door to the church opened. The cops tensed and aimed their weapons. Kelly raised her arm in the air. "Hold! Hold it!"

The priest flattened himself against the wall, put his hands up.

"FBI!" Dixon came around the parked vehicles and moved across the front lawn with his gun pointed down. Kelly, Orzo, and four deputies followed behind him. More cars were coming, racing down 34 with their lights blazing.

* * *

They found the phone after an hour of searching, hidden beside the pipe organ in the mezzanine. The priest knew nothing about it, had seen no one suspicious, and once Dixon got through grilling him outside, they let him go.

After the rush of everything, Kelly needed a moment to think. Dixon wandered back into the church and found her sitting in one of the pews, staring up at the giant crucifix hanging above the altar.

"You all right?" He slid in beside her.

"I'm good."

Dixon held up his phone for her to see the screen. "Adam Grumett is sixty-three years old, Caucasian, divorced with three children. Not much of a criminal record except for resisting arrest during a protest in 1975. Drives a 2017 Honda Fit, burnt-orange color." He flipped to another internet page. "Psychology Department at Wells College."

In his official headshot, Grumett had gray swept-back hair, a pleasant smile. He wore glasses and dressed in a brown cardigan sweater for the picture. She took the phone from Dixon and navigated the site — Wells had a total of two professors in the department, one adjunct professor and one chair — Grumett. He taught the introductory course and advanced level courses.

Dixon retrieved his phone from her and climbed back into the aisle. "You ready?"

"Everyone needs that photo. Do they have it?"

"I mean, do we want to put it out officially?"

She jerked her head toward the church doors, indicating the deputies standing around outside, the bewildered priest talking to Detective Orzo. "Just the people who were here for now."

"All right . . ." Dixon sounded skeptical but he took a screenshot of Grumett's faculty profile page and sent it around. It struck her that with multiple departments and the FBI involved on a serial killer case, this was how they were operating — texting screenshots to one another. Maybe this was what it was actually like in the field, just people doing the best they could in the moment.

When Dixon was done he gave her another look, but she didn't move. "Something's off," she said. She could taste it in her mouth, a kind of acid on the back of her tongue.

He arched an eyebrow. "Something's off? He calls Archer's phone, vindicating your theory that this guy is contacting the husbands, or at least one of them. Maybe he does it while sitting here at a midday mass, but he's got some software on his phone indicating it's being tracked, he dumps it and runs. Now we go pick him up."

Dixon put his hands on his hips and looked around the church. Giant stained-glass windows, exposed beams crossing the cathedral ceiling, everything awash in a buttery sunlight, dust motes twinkling in the air.

"Let's talk to Orzo," she said.

Outside, Orzo spread his arms, his face crestfallen. "We looked through everything with Tammy Haig's classmates and the faculty over there at Wells College. We interviewed forty people. Grumett had a solid alibi for Tammy Haig and was able to provide phone records that showed he was on a call with one of his kids when the murder happened."

Dixon looked at Kelly. "What do you want to do?"

"Let Cayuga County pick him up, tell him it's routine, we got a few things bubbling and are just going over familiar territory to make sure we've got all our facts straight for our timeline."

Orzo asked, "We tell him we got his phone?"

"Let's see what he says. If he asks about it."

Orzo checked his watch. "I'll get the guys." He walked off toward the deputies standing around on the front lawn of the church. There was little traffic but a van had pulled off the road and there were a couple of cars over on Breaker Street, one motorist brazenly standing outside his vehicle by the edge of the cornfield, watching.

Kelly got back in the Mazda with Webber, and they followed the caravan of police vehicles away from the church, toward Adam Grumett's home.

* * *

Fleming was a picturesque little neighborhood with a tiny post office and a hardware store and not much else. Kelly was sitting with Webber a few blocks away from Grumett's residence. "Not here," Orzo said over the phone. "We're going to try the school."

She followed at a distance. Wells was five minutes away, a small liberal arts college. A red brick Gothic bell tower scraped the sky in the middle of campus. Grumett's office was in a smaller building. Kelly waited in the car as Orzo went inside, his gray trench coat flapping, two deputies on his heels. Everyone was on edge. Even if someone was pulling their strings, you never knew.

Webber drummed the seat. "This is what he does — he does the texts, leaves the phone at the church, he wants us to come find him. This is all part of a game he likes to play. I mean this guy was a teacher to the first victim? He's got a doctoral or what?"

"He does." She showed Webber her phone. "He's also an author. Five books, all on psychology and even one on psychopathology."

Webber made a low whistle, like *there you go*.

She looked into the school some more. Apparently endowment revenues were down, faculty and programs getting cut. Grumett had large class sizes and had been taking on quite a lot. Bit busy for a serial killer.

She went back to his Amazon page. "This one's called *The Myth of You*. Sounds like something from JoJo Moyes." She read aloud from the product details section. "Published by Boxcar Press, sold exclusively on Amazon . . . Here's the blurb for it: 'In his ground-breaking work, Dr Grumett illustrates how the concept of individual agency — a sense of authorship over our lives — falls apart upon inspection. What we think, what we feel, even what we do are responses to environmental factors and physiological processes we have no control over. Healing, Grumett demonstrates, is possible when we stop heaping "blame and shame" upon ourselves, but seek to understand the conditions shaping our lives.'"

"Sounds like the kind of book that'd drive most libertarians nuts," Webber said.

It also sounded familiar. If she had Archer's notes from his call, she was sure she'd find something very similar. Maybe Grumett was their guy after all.

Her phone buzzed and she took the call from Blanchett, who claimed the internet links sent to Archer's phone pointed to two separate videotaped lectures from Grumett. They'd been uploaded to YouTube by a user called Storm Brewer.

"Both lectures are from his abnormal psych class and they're pretty dry," Blanchett said. "In the first one he talks about social pressure, or something. In the other one he talks about the brain — a billion neurons, a trillion connections, yadda yadda — scientists are finding more mental states with specific, physical correlates. I wrote this one down, he says: 'Nature is patterns and anything you let win the internal argument grows. You literally build yourself that way, forming new architecture in the brain via neuronal connections.'"

It not only echoed her own study of psychosis, but for the first time she thought she might have a clearer picture of the philosophy lurking in the cryptic words of Ted Archer's caller — the nature of the mind wasn't to be a source of liberation and individual agency, but to hold us hostage.

Blanchett said, "I can send you clean links from my own computer."

"Do that."

She skimmed the first video. Webber leaned close and listened with her. Grumett said, ". . . And so we're not as much the thinker of our thoughts as we are their observer. You're not selecting thoughts from some encyclopedia in your head — more like you're in the batting box and they launch at you like mechanical pitches."

"Huh," Webber said.

"Mostly we're guided by feelings," Grumett said on screen, "and the preponderance of our feelings has to do with social concerns, social connection, status, finding a mate. Our thoughts basically serve these feelings, cluster around them. But we don't select these feelings — they're coming from modules in the brain deeply embedded by millennia of evolutionary biology. Our thoughts comport in *reaction* to them, and then our actions follow our thoughts.'"

Kelly glanced at Webber, who said, "You know what my dad told me once? He goes, 'You're not going to figure it all out, so don't bother trying.'"

"And then you hooked up with the BU."

"Sons are supposed to trouble their fathers, right?"

She called up the second video. Same Grumett, maybe a few pounds lighter, hair a little lower around his ears, otherwise another classroom lecture.

"Understanding the role of identity is key to psychotherapy. We say things like 'me,' 'myself.' And really, I think, we truly believe that we're the authors of our lives. How could we not? That ethos is everywhere in society — the hero's journey. Right, so maybe we understand that there are certain things beyond our control — the weather, or maybe an illness we have — but for the most part we believe we're responsible for everything which happens to us. But now here's the kicker — there is a huge body of scientific evidence, countless experiments in social science, which show us exactly how easily we can be tricked, how we're influenced in ways we're not cognizant of, and how easily the mind can be manipulated . . ."

The video glitched as her phone vibrated with an incoming text. *We got him*, Orzo wrote. And a minute later they were walking out with a man in a V-neck sweater and pleated pants, his expression inscrutable as Orzo showed him to the back of an unmarked police car.

* * *

When Dixon arrived at Auburn PD, Kelly told him, "I want to bring in Chief Broward."

"Why?"

"I'd actually like him to sit in place of you," Kelly said.

Dixon's silence demanded a reason.

"He's less intimidating," Kelly explained. "We want Grumett comfortable. And if he wants to, to dominate. Let's give him that chance."

Broward said he'd be there in twenty minutes. She spent the time setting up the conference room the way she wanted it while Grumett waited in the lobby. Orzo wheeled in a comfortable swivel chair from his own office that she placed at the head of the table. She set the camera on the other end, collapsing the tripod legs down to their smallest length so that the apparatus sat on the table surface. Then she opened the blinds on the windows overlooking the parking lot and some trees beyond. Orzo would sit on his right, Kelly on his left a bit further away, and Broward across from her, beside Orzo.

She was in her element now.

"All good?" Orzo was watching.

She looked over the arrangement and then up at the ceiling. "Something we can do about the lights?"

"What do you want?"

"Dimmer."

"I can take out some of the fluorescents."

Orzo got a deputy in the room with him and a step ladder and spent several minutes taking two of the fluorescent bulbs out of the ceiling and closing it all back up. Dixon and Webber were on the other side of the one-way mirror.

She briefed Broward when he got there and they brought in Grumett. Kelly directed him to sit at the head of the table. He looked older in person, his face now filled with confusion as he took his chair and placed his hands flat on the table, as if he were about to take a lie detector. Which it might come to.

"Okay," she said. "Recording is on. My name is Agent Kelly Roth, with the FBI Behavioral Analysis Unit based in Stafford, Virginia. The time now is 2:05 p.m. We're presently at the Auburn Police Department in Auburn, New York in the department conference room. If I could just have each of you identify yourselves for the purposes of the digital recording that's being made." They completed the formalities.

"Mr. Grumett, I just want to state for the record that you've been presently given no caution and I want you to understand that your being here today is voluntary — that means if you don't want to talk to us you don't have to. You've waived counsel and are here on your own. We're interviewing you as a potential witness. Do you understand that?"

"Yes."

"The reason that we're here today is because your mobile phone was found. Do you know where we found it?"

He looked at each of them and said, "I have no idea. I thought I'd misplaced my phone Friday night. I got all the way home from the school and realized I didn't have it and I went back to the school. I asked the night custodian and he said he'd already been through my classroom and office and hadn't seen it."

"What did you think?"

"I thought maybe one of the students might've taken it. I hate to say that, but I don't know what else. I retraced my steps to the parking lot — twice. I turned my car inside out."

"Your car is a 2017 Honda Fit."

"That's correct." He glanced at the men again. "Where did you say the phone was found?"

"I haven't yet."

He shifted in his seat a little. "Was my phone . . . ? I don't understand why I'm here."

"I'd like to get to that in just a minute. First I just want to reestablish a few more basics. You're a psychology professor at Wells College, is that correct?"

"Yes. Correct."

"You were previously interviewed by Auburn police on April twenty-seventh. Has anything significant about your position at the college changed since then?"

"No, I wouldn't say so. I still teach the introductory course in psychology, an abnormal psych class and an upper-level course in psychotherapy."

"I've seen some of your lectures online. Did you upload those yourself?"

"I upload the whole lectures initially, but then some of those videos get cut up and reposted by other people since they're free to distribute."

"Okay. Again, you've been previously interviewed and provided a statement in April, but we'd like to just go over things again, so some of it may feel redundant to you." She folded her hands. "Could you describe for us your relationship to Tammy Haig?"

Grumett's back was arrow straight, his hands still palms-down on the table in front of him. He made direct eye contact with Kelly. "She was my student."

"For which class?" Kelly asked.

"Introduction to Psychology."

"And when was the last time you saw her?"

"On April twenty-fifth, during my twice-a-week Intro to Pysch evening class."

"What did you do right after class that day?"

"I went into my office, checked my email, packed up and went home."

"Where you live alone."

He looked at Orzo. "I'm sorry . . . I thought you checked my phone records?"

"We did," Orzo said. "Agent Roth," he said, turning to Kelly, "as you may already know, Mr. Grumett's phone records showed that he placed a phone call to his daughter in Buffalo at eight thirty-two the evening of the twenty-fifth and the duration of the call lasted twenty-eight minutes. That's a hardwired phone, a landline."

"That's right," Grumett said. "Wasn't that when she died? Eight thirty? I was on my home phone."

"Thank you. Yes, I'm aware. As I said, we're going to cover some of the same ground. I appreciate your patience. Anything unusual about that last class? Anything out of the ordinary?"

"No."

"How did Tammy Haig seem to you? Did she seem to be under any kind of stress?"

"No. Tammy was . . . should I answer more fully or just answer yes or no?"

"I encourage you to share as much as you like."

"Tammy was an active student, lots of class participation."

"Did you have any sort of relationship with her outside of the classroom?"

"No."

Kelly let the moment linger, watching him. "Not any sort of extracurricular activity? A school club or some sort of organization, nothing?"

"No, ma'am."

"Did you ever see her in your office?"

"She came in once. She'd been out sick for two classes in one week and she wanted to catch up."

"And she couldn't just do that from the classroom? Meaning, she couldn't pick up any assignments she may have missed in class? Or online?"

"No. I had to give her the notes which were back in my office. It was five minutes, maybe less."

"Did you know Mrs. Haig was pregnant?"

Grumett swallowed. His eyes seemed to redden around the edges. "I did not."

"And you never did anything socially with her — never got a coffee, never shared a lunch in the cafeteria, anything like that."

"I didn't hurt Tammy Haig."

She waited again, giving Grumett time to reveal something. He was trembling. "Mr. Grumett, you wrote a book?"

"Yes . . . I've written more than one."

"I have a digital copy here of one called *The Myth of You*. I'm going to show it to the camera a moment." Kelly pulled her iPad from her bag and faced the screen toward the camera, revealing the cover. She listened to the sounds of the people breathing and turned her gaze back to the teacher. "Can you talk a little bit about it?"

Grumett was caught off guard, as if he hadn't expected the book. "Would you like me to summarize it?"

"Please. That would be good."

He shifted in the swivel chair, unfolded his hands and gestured with them as he spoke. "Um, the basis of that book takes concepts from neuroscience and applies them to psychotherapy. From a psychotherapy perspective, we work a lot in removing layers from a person in order to get at a root problem, and this idea that identity is somewhat illusory is . . . I'm sorry, I'm a little nervous."

"That's okay."

He sighed and then he blushed. "I'm not very good extemporaneously. That's why I write. I'm kind of an introvert."

"I understand. Me too." She looked at the digital book cover. "I haven't had a chance to read much of it yet."

"Well, you bought it, that's what matters, right?" He grinned and looked around to see if the humor was appreciated. Meeting somber gazes he said, "Sorry. A little publishing joke."

"Please continue if you can."

"Okay. Ah, well, the title was really . . . a title has to be catchy. Of course, there's a 'you,' given a certain conventional definition of that. But it's also a bit mythical, in the Joseph Campbell sense of the hero archetype. That's where I took that from. And from the perspective of neuroscience, there's no 'you' actually in your brain, no little person in there riding around. There's a million things you're not in control of — your body makes white blood cells, digests food, produces serotonin, all of these physiological processes in your body you have nothing to do with . . . should I keep going?"

"I guess I'd like to know what the aim of the book is. Besides selling a few copies." She offered a smile.

"Well, okay — so there's the broader sense that you didn't choose your circumstances, your childhood, and these can lead to opportunities and challenges all on their own. So in the book I'm taking all of this and weaving it into the psychotherapy techniques established by Freud, Jung, and Breuer. But the ultimate idea is to call us to compassion. For ourselves and for others."

Kelly glanced at the other cops. Grumett's summary seemed to have had a sedative effect on them — Orzo looked sleepy, Broward a bit lost.

She swiped the iPad screen until she was back at the book blurb and read it out: "'Healing, Grumett demonstrates, is possible when we stop heaping "blame and shame" upon ourselves, but seek to understand the conditions shaping our lives.'"

Grumett said, "Exactly. A lot of the things that a person in crisis is going through — mood disorders, chronic behaviors — when they attach their identity to these things, the problems tend to compound, because then there's shame."

"So you're taking these concepts and applying them in a therapeutic way."

He blushed again and looked at his hands. "I was a therapist for fourteen years before teaching. I encountered many people who feel shame for not living up to expectations. The idea is to look at the factors driving our thoughts and actions. And in my clinical experience, it's worked. It's worked particularly well in cases of past trauma."

This was close to home and she felt flustered for a moment.

Grumett had found his rhythm. "Once we identify the trauma we can start to let go of repressed emotions. Let go of attachment. I think I was always building toward this book — to bring these concepts to the wider public."

"You must've gotten some criticism. Some of what you're talking about could sound a bit like you're saying there's no good or evil, just bad wiring that can be fixed. Therapy, even science, maybe, instead of religion. And then on the other side I'm sure there's a neuroscientist or two out there claiming you've hijacked hard science for something softer, more philosophical."

He was warming to her, relaxing his rigid posture. "Absolutely. I'm in the crossfire. That was a concern."

"Ever had someone threaten you?"

"No . . . not threaten . . ."

"Not a student or former student, or anyone upset with your philosophy? What about online?"

"Nothing in person. I get trolled online, sure — I've gotten my share of angry emails. Some of the harshest rebukes came from veterans, from writing about the military."

Orzo seemed to come back to life. "You write about the military?"

"As an analogy, yes. The military tends to strip a person of their individuality. Shave their heads, put them in uniforms, trains them to march and respond to commands, until all that's left is a number to distinguish them. When you deconstruct a person, when you pull away gender and race and creed, what's left?"

Kelly leaned back. "But is the point of the book to have people deconstruct themselves? Is that part of the — say, process?"

He scrutinized her. "The point of the book is to call us to compassion. For ourselves, for other people . . ." Grumett broke eye contact and looked at Detective Orzo.

"I'm sorry, I thought this was about my phone? Does my book have anything to do with what happened to my phone? Or Tammy Haig?"

"Mr. Grumett," Kelly said, "I appreciate that, and we're getting there. But we're doing well here. I like talking to you about this. Let's just stick with it for one more minute."

He focused on her again. "Okay. My apology."

"This notion that we don't have much control over our lives — doesn't that risk giving certain people a kind of license for bad behavior? 'Oh, it wasn't me, it was just the things that shaped me.' And they go on to assault, or maybe to murder, and they feel blameless?"

Grumett just watched her with his eyes getting wet, like he'd been wounded. He lowered his head and made a nod. "Okay . . . I understand now."

"What do you understand?"

He lifted his face toward her. "The ethics of criminology come into play here. And that's why I'm here — because of my book. You think someone might have read and misinterpreted . . . Or you think I did something?" His gaze flitted between the other detectives. "And I'm sorry, but — where is my phone?"

"It was found at Bogart Wesley church," Kelly said.

A blank expression. "Really? I live near there."

"Do you attend that church?"

"No, I'm not . . . No, I've never been there. I drive past it all the time, but . . ." He looked away, and Kelly thought he was questioning his own sanity for a moment, wondering if he'd somehow left it there and forgotten. But he shook his head, as if answering his own question. "That makes no sense."

"Do you know anyone in that congregation?"

He glanced up, then shook his head. "Not that I can think of."

"You've said you've gotten some angry emails — how about from a religious person?"

"Sure, yes, some of those. But not anything overtly threatening. Just warning me, I guess. Some people get uncomfortable when you look too closely at these things."

"Mr. Grumett, in the neurological study of serial killers, it's been shown time and again that many are dopamine deficient, or have suffered serious childhood trauma, including sexual molestation."

Orzo interjected. "Agent Roth, I wonder if—"

"—things they never asked for — just what you're talking about here — involuntary processes, past experiences and mental illnesses." Kelly hurried to the question. "How can you condemn someone with a mental illness? It's a neurological, biological problem. Would you say so?"

"Should I have a lawyer?" Grumett asked.

"I'd just like to know what you think."

"I was miles away from Island Park when that poor girl was murdered. I have records showing that I was on the phone precisely when they said she was shot and killed. If someone took my cell phone, I have no—"

"The Park Killer has expressed ideas similar to those in your book."

"Well? He could be anyone! Many people have read my book, or seen my lectures online."

"Do you think neuroscience and psychology give violent offenders a pass?"

"No! Of course not. But I do think the ideology that criminals have just made *bad choices* is undermined by research." Grumett had gotten loud, his face red now. "And the idea that they're somehow spiritually corrupt or going against God — these are becoming archaic concepts. Research has been done. We've seen people who rate high in psychopathy have problems with brain chemistry. Does that mean I endorse violent behavior? No."

She leaned toward him. "Should we still capture violent offenders and prosecute them to the fullest extent of the law? Because I've got to tell you, I'd like to take the man who did this to Tammy Haig, Danica Payton — to Megan Archer and her ten-year-old son, and now to Jessica Carter-Spence — I'd like to put him in a chair and pull the switch."

The room went quiet and the air felt heavy, everything cramped.

"You . . ." Grumett seemed to calm himself. When he spoke again he'd reverted to his more professional demeanor. "Do I think we need to reconsider some of the ways in which we deal with violent offenders? Yes. Is there room for criminal justice reform and can we include more science in our view and treatment of violent offenders? Certainly. But does that make me a . . ." His anger came back in a flash and he pushed back from the table. "I'd like to leave now. I'm not saying anything else unless you want to charge me with something and then only with my lawyer present."

* * *

Once Grumett was gone from the building, Kelly watched the recording. She studied his body language. His eyes were on her and Orzo or he looked at the table or his hands. She was on the fence about how to judge his anxiety. He was most nervous when talking about his book. He'd displayed nervousness even before that, but being interviewed by three cops in a closed room was uncomfortable for anyone. So she'd made him comfortable, got him to elucidate, feel kinship.

Then when she'd pushed, he'd become agitated and pushed back. Also normal behavior, especially for the innocent. Rather than controlling the conversation he'd allowed himself to be led right down Kelly's path, and was triggered when his character was implicated.

"And like he said, anyone could have read that book," Orzo said later as they sat in the conference room to debrief. Dixon stood against the wall, arms folded, listening. Orzo continued, "I think he pissed someone off and they tried to incite Archer to go and kill him, thinking he was the murderer — Tammy Haig being his student is not a coincidence, because this guy is the target."

"But it leaves out the others," Kelly said.

"It does and it doesn't," Orzo said. "If maybe each of these victims were picked because there's some other target, something he's trying to get the victim's husbands to do in each case . . ."

"Or this is for our benefit — *we're* the ones he's messing with now. Grumett is a nice piece of bait for us."

They all thought about it quietly until Kelly said, "At any rate I'd like to take another look at all of his students."

"Tammy Haig was in his spring class," Orzo said. "He's got a whole new crop of fall semester students. Maybe one or two failed or something and has to retake the class but otherwise they're all new. If someone from his current class took his phone, we haven't seen any of those people that we know of."

"Then we look at anyone repeating the class."

"And he teaches multiple courses. So we're talking about a hundred, hundred and fifty people. New faces we haven't even looked at."

"Let's stick to the Intro to Psychology class she was in. I'd like to look at the student interviews from the fall. How did you do it?"

"We did it over a two-day period starting with the next class, that Friday after she was killed. Grumett let us take them one at a time. It's a two-hour class, we got half the first night, then we followed up with the rest the next week, on the Wednesday class."

"And every student enrolled was in attendance both days?"

Orzo blew out some air. "Ah, it's been a while. If memory serves, two women were absent on the Friday. The next week they showed up, we got them, and one male student was out. But we'd already got him. We got them all. Thirty-eight of them. Twenty-five women, thirteen men. Since they were all the last to see her alive, we got statements from every one of them and it's all on video."

Dixon looked at Orzo. "Grumett could have had someone place the hardline call. Did you ever contact the daughter he was talking to?"

"No. Look — you heard the guy. He pissed off the military with his book. Goes back to what I said all along: he's ex-military. He gets a hold of Grumett's book and all these ideas about people being helpless . . . whatevers. Victims of circumstance, all that. He sent links to Archer's phone! Said, *this is who I am.* He wanted Archer to go after Grumett."

"What does Tammy Haig have to do with that?" Dixon asked. "She's just a student. A pregnant young woman. She didn't write the book, she's got nothing to do with Archer."

"Because reading that shit flipped some switch in the dark part of his brain," Orzo said. "You know, I'm not saying this guy was just minding his business and knitting sweaters and then the book sent him off into psychosis. Maybe he's got PTSD. Shit, maybe he lost his family when he went over to Iraq. Or Afghanistan. Like Agent Roth said, he's had his own major loss and he's acting out. Tammy Haig happened to be the perfect first victim because of what Roth has been saying all along — her routine, her period of vulnerability, going alone to Island Park."

Orzo's brown eyes were big and watery, his color high. Everyone was getting agitated.

Calmly, Kelly asked, "What about someone auditing the psych class?"

Orzo waved his hands in the air. "I asked about that. If someone came in, sat in the back, Grumett didn't notice. Anyone could have walked in off the street."

"Well, let's make sure the phone call to his daughter is solid," Kelly said. "But I've got to tell you, I think this is a chalk outline Grumett is supposed to lie down in."

"Me too," Orzo said. "I don't see this old guy for it." He shook his head. "Sorry, but nope."

She looked at the frozen image of Grumett with his hands on the table. The text had been sent just as she and Dixon got going on the mall. Like they were getting close, and the killer threw them a red herring. If it were true, he was somehow privy to the FBI's moves. Which meant discretion was even more important.

"Check with the school," she said to Orzo, "find out if anyone could have slipped in and audited that class, check the registry, check video."

"Can do. And I can get a list of all students from each of his classes and see who drives what. And I'll check it against arrest records, too."

"That's good. But we're not looking for drunk and disorderly, I don't think. Our guy is quiet."

"He's ex-military," Orzo repeated, and flicked a look at Dixon.

Dixon paced the room. "But why point to Grumett? Why are we saying someone else pointed to him? Why can't he be our guy? Because he's older? I know I'm not the expert here, but I think Grumett looked about ready to have a heart attack. Maybe I'm out of line, but I can pretty easily picture him sitting somewhere, sipping his coffee, watching people he's going to kill."

Broward, sitting in the back, spoke up for the first time. "I don't think he was talking to Archer, or thought he was. He knows Archer is dead. This is him talking to us directly. This is him saying, 'Poor me, I'm a victim of my biology.' He's saying he can't help himself. He does this and it puts the men in the same boat — they've got this monumental thing they can't control now; they've lost their wives, their kids. Like he's preaching."

Kelly kept her eyes on the frozen image of Grumett. "Maybe he slept with her," she said.

CHAPTER FOURTEEN

Grumett had been thrown in her path. It wasn't a killer giving himself away, it was a game, and she'd felt it in her bones from the moment the priest had stepped out of the church and flattened himself against the stone wall. The real lead was still Destiny. But she and Orzo were mostly alone in their thinking.

Dixon had posted twenty-four-hour surveillance on Adam Grumett. Two agents just to track his movements. He didn't want them to tag the professor's car with a GPS, he wanted eyes-on the entire time. He'd sent Grumett's phone to the lab in Quantico. No one, not even Dixon, expected prints. But the lab would feed them information on his outgoing and incoming mobile calls for the past year.

"You suggested he could have slept with Tammy Haig," Dixon said as they rode the elevator to their hotel rooms. "His phone was at the church — the texts from this morning can be traced to it. He taught one of the victims — the first one. I mean, what more do you want?"

"Motive."

Dixon threw up his hands. "He's in love with her and she won't leave her husband and so he kills her. Motive. He's got crazy ideas about how she's a victim of her own conditioning or some shit. Motive. I mean when he calls the Archer guy he spouts lines from his book."

"From the *blurb* of his book. On the Amazon page. Anyone could have seen that or parroted that. And that's a different case you're talking about — Megan and Colton Archer. Then there's Danica Payton. Is he sleeping with all these women? I'm not seeing this tweed-wearing sixty-something college teacher going around shooting people, Mark. He's bait."

"But why him? Why throw it on him?"

"To screw us up."

"You're giving out too much credit. Like I said, our killer is just a man."

"And maybe you're not giving him enough."

Dixon fell silent after that. He shook his head. "I don't care if Grumett denies the affair — I mean he denies it, right?"

"Orzo went back to his house a half hour after the interview with Ingram and they asked him and yeah, he vehemently denies it."

"Well maybe because he teaches at a college that's out of money and he's clinging to his job by his fingernails, tenure or not. It gets out he's had an affair with a student — you know how this goes — ten more former students will come forward — this guy is done. Publisher drops his book, he resigns from teaching, he's over. Spends the rest of his life dealing with the shame he likes to write about."

She looked at her reflection in the elevator doors, then watched herself split in two when they opened. "You could be right," she said, stepping out into the hall.

Dixon looked around to make sure they were alone. "And what about Blake Haig?"

"Same problem. He's got tight alibis, and he's been out chasing down his own suspects with the Harbaugh brothers."

"Well, it sticks," Dixon said. He opened his room door. "We move all available surveillance onto the professor and watch him like a hawk."

"With two agents on Grumett, three more working the tip-line calls, local cops busy following up on Grumett's alibi and Wells students, it leaves little manpower for the Destiny watch."

Dixon only looked at her then went into his room.

She sat on her bed with her head in her hands. Took off her boots and rubbed her feet. The sleeve of her shirt was somehow torn at the elbow and she changed clothes. The day had started at 3 a.m., talking to Dixon in his room. A morning briefing, a trip to Destiny, then the texts to Archer's phone, subsequent rush to the church and interview with Adam Grumett. It was going on 7 p.m. But she couldn't rest now.

Back at the command center, Kelly read the Destiny reports from the past six hours — a dozen people flagged. Men lingering alone on a bench in a baseball cap, two of those. A man taking pictures outside the Build-A-Bear Workshop. One sitting alone by the play area for a half an hour, no kids of his own. They'd been pulled aside by Apex's security people, questioned and released, told that cops were searching for a missing man fitting their description.

Kelly shook the papers at Dixon, who'd returned half an hour after she had. "I need to have a look at these before they get cut loose."

Dixon leaned on a desk with his knuckles, reading something to himself off the computer screen and not looking at her. "You want to chase down all the tip leads, too?"

"I'm not interested in what someone thinks of their neighbor."

"Neither am I. But we've got mall security — twenty-five on staff, plus a half dozen off-duty cops, three agents, and there's no way we can cover this on our own."

"No Jeep or Taurus in the lot?"

"We've run seventeen through DMV. But we've got nothing to cross-reference. Why is our guy middle-aged? Grumett is in his sixties. And if you don't think it's him, why couldn't it be a student at Wells College? There're over two hundred thousand university students within the trade area of this place. Even that would be better than a pool of millions. Any school, any student. Give me something, Roth. Please. Because right now I might as well be watching static on a TV and looking for alien messages."

* * *

Kelly retreated back to the hotel at 11 p.m. She booted up her laptop and stuck in the thumb drive containing interviews with the students from Grumett's spring Intro to Psychology class.

Thirteen men, ages 19 to 43. The Auburn PD interview room was typical for local departments — cramped and over-bright, which was why she'd made her adjustments to the lighting and arrangement of seating. Narcissists had similar tells: they acted bored, studied their fingernails, toyed with the police, tried to dominate and direct the conversation. When she interviewed, she wanted the suspects to think that the cops were inept, all thumbs and guesses. And a seat at the head of the table made them feel important.

Orzo wasn't bad in the box, but he had a way of posturing, like most cops did, acting like he was on top of everything. She watched his first interview with a student:

"What's your major?"

"Uh, undeclared."

"What are you interested in?"

197

"You know. Lotta things." The twenty-two-year-old student looked like his main interests were pool halls and drinking.

Next. She skipped ahead.

Overweight and shy, this twenty-year-old student wanted to be a counselor someday. "In what capacity?" Orzo asked.

"Maybe high school guidance counselor. But I could also try to go all the way to Master's and get a job with the county doing licensed mental health counseling. I'm not sure yet." Kelly squinted at the grainy image and heard the shakiness in the student's voice.

"Do you remember Tammy Haig?"

"Yeah. I mean, she sat in front of me most days."

"Ever follow her home?"

Come on, Orzo. Kelly thought. *Easy, hot stuff.*

The heavyset student's flushed cheeks showed on the video. "What? No. Not at all. No."

"Where do you live?"

"Ah, I live with my parents."

Next. Kelly advanced to another digital file.

Eighteen years old, slouchy and doe-eyed, looking like he'd never seen the inside of a police station before. She watched for a minute until he inadvertently farted on camera, then excused himself and looked mortified. *Next.* Following him was a twenty-one-year-old African-American who was a bundle of nerves. *Next.* The forty-three year old was enrolled part-time and had taken the psych 101 class as a required humanities course. "Mr. Keesing," Orzo asked, "what do you do for a living?"

"I sold my business, decided to go back to school."

"What was your business?"

"Cleaning company."

"And what are you studying at Wells?"

Keesing looked fit, in a crisp white shirt and blue jeans, he acted casual, leaning back in the chair. "At the moment I'm just taking the basics. Trying different things."

"Are you a hunter?"

"Am I a hunter? No, sir. When I was little I had a BB gun. I shot at some squirrels. Does that count?"

Kelly looked closer and caught his sly smile.

Orzo continued, "Did you have any sort of relationship with Tammy Haig outside of the psychology class?"

"Huh? No."

"Did you share any other classes with her?"

"I don't think so."

"You don't think so?"

"I don't know. You got my schedule there, right? In the file? What does it say?" He brushed a thumb over his lip and acted like he was waiting for Orzo, off camera, to look.

Finally Orzo muttered, barely perceptible. "It doesn't appear so."

"All right then."

"Looking at your schedule, since you brought it up — what are you in school for?"

"To get information. To learn something practical I can put toward the next part of my life."

"And what is that? It's not psychology?"

"Nah. People spend all of this time analyzing themselves, trying to figure everything out instead of just living life. I'm not in school for that."

"I'm sorry but you still haven't said what you're in school for."

"Does it matter?" Keesing seemed to tense up. "I never finished high school. I dropped out at sixteen and got a job. By twenty I had my first business — I sold vacuum cleaners, door to door. By thirty I had my cleaning business and I ran that for twelve years, franchised it, and then sold it. I don't really ever need to work again, but I

want to do something else with my life. So I got my GED
and here I am."

"Fair enough. Did you ever see Tammy Haig with
another student outside of class?"

"Honestly I didn't really notice her until this whole
thing happened. She was just kind of . . . you know.
Whatever. Then I remembered her."

Orzo kept along his line of questioning. "Mr. Keesing,
on the night of April twenty-fifth, you left class and went
grocery shopping. You said you used a debit card and
we've asked you for your bank records to verify this, but
you have yet to turn them in."

"That's my bad, I'm sorry. I can get that over to you."

Kelly made a note beside the laptop: *Keesing, bank
records, grocery store.*

"As soon as possible," Orzo said. "We just need to
cross you off our list."

"Yeah, that's the line, right?"

Kelly's attention sharpened.

"I'm not sure I follow," Orzo said.

"You want to cross me off your list, you say. And
how are you going to do that? You'll ask me the same
questions three or four times, see if I change my answer.
You'll act like you're my friend, get me something to drink.
You ask me if I'm interested in psychology. You're poking
around, looking for the spot. If I have any ideas that are,
you know, shapes outside the cookie cutter, then I'm a
suspect, right? That's like thought police."

Kelly felt a sweat break her skin. Most people were
scared of authority but Keesing was ticking the right boxes
— egotistical, belligerent. He oozed disrespect.

"For someone uninterested in psychology, you sure
talk the talk," Orzo said.

Good for you, Orzo.

"That course is a requirement," Keesing said. "If what
you're saying is I sound intelligent, I'll take the
compliment."

"I'm glad."

"It's a basic, freshman-level course, but most if it goes right over their heads. I don't know about the youth these days. You see that video? About people being asked to name a book, just any single book, and no one can? Society is going *down*."

Orzo said something inaudible. He was sputtering out. Keesing had taken over the interview and had control of the conversation.

"What's that?" Keesing asked. "Do I own a rifle? No. You already asked if I hunted. I said no. If I don't hunt, why do I need a rifle? Unless you mean for home defense. Nah. I can take care of myself. I don't need a gun."

Kelly suddenly wanted to ride out to wherever Keesing lived and tear through his house. Find the Winchester hidden in the walls or beneath a floorboard and put this guy in chains. But she kept watching. A cocky middle-aged student didn't necessarily mean a killer.

Yet.

Orzo was still trying to recover. "Can you explain what you mean?"

"You need me to explain that? That I can take care of myself? I'm not surprised you guys don't get it." He sighed and looked at the walls. "That's the point, anyway — endless talking gets us nowhere. The things that change people are raw and real."

She didn't even hear Orzo's next question — she had her phone out, keying his number. When he answered she said, "Why haven't I heard about Taylor Keesing?"

"Keesing?"

"Yeah. The Charles Manson-type forty-something student from Tammy Haig's psychology class."

Orzo took a moment. "Keesing?"

"I'm looking at your interview with him right now. Seven months ago. You had him in the box and he's dishing it right out."

"I remember him. He checked out."

"Most cocky and aggressive suspect interview I've seen — wait, checked out how?"

"Debit card transaction. Keesing was buying beer at a store forty miles in the other direction during time of death. We pulled video from the store. We were quick enough and they still had it and Keesing was on camera."

Kelly stared at the screen, feeling her stomach sink.

"Plus, Keesing's an addict. He was all coked-up in that interview. Guy's a mess. We busted him."

She leaned in toward the laptop, studied him, looked at his clenched jaw. His fingers tapping the desk. How had she not seen it? She felt a wave of denial. "What about his phone records?"

"Yeah. We got those, too. He was between a rock and a hard place because his alibi led us to the grocery store — or I guess you'd call it a bodega — down in the city. He went in and bought a forty ounce but he'd been getting his dime bags down there. That whole place went down — drug taskforce between Syracuse and DEA."

The video continued to play on her computer.

"Right now," Kelly said, feeling edgy, "*right now* he's daring you to accuse him of murder. I mean, you *sure* about this guy? Listen to him."

She put the phone to the laptop speaker. "That's an indirect question," Keesing was saying. "All of these are indirect questions. There's only one question that you want to ask, one question that means anything. I'm just trying to get you to come to the point so I can go home."

She put the phone back to her ear. "I mean . . ."

"I wish I could tell you otherwise, but you're not listening. Keesing couldn't have done Haig, and he couldn't have done Payton or any of the other murders after Haig either — he's been in county for the last seven months waiting for his day in court," Orzo said.

She slammed the laptop closed. "Fuck."

"You probably can't see it on the video," Orzo said, "but he was sweating like a pig."

She stood up abruptly and knocked the desk chair backwards onto the hotel room floor. "That's why I want to do these in person."

Calm down. Keep it together.

Orzo picked up on her frustration. "Not one of those spring semester students admitted to owning a hunting rifle. And I checked since this morning — not one of them owns a Jeep Cherokee or a Ford Taurus. Nobody on the new list, either. But I'm only about halfway through it. And nobody failed and took the class again."

"It's not Grumett. And if it's no one from his spring class, could still be any student in that school. Someone who shared other classes with her."

"Yeah, maybe . . ."

She could hear it in Orzo's voice. He was humoring her because she was reaching. She stared at the closed laptop, thinking until a noise on the phone distracted her. "What's that sound?"

"Sorry. Got an impacted molar. I can't seem to stop poking at it."

"The press is all over us now. Someone took a cell pic of all of us outside the church like it was Waco and it's gone viral."

"I can see why you liked Keesing. Unmarried, no kids, financially independent."

"He was just high."

"No, you saw it — he was enjoying himself. Right up until I asked him about the purpose of his education or something then he went off on this jag about being a self-starter. You know who he reminded me of, a little bit — Billy Bath."

"You worked that case?"

"I kept up on it like everybody else did. Some guys you can just tell, they've got this hate in them. I don't think it's directed at any one type of person or group. I'm Mexican-American, so I know all about that. I remember Bath coming out, they did the perp walk with him, and he's not hidden under his jacket, he's got his head up, and there's just that poison in his eyes. You were probably a kid then."

"Yeah. Fourteen." She took a deep breath, let it out slow. She needed to relax. "You got kids, Orzo?"

"All grown up now. Genevieve teaches second grade over in Rockland County."

"That's a beautiful name."

"Rockland? Yeah, it's got a ring to it."

Kelly laughed. Talking to Orzo was calming.

"My wife is French-Canadian — Eugenie." He pronounced it *ooh-shenny*. "I call her Jeannie. She's the one made the appointment for me to go see the dentist, figure out this thing in my mouth."

"Probably a good idea."

He grew wistful. "I used to hate going to work when they were little. We had our kids quick — bang-bang — two years apart. In the morning they'd be sitting around the kitchen table, Genevieve would spill her orange juice and Sasha would walk in it. Or she'd hide beneath the table and poop in her diaper. Don't ever tell her I said that. But you'd lose track of her for a minute and look under the table and she's got this look of concentration on her face because she's taking a big dump right there."

Kelly laughed harder, got up from the bed and opened the mini-fridge. She pulled out a bottle of water and drank. The laughter died in her throat when she thought about the killer, choosing young families. Families just starting out in the way Orzo described — full of potential and curiosity. But also busy, frayed, emotional. By the time her brother Rick had a job and she and Raquel were busy with friends and boys, her father's melancholy had rooted down. Whole meals would pass without a word from him. He'd eat his food and drop his plate in the sink and retire to his study for most of, if not the rest of, the evening. He'd been in that study when the heart attack happened.

Striking them down in their prime, maybe that was the killer's objective. Take a family full of promise, who displayed happiness and hope, and snuff them out. Leave the husband shattered and bereft, and then go to work on him. Drive him to suicide. Turn him into an unfeeling robot like Haig or a single parent like Spence. Make him an exile like Roger Payton.

She wanted to climb inside his mind to see what he wanted, where he was going with this. Because she had the sense — from the beginning really — that he had a plan, a purpose. Whether Dixon agreed or not, this was more than pathological need, more than faulty wiring. This guy had something to say; he was just about bursting at the seams with it. Grumett wasn't just misdirection, no — she thought the killer really believed in the professor's ideas, or at least thought he did.

After ending the call with Orzo she plugged in her speakers and opened iTunes, flopped onto the bed and let the music wash over her as she went over the case. Something they'd drilled into her at Quantico: always go back and review. Old things take on new meaning.

Number one, contact from the killer: Blanchett's gear remained hooked up to Ted Archer's phone but there'd been no more calls, and there probably wouldn't be. He'd stolen Grumett's phone and the cops had jumped for it. Archer's suicide wasn't public, so the killer had been watching the house. Maybe surveilling it — he didn't need to know about the FBI putting a net around Destiny, only that they had the phone. He was improvising as events developed.

Dixon was monitoring persons of interest. Agents were sifting through the gun ranges, following tips from the hotline. The bodies of the victims had been taken apart and put back together, the crime scenes scoured for physical evidence, the projectiles analyzed.

Maybe Cal Wagner didn't think he was military, or an expert marksman, but even with a scope the killer was pretty accurate. It made her think of safari hunters, big game hunters who went to Africa to shoot elephants and tigers from the safety of their Range Rovers. It also reinforced the idea that he'd taken a bigger chance on Jessica Carter-Spence, his furthest shot placement yet, like he was making do with unideal circumstances, finishing one task in order to move on to another. He'd almost missed his mark, too; another millimeter or two and the bullet might've just traveled around outside Jessica's skull, leaving her alive.

Kelly mentally auditioned a new psych profile: you didn't have to be ex-military to be a gun nut with surveillance capabilities. There were enough doomsday-preppers in the States and the FBI had a list of over 500 militia groups. Plenty of men had the means to carry out strategic serial killings with a professional's touch. The shooter in Las Vegas had packed an arsenal into his hotel room and fired on a crowd of thousands like a sniper. Teenaged gunmen walked into schools with little more than hunting and target-shooting experience. Or even video games.

The killer had sat in a car to shoot his victims. According to the medical reports, each victim was killed instantly except for Jessica, who'd lived for another fifteen minutes. The bullet casing from the projectile which eventually killed her had been found thirty yards away from her body, plus the additional twenty yards from the parking lot — he'd retrieved the casing and thrown it into the park. Forensics were quick on the scene and bagged it before press arrived.

Casings had been left behind at all the scenes. They meant something. Either to taunt authorities or they held some other function.

Maybe to prove to the men he was speaking to that he was the real killer?

She sat up in bed, feeling her heart race.

Probably one of the things the killer wanted most was to be legitimized. And he needed to be, if his manipulation of the men and his poisonous words could take real effect. Knowing something the public didn't proved he was who he said.

But had he told Archer about the casing? If he'd told Archer then Archer would have relayed that to the cops, who were doubting his story. Maybe that *was* the point then, after all — torture Archer by not giving him proof, but igniting his blind need for closure, for blood. The killer could have also wanted to see what Archer would do, see if he'd involve police.

If she was right, he'd called the other men — Blake Haig first, then Roger Payton.

She had no proof of that, though, and neither of them were coming forward with it.

She called Dixon and told him she wanted to talk to Roger Payton.

"I think it's a good idea you talk to him. Who do you want to take with you?"

"Broward."

"The chief? You two have really taken a shine to each other."

"He knows Payton personally. And Broward was the one to fire the detective — Faber — so maybe that gives him a little leverage. Maybe Payton will talk to us. We'll go tomorrow."

"Sounds fun. Talk to you in the morning."

* * *

The killer watched a few videos on YouTube before he clicked on the Channel Five coverage of Kelly Roth coming out of the police station in Liverpool and the intrepid reporter who wouldn't let her off the hook.

The reporter had a round, pixie-like face and big fuck-me eyes. "Can you confirm an FBI presence here in Liverpool?"

Roth had harder features — still pretty though. "I am an FBI agent."

"Is the FBI here because of a serial killer? Are you linking the Payton murder with the Archers and Tammy Haig? Is the Park Killer official?"

"As I said, we'll have all that information for you soon."

Pretty, sure — even looked like Tammy a little bit — but full of shit. Typical FBI, typical cop, placating the public. He paused the video and touched the screen, running his fingers across her face. Something about her though. He stared into her eyes as she looked off camera — calculating her escape, probably, or maybe seeing someone or something she recognized — and let himself enjoy what he knew about her, what a little bit of Google-searching had yielded without much effort at all.

A father dead when she was in her teens. That was one thing. An attempted rape not long after — that was another. Driven into the life of an FBI agent, probably by a need for control, a need to make sense of a world that had become alien and hostile in her youth.

She didn't seem to ever have a man with her. She was alone in the universe, and she made the perfect match for him. They were the same. Fathers gone, mothers distant, abandoned to an indifferent world. The realization of that was so deep as to be arousing — she was the ultimate result, the effect of his cause, of events *he* had set in motion. Like a message in a bottle, and now he was found.

He couldn't say when for sure he had started thinking like this. The first couple of eye-opening books in his youth had felt like secrets; he was coming to understand what almost no one else did.

All of these reporters and FBI agents and local police all running around, these medical examiners and forensic technicians and doctors and lawyers and whoever the fuck else cashed in on these kinds of things, they were all buzzing with ideas *he* had ignited. And just like everyone else on the face of the planet, each of them was ignorantly unaware of that fact, blithely believing that they were getting up each morning and deciding about their day, authoring their lives, being the heroes of those stories.

He switched to another website and read the headline from the *Syracuse Herald*. "Park Killer Strikes Again." The article featured pictures of the playground and the people standing back behind the crime scene tape and police gathered around by the trees. All of those people there because of an external event setting them in motion. They would never forget it, either — for the rest of their lives they'd have that memory of the Park Killer, they'd look back on The Day The Woman Lay Dead Behind The Swing-Set, they'd be forever affected and influenced by it.

This whole thing probably meant he had a screw loose somewhere, there was that. And not just some cross-threaded bolt or bad switch, but major problems with his internal fuse, a busted surge arrester and he was unable to stop hunting and killing and disintegrating the people who were left behind. But nothing was more pathological than believing in your own free will, as if you lived in a vacuum, as if nothing and no one affected you beyond something you could brush off, choose to ignore.

Cause and effect. This was cause and effect, and it was set out when time began. From that very first spark of all — once things had started everything in motion, nothing would ever stop until it all ran its course. You couldn't mess with that, no one could, not even him.

A little later, then, he went to the range. He took the first earplug and pinched it between his thumb and forefinger and squeezed and rolled it and then stuck it in his right ear. While it expanded to fill his ear canal he took the other plug and squeezed it the same way and put it in his ear. He waited, swiveling his head, until the world of sound closed down to a hushed rumble. Then he pulled the earmuffs out of his bag and spread them and lowered them down over his head and gradually let go so that the tension held them against his ears. Now there was nothing. He tapped the right earmuff with his middle finger. Like someone tapping on a dock when you were six feet down in the water.

Good — you couldn't be too careful about that sharp report from the Winchester. Going off like that next to your ear, no protection — too many of the old guys had tinnitus.

And when he was done he packed up his rifle in the rifle case and walked out. Coming in was a guy he recognized who said hello and he raised a hand and said to him, "Howdy," and then he kept going out to his white Jeep Cherokee and got in it.

CHAPTER FIFTEEN

Monday, December 3

The dream was the same — she lay helpless on the ground, a yellow puddle near her head that smelled of garbage and copper, grit beneath her grasping fingertips, a rectangular cut of gray sky above. Then the people materialized, surrounding her, looking down at her, but this time their normally blurred faces took the features of Orzo, Dixon, Broward. Even Webber watched and smoked and laughed.

When Kelly woke up the room was dark, a pale violet dawn tinging the windows. She rose and showered with the dream still buzzing in her mind.

She strapped on her belt and gun and holster and drove to the command center in Somerville. The only other agent there at the early hour was Webber, sitting by the monitors, head nodding in a doze.

Kelly sat down beside him. "How we doing?"

He snorted awake. "Roth." He blinked his eyes. "G'morning."

She checked her emails and found one from Orzo on Adam Grumett and turned back to Webber. "Heard from Dixon yet?"

"Uh . . . I don't think he's back."

"I knocked on his door and there was no answer. Back? From the hotel?"

"Back from . . ." Webber looked nervous. He pointed to the monitors which cycled through the various security cameras in the mall — this time of day there were metal grates drawn over the storefronts, a custodian polishing a floor on level three with one of those big riding buffer machines. "Dixon took a call last night," Webber said. "Security stopped a guy about one a.m., coming out of the movies. A guy alone and they thought he was carrying."

She stood up, unsnapped her phone and dialed Dixon.

"Kelly," he said after a few rings. The noise in the background sounded like he was driving.

"What happened?"

"Some widower going to the movies to see an action flick. He's got a concealed carry permit, no record, alibis for most of the shootings. He couldn't think back to April or August, but he's not our guy. We let him go."

"What was he wearing?"

"Blue jeans, sweatshirt. Baseball cap for the New York Mets."

"I'd like to know if—"

"Listen, we get someone who's hot and bring him in, you get him in the box, and if there's something that can stick, you make it stick. That's your end. My end is to run around in the middle of the night harassing law-abiding citizens. You want to switch?"

She ran a hand over her face and looked around the Quonset hut at all the desks and computers and monitors. Other agents were filtering in and the phones were starting to ring with tips on the hotline. Running a command center like this was costing tens of thousands of dollars a day. Neither she nor Dixon were bean-counters, but the expense of it loomed. "I want to talk to you," she said.

"You got something?"

"How far out are you?"

"I need to get something to eat, take a shower. Haven't been to my room since yesterday. What's on your mind?"

"Adam Grumett's got office hours for two of the other murders — the two Friday afternoons. I'm looking at the email from Orzo and Ingram right now. They just got through each time of death. Sometimes Grumett comes in again on weekends, catch up on things. He claims the Saturday Danica Payton was killed he was down visiting his daughter and she's corroborated."

"Fine. So Grumett is out."

"I just wanted you to know."

"Okay." Dixon was acting cold, angry with her.

She sighed. "I'll talk to you in a bit."

Before he could say anything else, she hung up. She moved away from Webber and phoned Broward.

"Hey — was just going to get in touch with you," he said.

"Something happen?"

"No, I mean I was going to check in, see how you're doing."

"Medical records on all of the husbands. Anything there?"

"I mean not without a subpoena. Faber tried with Payton but the judge wouldn't lift the doctor-client privilege. What are we looking for?"

"Health problems, any pills or prescriptions."

"Roger Payton had health problems."

"Like what?"

She heard Broward moving around. "I mean he's out of shape, he's older. I know he's got high blood pressure. And if you take a look at it — you know, I've been wanting to say this for a while — Danica Payton is the only victim without children. Jessica Carter-Spence left behind two, Megan Archer was killed with her son, Tammy Haig was pregnant. Danica Payton — no kids."

"And what does that say to you?"

"Well, to be honest, maybe Payton was unable to perform in that department."

"You have anything that could help show that?"

"No, not without the medical stuff. But it's . . . I mean, for what it's worth, there's always been a little bit of talk about that. Just people in the area that knew them."

"I appreciate it. Give me a little bit and I'll get back with you."

She went through the police report on Blake Haig. Medically there was nothing but a past work injury — a laceration on his hand he'd had stitched up, paid for by Xylem.

Ted Archer had been in fine physical shape, though she knew Severin questioned his mental health. There was no indication of him seeing a therapist or being medicated.

Outside, sitting in the Mazda, she called Broward again. "Where is everything at with Detective Faber?"

"Well, he resigned, but Internal Affairs still have to close their books on it. He'll face charges if it looks like he tried to coerce a confession with falsified evidence. The last I talked to him he was sitting at home, not doing much of anything."

"I'm going to talk to him about Roger Payton."

"Well, let me apologize to you in advance; he's on the cranky side."

"Thanks. Can you meet me at The Post? I'll text you when I'm done with Faber — shouldn't be long."

* * *

She drove with the windows down, putting her hand out the window to feel the raindrops, letting them cover the windshield for a time before she turned on the wipers, thinking about Billy Bath.

Are you truly a good person, or are you merely afraid? Maybe it's men with heroic courage who eschew society to become outlaws while cowards follow the rules.

Bath liked to write about his exploits killing prostitutes. He also thought he was enlightened.

I'm not a maniac, I'm what the kids call 'woke.' Once I realized the illusion, I was able to transcend any social constraints of civilized life. I learned what a gun truly was — the ultimate equalizer. The perfect tool to crack open the façade of society.

She wanted the killer to have a reason. A history of abuse. A brain tumor. Maybe, like Roger Payton, trouble performing sexually. She didn't want him to be like Billy Bath, from a middleclass suburb with two loving parents.

She let the rain come in the open window and spit against her face, until she pulled away and rolled up the window.

Chittenango was quaint, with squat brick buildings and a dwindling population, the birthplace of L. Frank Baum, of *Wizard of Oz* fame. Fitting. Oz never wanted people to see who was behind the curtain, pulling the levers. That was her job — to look.

Faber lived on Lake Street, which sat on the edge of Sullivan Park. Kelly got out of the Mazda and stood looking across the street at the park. It could've been farmland, with a vast green lawn, a forest of maples and birch over a hundred yards away. Faber's house was small, yellow, with a pickup truck in the driveway. She walked up to the front door and knocked and about two seconds later someone spread the blinds and peered out, like he'd heard her pull up. Then the door opened.

He was in his late fifties, dressed in sweatpants and a Syracuse Orangemen hooded sweatshirt. "Help you?"

She could hear a TV burbling in the background and smelled cigars. "I'm Agent Kelly Roth with the FBI."

"Yeah, I know." His voice was gravelly, a smoker's. She recognized the look in his eyes, the wary suspicion of an older cop.

"Can I come in?"

He looked past her, as if expecting more company. "I guess."

Faber muted the TV. He sat in an upright easy chair and didn't offer her a seat or a drink or anything else.

"I'd like to talk to you about Roger Payton," she said.

"On the record?"

"Just an informal chat. One law enforcement agent to another."

"My union rep and lawyer told me to keep my mouth shut until the hearing. I don't know what I can do for you."

"You have my word it will travel no further than this room."

He gave her a look that lasted a second past comfortable. It looked like he hadn't shaved in a few days. "How long you been with the FBI?"

"Eight years, all in."

"You're not used to the field, though." The air grew heavy with aggression.

"I'm happy to discuss my career with you."

"But," he said.

"But there is someone out there killing women and children and I want to stop them. Can you help me?"

He looked at her some more, and then he laughed. Reaching down, he grabbed the handle of the recliner and pushed himself back and laughed some more.

If he wanted to be an asshole first, then she had to wait it out. She thought he had something to offer.

He squinted at her. "They teach you that at the academy?"

"I don't know what you mean."

"That sucking up. 'Can you help me?'"

"I'm asking if you think you can help. There's nothing more to it."

The humor drained from him, he snapped the leg-rest back into the chair, and jabbed a finger at her. "I was doing my job. Before all of this politically correct bullshit came into play, I used to be pretty good at it, too."

No matter how she reacted — calm and collected or offended and emotional — Faber wouldn't like it, but she stayed measured. "Broward said you were a good detective."

"Oh did he? Was that what he said?" He made a dismissive sound with his lips. "Broward. Another one for the cause." He looked at her again, his eyes hooded.

As long as he was talking, maybe she'd get somewhere. "The cause?"

He was ready for it: "The politically-correct, nanny-state bullshit. Sorry, but the feminist manifesto. We all have to be nice and hold hands now. There's someone out there killing women and children? Oh yeah? That right? We gonna catch him by gathering around and doing therapy?" He sat forward. "You know, you've got all this psychologizing of criminals now. What you do. I saw you in the paper — Behavioral Analysis Unit. Guy takes a .30-30, gets out of his car, pops a woman in the back of the head while she's watching the ducks. You want to analyze that? Here you go: Either it's the husband, or it's a lover, or it's some random psycho and *why* he did it doesn't fucking matter."

"You said the killer got out of the car . . ."

Something passed over his features. "Yeah. He was close. I always said he got out of his car. Ballistics corroborated it."

"Ballistics didn't corroborate it, actually. And even if he had gotten out — why didn't she turn around? Why didn't she move away when a strange man was walking toward her with a gun? No drugs in her system, she wasn't intoxicated — her BAC was .06. If it's Payton, she's going to look, see her husband coming. Or anyone else — someone he hired, someone random — they get out, they walk toward her, she's not going to just stand there."

"Because she knew him."

"She knew him?"

Faber looked away. He pulled a cigar out of the humidor beside the recliner and lit it.

"You thought Payton had hired someone," Kelly said.

"I never said that. I was poking at the guy, but I never said he hired someone. I never thought he did, not really. The whole thing got twisted around. I tried to lead him, yeah. I tried to get him to admit it, but — what? I can't do my job now? I think a guy is good for it, I'm going to get him to try and cop to it, plain and simple. Sometimes blood, DNA, you don't have those things. We didn't have those things. I needed a confession."

"But you *did* think he was in contact with someone. If not someone he'd hired to kill his wife then someone else. Correct?"

He just stared at her, a nerve firing beneath his right eye. He took a drag and squinted in the smoke. "I got pulled off the case."

"Is that a yes or a no?"

"That's a fuck you."

She cleared her throat, stood her ground. "Maybe I need to remind you—"

"Yeah, yeah, yeah. So arrest me. Yeah, Roger was talking with someone."

She felt a release of something, like a pinch letting go in the back of her neck. "Do you know who the person was?"

"No."

"How do you know? What's your proof?"

"He told me."

"Roger Payton told you *someone* was talking to him. Before or after the murder?"

"That's what I said. After."

"When, after?"

"When I interviewed him."

"It's on record?"

"No. It comes after the part he asked me to stop recording. Didn't you watch the interviews?"

"They go on for almost nine hours. I didn't watch all of it. I shut it off when I sensed coercion."

He looked like he wanted to snap at her again, but it passed, and he chuckled and blew smoke.

"What did he say?"

"Hey, listen. Guy like that — you want to figure him out? He didn't know whether he was coming or going."

"In your opinion, did Payton have some underlying condition? Did you find anything to suggest he was ill, mentally or physically?"

Faber waved a hand. "Well, he was a drunk for years, how about that? But none of that matters anyway, just an excuse. If he lost his shit it was afterward, and it was the guilt. Because he says to me, he says that someone talked to him. For all I know he's talking about a voice in his head, or he's already angling for an insanity plea. See what I'm saying? *That's* the end result of all this whiny, hand-holding sensitivity training — stone cold killers walking free because they act like a victim themselves. So? That's his move, and I play right back at him. I tell him I know he did it and that he was too much of a pussy to pull the trigger himself so he had someone do it for him." Faber grunted to himself and stared off into the room, sniffed and wiped at his face.

"Maybe this, though — and I'm just playing my own hand here — maybe you thought it was Payton and you looked for evidence to support that instead of the evidence leading you."

His eye was twitching. "Yeah? Well you weren't there during the interview, were you?"

"He doesn't own a rifle. Twenty people confirmed he was at work at the time of her death. I came here to ask what you knew about his physical and mental health prior to the murder, and you've answered, so thank you."

Faber glared at her. "You can look at the video all you want but you didn't *feel* that room. I bluffed him that I had information he'd hired someone to kill her and the temperature went up ten degrees. I'm sweating, he's sweating, right down to the balls. Then he asks me to shut the camera off. I'm thinking, here we go — payday. I shut it down, he tells me that someone called him. I says, someone called you? He says, yeah — they told him that if he listened to them, the whole thing would go away. The pain would go away. So that's when I'm thinking, okay, this guy is already angling for an insanity defense. I turn the camera back on and ask him to repeat what he's said but he just goes quiet on me. And by this time — you know, we got all of these rules about how you can't grill a suspect for too long, all of this ACLU bullshit, so I let him go. And I never got a chance to follow that up because I got pulled off the fucking case. Meanwhile, Roger Payton goes up to his little cabin in wherever the fuck it is."

"You told Broward what he said?"

"I told Broward I thought Roger Payton was trying to pull a fast one."

"Did you look at his phone?"

"'Course I did — there wasn't anything on his phone."

"Maybe he deleted it."

"Maybe he made the whole thing up. Anyway, then Broward reviewed the tapes and called in the IAB and had them investigate me. This is what I'm telling you — cops aren't even allowed to do their jobs anymore."

Faber's eye kept twitching. He was lying about something, maybe covering his own ass. "You ask me, the whole thing was a big show for Broward because he's running this little department and can't handle the case, there's no one in cuffs, those brothers of hers keep turning up and demanding a suspect and so he throws me under the bus. Period. Throws me right under the bus. Like I said, Broward's just another hand-holder, just wants to keep the pressure off of himself."

"I've spent some time with Chief Broward and I don't think he'd make decisions based on social pressure."

"Oh — you don't? In all your books, they don't teach you about social pressure? Even I know that people fear social awkwardness more than they fear actual physical pain. Even I know that."

"Not cops." But she didn't believe her own words.

* * *

Broward was sitting outside The Trading Post in his Liverpool police car. She knocked on the window and he looked up from his phone and smiled. She was thinking about him hiding something Faber did or said during the Roger Payton interviews.

Payton's restaurant manager sat at the bar hunched over some paperwork and a coffee within arm's reach. She climbed down from the bar stool as they approached. "You again."

"Hey, Eileen. Can we get into Roger's office, please?"

A bus boy swept the dining room around tables with overturned chairs. Pots and pans clashed in the kitchen. Eileen took them into the back and pushed open a door to a cramped room with no windows. She moved some things around to clear a path to Payton's desk. "Roger hasn't been here in a while. Excuse the mess."

"Thanks Eileen," Broward said. "Can you stick close in case we need anything?"

"Uh, sure." She pulled the door shut.

Broward sat behind Payton's desk. A few boxes were filled with framed pictures. There were oily marks on the walls where the pictures once hung.

"So what are we doing here?" Broward said.

"I think Payton was telling Faber the truth. I think he was contacted by someone, just like Archer."

221

He seemed disappointed. "I thought you wanted to take a run at him. That's why you're asking me about his health? Like I said on the phone, how it looks — Danica Payton is the only victim without kids."

"Were they trying? In Faber's report he says he asked Danica's mother and she said no."

"Some other family thought maybe. The brothers thought she was."

"I doubt she's going to talk to her brothers about something like that."

Broward shrugged and turned his head.

Kelly looked around some more at the filing boxes and stacks of papers filling the room. "Your County MCU took most of this into evidence, gave most of it back, finding no indication that Payton's business was in the red, or he had any financial motive. And her life insurance policy wasn't huge, either."

Broward fixed her with a look. "Yeah but he ran."

"He could have run to escape the TV crews and newspapers. And her brothers, constantly showing up, asking him questions. And with all due respect, you let him go. You couldn't have liked him for it too much."

He raised his arms. "What am I going to do?"

"You get the state police, you have him arrested when you have something to charge him with. But you didn't, and you still don't, and that's my point."

Broward looked hurt. "So what are we doing here if you think he's innocent? You're the one who called me, Kelly. Asking about Payton. I thought maybe because of the childless thing . . ."

"I think he's been in touch with the killer just like I said from the beginning."

Broward seemed to decide something. It was good enough for him to get to Payton even if they were coming at it from different angles. "So let's go. I'll go with you."

"You and me? Don't you have a department to run?"

"I have capable officers. Just give me an hour to clear the deck."

CHAPTER SIXTEEN

Broward was ready at 4 p.m. and they left Liverpool, headed for the Adirondacks. Dixon knew where she was going and had state police on alert in case anything jumped off. Even though the state police reported that Payton had been at his cabin every day for the past two weeks, he could have been using a second vehicle to get around if he was up to something. And there'd been only one victim since Payton had fled to Green Pond — Jessica Carter-Spence, so it was possible Payton had slipped the casual surveillance for just that one event.

They drove into the silvery evening, turned at the junction for 81 and continued north.

Kelly turned on the stereo and found a radio station.

Broward listened. "You're a country girl? I wouldn't have thought it. What is this? Waylon Jennings?"

"I never listened to Tori Amos."

"I'm still in the same Dave Matthews Band phase. Sorry."

She felt herself grinning, and realized it was mostly out of relief Broward wasn't still stewing about her comments in Payton's office.

They fell into silence and the odometer ticked off the miles. As they came into Watertown Kelly said, "This is where William Bath was born."

"Billy Bath? He's not from the 'Cuse?"

"He was twenty-seven when he killed a young boy and a girl here. He took a plea bargain, did twelve years for one charge of manslaughter and got paroled. He stayed in the state like he was supposed to but relocated to Syracuse."

"I didn't know that. Jesus, bet the parole board caught hell for that one. He wound up convicted of eleven more, was that it?"

"Mostly street workers. Never really had anything we could point to, no real reason for his crimes. And he writes to us."

"Writes to you?"

"To the FBI. Like he wants to be heard."

"What's he write?"

"It's similar in some ways to the stuff our killer is saying. The stuff in Grumett's book. That's there's no real identity, no true free will."

"So he's a socialist."

Kelly's smile quickly faded. "Only thing you could say stood out about Bath was that he was tall, six foot five. That's why everyone called him Billy Bath — it sounds like a basketball player, I guess. His real name is Clarence William Bath." She turned on her headlights now that it was full dark.

Broward thought about it. "So when he got inside, he starts writing — writes this manifesto about seeing beyond the pale, seeing the falseness of society. Sounds like our guy. Yeah. Has this need to preach. These killings are his sermons. What got Bath into it? There had to be something that set him off. Maybe you just never found it."

Or, maybe Severin, Faber, even agent Webber, were right — the why didn't matter. "Bath was narcissistic.

Hence the writing. But where that narcissism came from . . . born with it? A reaction to something that's too hard to see? Anyway, if there's a reason our guy is espousing the ideas found in Grumett's book it's because he's identifying with it. Using it almost like a religious text."

"A religious text . . ."

"I remember a lot of Bath's ideas. He says if you see yourself as an individual, if you identify with a group or cause of an idea, then you become resistant to change. He says it's the source of all conflict in the world. That identity is the true Original Sin. Eve became conscious when she ate the apple, and so began suffering."

"Poetic," Broward said. "So he's saving all of us, huh? And if we find a copy of Grumett's book in Payton's cabin, dog-eared and underlined? What then?"

"Then I call Dixon and we treat Payton as a threat and get state police Troop B behind us and we arrest him."

He was quiet a moment. "You go around with all this in your head?"

"Comes with the job."

"And you want to know why these killers do what they do."

She thought about her answer but didn't speak for a while. "To be honest I think it helps me to help others."

But she hadn't been able to help Jessica Carter-Spence.

And there was someone else he was after now — this killer was always working. The thought made her feel sick.

"I need to pull over."

She pulled off onto the shoulder and got out in the dark. A light snow was drifting down from a starless, black sky, revealed in the cone of headlights stabbing out into the cloak of darkness.

She stretched her legs and took in the fresh cold air.

Broward got out. "Okay?"

"I'm good." She hurried back to the car and started rolling again as Broward closed his door.

* * *

Payton's cabin sat back a ways from route 30 in a grove of pines and aspen. The place was unlit but a trail of smoke issued from the chimney. They rolled to a stop in the dirt driveway and a pair of flood lamps on the corner of the cabin snapped to life, bleaching everything in a cold white light. Kelly grabbed her gun in its holster and fastened it to her belt. Broward got out and opened his gun — he carried a revolver like an old-time lawman — checked the cylinder and then snapped it closed.

A light turned on inside the house, then another. The surroundings were so quiet Kelly could hear the wood creaking as someone came toward the front door. Water lapped against a hidden shore — probably Green Pond.

She and Broward stayed in the driveway between the car and the cabin entrance until finally a lock was drawn and the door opened. Roger Payton, large and sleepy-looking, darkened the doorway.

Broward stayed where he was, holding his revolver with the barrel pointed down, his trigger finger against the action. "Hey, Roger."

"Hey, Chief."

"How you doing?"

Payton raised a hand to shield his eyes from the area light and looked at Kelly. "Can't complain. You brought the FBI?"

"This is Agent Kelly Roth. We'd like to have a quick talk with you, Roger. Can we come in?"

* * *

It was a mess. The cabin could have been cozy — timber framed with exposed beams and knotty pine walls, scratched-up wood floors covered with braided rugs, a large woodstove, comfy old furniture in the living room, a large farm table in the kitchen. But after two weeks of living there on his own, things had deteriorated. The

227

kitchen smelled like rotten meat, the floors were dirty, and what looked like mice shit covered a little bit of everything.

They'd holstered their weapons and Broward sat across from Payton. Kelly remained standing. "So," Broward said. "What's new?"

Payton unscrewed the cap from the bourbon and poured some into a tumbler. He looked at it a moment then raised it to his lips and drank. He set down the glass and stared at the bottle.

"I used to not drink. I had nine years not drinking. Now I am. That's new." He turned his attention to Broward and kept it there. His skin was pockmarked but he wasn't an ugly man. Life had been ugly to him. "I didn't do AA. Probably should have. You know what they say — they say someone who isn't going to AA is only a dry drunk, doing it white-knuckle. But with Dani and the restaurant, it kept me sober." He looked around a minute and then poured another drink and held the glass and his upper lip started to twitch like he was getting angry. "The night after she was killed, I didn't even think about it. I just went behind the bar and took down a bottle. There were people around. No one said anything. What could they say?"

"Nothing," Broward said.

Kelly spoke up after they'd fallen into an uneasy silence. "Mr. Payton, I met with Detective Faber earlier today."

"Sorry to hear that."

"Why?"

"Because he's an asshole, excuse the language."

"What do you think he told me?"

"Ah, come on . . ."

"Help us to understand, Mr. Payton."

"Help you to understand . . . Help you to understand . . ." Payton took a drink. "Well, if you talked to Faber then you know what I said to him."

"You told him — off the record — that someone had contacted you."

Payton turned his face away and stared into the kitchen. "Dani was a good wife. A great wife."

Kelly shared a glance with Broward as Payton continued.

"But I think something happens to a person when they have what happened to her, losing her ticket to ride like that, getting injured. She had this whole plan, this whole map of her life, and then it all went away. And she never really felt she could measure up. Not again." He smiled and looked down and laughed softly to himself. "That's how she wound up with me, if you want to put a point to it. She settled."

"Mr. Payton, could you talk about this person who called you? Or texted you?"

He looked at Kelly for a long time. His dark hair was curly, greasy from being unwashed, gray around his ears. "Dani was taking meds, too. But you probably know that. We had this thing, right, where I'd say that Dani had gone slumming with me, you know? She'd dropped a weight class. I mean, you've seen her. She was just a knockout. Smart as hell, funny — could've had any guy."

"She was a beautiful woman," Broward agreed.

After another silence, Kelly sensed their talk was over. "Mr. Payton?"

"Mmm?" He stared past her, lost.

"Did the man who killed Dani call you?"

Payton took a drink. "Yeah, he called me."

She looked at Broward then back to Payton, her stomach clenching. "When did he call you?"

"He texted me not long after he killed her." Payton nodded slowly to himself then drummed the table with his fingers and bit his lower lip and looked around.

Broward leaned forward. "Why didn't you tell me?"

"Tell you? Because I saw you one time for about five minutes before you left me alone with Faber in that room for three days. And when I did tell him, he said I was crazy."

"Why did you ask for the recording to be shut off?" Kelly asked, but she knew the answer.

Payton jammed a look at her. "Faber had been trying to label me as the guy. He kept saying, 'we're just trying to eliminate you,' but then he was coming at me with all this about how I might've had her killed for the insurance."

"Okay, but—"

"You want to know why I didn't tell anybody? Because the guy who killed Dani said he was going to give himself up. To me. He swore up and down he was going to tell me who he was and I thought, what if it's true? But I couldn't say anything. That would break the deal."

Kelly's mind raced. On the one hand, Payton's story fit with the texts on Ted Archer's phone and what she'd come to see as the killer's signature — his manipulation of the men. On the other hand, Payton seemed disturbed on multiple levels. An unreliable witness, crazy or not. But if he was mentally disturbed it was possible he'd lied about receiving messages from the killer and instead been the one to contact Ted Archer. Maybe he even believed his own delusion, like Faber thought.

"Do you have any record of your communication with this person?"

"I erased it all."

"Since then, since Faber, since you've been up here — has he been in contact with you?"

No answer for a few seconds, then he looked down and nodded. "He called."

"When?"

"But I didn't have any way to record it or anything."

"When did he call you?"

"Just recently. Few days ago."

"I'd like to see your phone please."

"Yeah, I'll go get it. Just a second."

Broward jumped in. "So he says he'll give himself up, you can't call us, and you go with it — just in case. But did you believe it? Do you? Do you really think you've been talking to Dani's killer?"

"He said things that weren't in the papers."

"Like what?" Broward snapped.

And Kelly knew before Payton answered.

"He said that he left behind bullet casings," Payton said. "He said that the first time we talked. They said '30-30 WIN' on them."

She moved a little closer to Payton. "How did you know that was true?"

"I asked. I pulled it out of Faber. When the guy first called me, it was right in the middle of all these interrogations. I told Faber I needed to know if there were any leads. And he told me about the casings."

"Bullshit," Broward said. "No way. Sorry, Roger . . ."

But Kelly believed him — she'd felt Faber was hiding something. She put a hand up to silence Broward and focused on Payton. "Why would Detective Faber tell you that?"

"He thought he was going to catch me in something. I don't know."

"Kelly," Broward said, sounding upset. "This is—"

"And that's when you told Faber about being contacted?"

Payton was only looking at her now. "Yeah."

She could smell the alcohol. And musty woodwork. And Payton, a sour sweat like he hadn't showered for a while. "Has he ever told you who he is?"

"No."

Broward got up from the table. "Kelly, can we talk for a minute?"

She told him to hang on. "Do you have any ideas?" she asked Payton.

"I don't."

"So you're being contacted by your wife's killer, he warns you not to talk, you're sure it's him because of what he knows about the casings, then you have Faber turn off the camera? Now there's no proof . . ."

"Here's what I thought, okay? I didn't want a record of it. *Of course* I wanted to tell someone. This guy said if I said anything, he'd never give himself up and never be caught. That he'd do it again to other people. So I asked Faber to shut the recording off. I thought Faber would help me. But he didn't believe me. How's that, huh? How's that for police work?"

She performed a quick review — Faber had disclosed the information about the left-behind casings to Payton, then Payton said someone contacted him who knew about the casings, too. But Faber shoved it all aside when he realized he'd screwed up and given critical and confidential police information to a suspect.

Or Payton's story was a convenient way to hide his own lie.

"The person contacting you said specifically he was going to do it again? To whom?"

"Not like that — he said it was part of something. Part of a larger picture. And it would be over if I did what he said. Then he started talking about all of this—"

"This is all one phone call?"

"There were three times. The first was texts, just before that interrogation. The next one was . . ." Payton squinted and glanced down. "Ah, it was maybe a week later. Not quite. He called and started talking about how all of this was just in my mind. That I was bringing myself pain because I kept thinking about Dani. What do you do when someone starts talking shit like that? I didn't know what to do."

Broward went over to the sink. "Can I get some water?"

"Sure. Yeah — glasses are right there above you," Payton said.

Broward got a glass down and ran the tap. "Water any good here?"

"Yeah. Well water. Better than Liverpool."

Broward took a long drink, his back to them. Kelly felt her heart pound. Something was wrong. Broward was off. She took a step back from the table so she could observe both men.

Payton resumed the story. "And this guy knew things. Knew things about me — my past, my business. I started getting paranoid. I swear to God every day I thought about it and I said to myself, 'Just wait. If this guy is so fucking crazy he's going to admit who he is, then you got him.'"

Broward finally turned around, set the empty glass beside him on the counter. He hooked his thumbs in his belt and watched Payton. He wasn't making eye contact with Kelly.

"It's the weirdest thing," Payton said. "I mean, the weirdest fucking thing. And you know, the funny part is, it took my mind off her. Thinking about this guy, waiting for him to call, it took away the pain, a little bit. Gave me something to occupy my mind." His rheumy eyes searched the space. "And I came up here. I didn't want to talk to the cops again, or Dani's brothers, or any more journalists. I had to get away. But I see the troopers going by my house, driving slow — I know I'm being watched."

Kelly spoke. "Mr. Payton, I'd like you to come in for a formal interview. I have a couple of recordings that I'd like you to listen to. You need to sort out your recollections, try to get everything as straight as you can, and then come in. Can you do that? I'll need you sober, too."

"I don't know. Wait — you got this guy recorded?"

"We have something we'd like you to listen to."

"You got it on you? On tape or a CD or something?"

"Mr. Payton, we need to speak to you formally." She looked at Broward, who was still avoiding her gaze.

"And you'll arrest me for withholding evidence or something like that. Anyway, I'm selling the restaurant.

Not because business is bad — business is good. I'm just done. Done with the whole thing. I'm going to be free."

"I'm not interested in whether or not you came forward before. You're doing that now, voluntarily and informally, and that will factor in to everything. But you've kept this to yourself on the off chance this guy would stay true to his word. Because now we have a real shot at getting him."

"You have a suspect, don't you?" His heavy eyes, the way he slightly swayed, Payton was already drunk. Unreliable. "You have someone you're looking at. That's who the recording is. Let me hear it."

She needed him sober. She needed his phone. She needed to call Dixon.

Broward stepped forward, hands on his hips. "What about a book, Roger? *The Myth of You*. Have you read that book?"

"The what?"

"Do you have a copy here, by chance?"

"You still think I did it. I was at the restaurant! Everybody knew I was there, all night. I never left. I never *hired* anybody. For Chrissakes — I wouldn't know who to hire. Who knows murderers?"

"Stay calm, okay? Keep it calm, Roger."

"Let me hear the recording. I'll tell you if it's him."

"Kelly." Broward jerked his head. She moved toward the front door. Broward was acting so strangely that if they were going to talk, she wanted to be near an exit. Her chest tightened as he walked over and opened the door and stepped outside. She glanced back at Payton, who sat staring into an empty glass.

The night was frigid and dark as coal. The fresh air was a welcome relief after the stolid, boozy air inside the cabin but she started shivering and couldn't stop. Stafford, Virginia felt a world away.

She faced Broward. "What's going on with you?"

His faint outline barely showed up in the light from the windows. "Nothing is going on with me. I can just see you getting taken in by him. He's trying the same thing on you as he tried with Faber."

She kept her voice down even though they were outside. "If Payton is our guy, at least a dozen people lied for him or were mistaken. And Faber wasn't able to prove he hired someone — he admitted to me that he made it up."

"I don't think Roger hired someone."

"Then what? He killed his wife — how does it relate to the other victims?"

"It doesn't. He killed her the same way as Tammy Haig was killed. To hide it. To make it look like part of a series. He copycatted."

Broward was beginning to sound like Severin.

"So then the killer just resumed as normal with the Archers and the Spences?"

"I think it's a possibility. I mean look at this guy."

She viewed Payton through the window, still sitting at the table. Why had Broward suddenly elevated him to a prime suspect? What had changed? Maybe the real reason Faber got fired was because he'd disclosed evidence of the murder weapon to a suspect — Roger Payton. And Broward had been trying to keep that disclosure covered up, make it look like Faber's real infraction was ginning up a story about a hired assassin. For his own sake, Broward needed Danica Payton's killer to be her husband.

"The only way he's coming with us is in handcuffs," she said. "But we don't have enough. He's still got a rock-solid alibi. He's got no motive—"

"The evidence is that he knows the caliber of bullets." Broward spoke in a harsh whisper. "What more do we need?"

"Rob, listen . . ."

"I know what you're thinking and there's no way Faber said anything about the casings. No way. It's not in any of the recorded interviews. He may have played bad cop but he stuck to procedure. And if this guy is telling Roger about the murder weapon, why didn't he tell Ted Archer the same thing? Archer had no idea about that or he would've passed it along to Severin. It's not in Archer's notes, not in the texts, nothing."

Broward had a point.

He glanced inside. "The only way Roger knows about the bullets is because he fired them from his own fucking gun."

She huddled in the cold.

"She's the *only one* without kids," Broward said. "They didn't have any children because he couldn't get her pregnant. He did it out of shame. And he did it the same way the others were done to hide it. To hide *himself*."

"It's still all circumstantial. You know how this works."

"Then let's play him the tape. While he's listening, I'll have a look around. Get his phone, see if he's got Grumett's book, see if he's got a prescription for Cialis or something — see if there's a fucking Winchester in there. Then we call the state police, we call Dixon, we call everyone, we take him down."

She took a deep breath. "Even if he killed his wife that still leaves someone out there."

"Well, listen — he was in Liverpool when his wife was murdered. And he was in the area for Tammy Haig and for the Archers. Maybe he *did* do the others. Maybe he's got a second car, drove down and did Carter-Spence, too."

"And Grumett's phone? You think he stole it and left it at the church? After texting me?"

"Or he's working with someone."

She'd expected to come up here and get Payton to admit he was talking to the killer and at least establish a clearer picture of what the killer wanted, or who might be next, and now they were considering Roger Payton for the whole thing. Him and maybe an accomplice.

"Play Grumett's interview for him," Broward said, "play the Taylor Keesing audio, too."

"The cokehead?"

"That will give me some more time. In fact, play Keesing first. Then when you play Grumett, if this goes how I think it's going to go, Roger will positively identify him."

She didn't expect it to work. Grumett wasn't the killer and Payton wasn't about to identify him. But it was a compromise that cooled Broward's heels and bought them a little time to search the place — they had enough to cite exigent circumstances — then either bring Payton as a cooperating witness or have enough probable cause to arrest him on the spot.

She pushed open the door with her hand on her weapon. "Mr. Payton? You got a computer? Something we could use to listen to this interview?"

His eyes lit up as she walked into the room. "Dani's old one. Hang on." He got up and staggered away and came back a few seconds later with a battered Gateway laptop, opened it up and said, "Just needs a second." Then he belched.

When it was ready he pushed it toward her and she dug the thumb drive from her pocket, snapped in the drive and clicked on the audio file.

Broward interrupted as she fiddled with the volume. "Hey Roger, can I use your can? It was a long drive up."

He jerked his thumb over his shoulder. "Right back there on the right. You have to jiggle the handle after you flush."

"Gotcha. Sorry, be right back. Just go ahead and play it, Kelly."

Broward walked off, his footfalls fading into the back of the cabin, and Payton didn't seem worried about it. She hit the play button on the audio, hoping to cover any noise Broward made as he looked around.

Keesing was in mid-sentence. "*. . . to cross me off your list, you say. And how are you going to do that? You'll ask me the same questions three or four times, see if I change my answer. You'll act like you're my friend, get me something to drink . . .*"

She watched Payton closely as he listened. He frowned and shook his head. "That's not it. That's not him."

"Keep listening. Just maybe focus on the content — what he's saying, not necessarily how he sounds. Between cameras and computers and phones it could sound different. That's why we need you to come in. Here, let me skip ahead to another part."

"*. . . a basic, freshman-level course, but most if it goes right over their heads. I don't know about the youth these days. You see that video? About people being asked to name a book, just any single book, and no one can? Society is going* down . . ."

She watched Payton for a reaction while tuning in on Broward's movements. The toilet flushed and water ran through the plumbing, rattling the pipes.

"It's a different guy." Payton poured another drink. "This guy is cockier, or something. Too keyed up. The guy who called me was much calmer."

She switched to Grumett's recent interview and played the audio. "How about him."

"*. . . before teaching. I encountered many people who feel shame for not living up to expectations. The idea is to . . .*"

Payton straightened up a little. "That's interesting. Yeah, I mean, talking about the same stuff." He cocked his head, listening, then leaned back in the chair. "But he's too old. Sounds like my uncle or something."

There it was. Broward thought Payton would pounce on Grumett but he was calling it dispositive. A little warmth started to circulate through her body. Things were going to be OK. She just needed to give Broward another minute or so to finish looking around. "All right, try one more. The voice might sound a little different here, different emotions."

She listened out for Broward again. He'd turned on a faucet now — he was coming and going from the bathroom, using the sound of water to mask his movements. Then she hit play.

"*. . . think the ideology that criminals have just made* bad choices *is undermined by research. And the idea that they're somehow spiritually corrupt or going against God — these are becoming archaic concepts. Research has been done . . .*"

Payton slowly nodded and she felt gooseflesh break out on her arms as she watched the recognition dawn on his features. "Yeah . . ." He nodded more vigorously. "Yeah. That sounds like it could be him, the more I listen. And, you know, all the stuff he's talking about . . ."

When he looked up at her she inspected his expression for any trace of guile but it was hard to tell. "You sure?"

"I mean, yeah, that could be the guy."

"But does he *sound* like the man you've been talking to? You said he was too old."

"At first, maybe. But now . . . yeah, I think it's him."

Broward came walking out of the back. "So what do we think?"

Kelly closed the laptop and put her thumb drive back in her pocket. "Mr. Payton has suggested the second interviewee sounds like the unknown subject who's been calling him." Her tongue felt numb. Payton suspecting the psychology professor could mean Payton was the killer, looking to frame Grumett after all. "It might just be the content that rings familiar, though," she added.

"I mean," Payton said, "If I could hear them back-to-back — you know, the guy who called me and this guy, then maybe I can totally confirm it. But it's close. I think it's close. Who is he?"

"We can't tell you that," Broward said. He came up behind Payton and placed a hand on his shoulder. "You know we can't. Not right now. But that's good work, Roger."

Payton drank from the glass, his gaze unfocused, still nodding a bit. "The guy told me that all my suffering was in my head. I was making myself sick thinking about Dani, over and over again, like a broken record. That there's an addiction to the pain. An attachment. Thinking I had to be someone for Dani, thinking I had to be a certain way. Be the best husband. It's just beliefs. What we think we are — just beliefs."

Broward gave Payton's shoulder a squeeze. "Like having kids, right, Roger? You believed you were supposed to give her children."

She needed to call Dixon right now. They had to take Payton down the hard way. She took her phone out as Payton turned his face up to Broward. "No, not that. Dani didn't want kids. If she did, I would have."

Her finger hovered on Call as Broward said, "We need you to come in, buddy." He walked around the table and sat next to Payton. "That's all it is right now. Okay Roger? We need you to help us. We can stop this guy from hurting anybody else."

At last Payton stood up. He took the bottle and glass and brought them to the counter and set them down. Keeping his back to them, head lowered, he said, "Yeah, okay."

She slowly put her phone away. Payton poured himself another drink. Any more bourbon and he was going to be unconscious, big as he was.

"Mr. Payton, we need to do this now," she said softly.

He nodded. "I appreciate that — you acting like I have a choice."

"You *do* have a choice."

He rotated around and pointed at the holster where she kept her phone. "If I don't come with you right now you're going to call someone and they'll come get me. That's not a choice."

"We need to have this conversation on the record, in front of other members of law enforcement and the US district attorney."

He sucked at his lips for a moment and looked into a corner. "Tell you what," Payton said, slurring his speech a little. "I'm meeting with a buyer for the restaurant tomorrow. I've had people in place down there to keep the restaurant thing going — you know, Eileen is great, she really keeps it together — but I gotta go down and sign the papers. I'm not packed yet, so let me just get a few things together . . ."

He moved out of the room before they could object. Kelly and Broward looked at each other and Broward gave a small nod and then followed Payton. Broward hadn't turned up a gun, or given her any indication that he'd found one. But once Payton was in custody they'd come back with a search warrant and pull apart every board.

Her ears were ringing. Maybe Broward was right and they had their man. But she was reluctant to jump to another conclusion. Either way, they had a long road ahead.

She heard a strange noise, then a thump. She pulled her Glock and stared into the back hallway. "Chief Broward?"

Her heart was in her throat. She listened, staying where she was beside the kitchen table. She aimed the gun toward the back rooms. "Chief Broward? Mr. Payton?"

There was labored breathing, someone grunting, then a final thump.

Keeping the gun in one hand, she pulled out her phone as Roger Payton emerged from a bedroom, at first slowly, then building speed and charging down the hallway toward her. She dropped the phone and aimed the gun again but it was too late and he crashed into her. The back of one of the dining table chairs barked against her side just under her ribs and she lost her footing and tumbled to the floor, her gun clattering away across the table.

Payton had hit her like a battering ram and she'd smacked her head hard enough that her vision blacked out for a second before coming back into focus.

He loomed over her, holding an axe. His hair was sweaty and messed, eyes glassy. There was spit hanging from his lower lip.

She tried to find her voice. "Don't . . ."

He lifted the axe over her and hit her with the handle. This time everything stayed black.

CHAPTER SEVENTEEN

The water shocked her awake. She jerked back and tried to get away but she was tied to something. Payton stood there with a phone in one hand and an empty glass in the other. The water trickled down her cheek and pooled in her ear. She was in a bed and the windows were still dark.

"How are you feeling?" he said.

She could only stare a moment, unable to speak. "What time is it?" Her throat was dry, voice scratchy.

"You've been out of it for a little bit. Sorry I had to do that — throw water on you. But you need to get up now."

"Where is Chief Broward?"

Payton came closer. He held the phone out, facing her. Her vision remained a little fuzzy but it looked like a call was connected. "He wants to talk to you," Payton said.

She was confused. Broward wanted to talk to her?

Payton came closer, set the glass on the bedside table and scowled as he tapped the phone screen. "There. I put it on speaker. Okay?" He laid the phone beside her head and stepped back. "Go ahead and say something."

"This is Agent Roth."

Nothing. She looked to Payton for an answer. He just stood with his hands clasped.

Kelly raised her voice for the benefit of the speaker phone. "Broward? Rob, are you there?"

"It's nice to finally speak to you," came the reply. A male voice, not Broward's, but vaguely familiar.

She didn't respond.

"You better talk to him," Payton said.

"I'm here," Kelly said at last. "What should I—"

"Do you ever forget?"

She hesitated. Best to play along, see where it led. "Everyone forgets."

"Something just blips out of your mind, right? You're in the middle of a conversation — has this ever happened to you? You're in the middle of a conversation and you have something to say, it's right there in your thoughts and then poof, it's gone."

"Is this what you talk about? To the men you call?" The pounding of her heart made her own voice sound strange.

"Then it just shows up on its own. You're sitting there ten minutes later or an hour or a day later and go, 'oh there it is — *that's* what I wanted to say.'"

The more he spoke the more she put a face to the voice. She saw him sitting on the couch in his living room, the books on the inlaid shelves behind him. She remembered him on the video tape, the checked racing shirt he wore, the way he seemed shocked and numb.

"Sounds like something Grumett talks about in his book," she said. "I haven't been able to read the whole thing."

"That book turned out to be pretty good. Not the best, but you know it when something speaks the truth. A truth you'd forgotten. Thoughts just happen, memories come and go, and you're not in control. We're slaves of our minds."

"Why don't we get together?" She'd finally been able to form a few coherent ideas despite the pain in her head. Blanchett had her phone tracked and Dixon would be expecting a check in. Any minute now the state troopers would be alerted and bust into the cabin. "I'd like to talk about it. Did Tammy have a copy she got from Grumett's class? Or did you order one yourself?"

"She had one. I leafed through it a little, thought it was pretty rudimentary at first, honestly. But then later, you know, I went back to it," he said softly.

"After you killed her? Or did you need a little more justification first?"

"You know, I thought, *he's right*. We don't have any sort of control at all. Not even a little bit. It's predetermined."

"You thought your wife and Grumett were sleeping together."

"That doesn't matter," he said after a moment. "Not now."

"Because after Tammy, you got a taste for it."

"Yeah — you'd like that. You'd like me to fit into your neat little personality box."

"There's no box. You come in all shapes and sizes." She grunted and shifted her position, feeling aches and bruises from Payton's attack regardless of the adrenaline now surging through her. Payton watched from the doorway, looking like he'd sobered up a bit. She wanted to know how much time had passed. The windows were still dark. It had to be later the same night. But she was so thirsty, even hungry, and her muscles felt stiff, like more time could have passed. Where was Broward?

Blake Haig's disembodied voice rasped from the phone. "We don't have any control over what we forget — or what we remember. Like what happened to you."

He knew about her past — big deal — he could've gotten the information from anywhere. "So you call up the men whose wives and children you've killed, and you try to

— what? Enlighten them? That exaggerated sense of purpose puts you right in the narcissist category you're trying to wriggle out of."

"You couldn't stop it when that happened to you. When those guys came after you, when they got on top of you. You hadn't done anything wrong and yet there it was. And everything you've done since that moment has shaped your life. See? We're all just reacting."

"And you're reacting to what happened with Tammy. But I've got to tell you, with all respect to her, that's exactly the type of woman you'd attract, isn't it? You knew she'd do this."

Haig laughed. "Everything you've done since you got here was entirely predictable."

She felt the fear and fought against it, talking over it. "You're a big man, huh?"

"You want to call me the bad guy. That makes you the good guy, or girl. Have you been listening to a word I've said? Despite overwhelming evidence to the contrary, we continue to think we're writing our own stories, that we have a choice. *That's* pathology. *That's* sickness."

"How about this — I don't give a shit what you think. And probably most people don't, either."

"I give people the chance to awaken."

"They only listen to you so they can capture and kill you. And you're only doing this because your wife cheated on you. Everything else is a justification and I don't think you even really understand the shit you're talking."

"Oh, I understand it. We actually think the same things, you and I. The difference is, you're trapped in the illusion because it's nicer to think we mean something. It feels better to think we're in control." He fell silent a moment. "Look at poor Roger. Look at him standing there — I assume he's still standing there. Roger? You there?"

Payton came out of his stupor when his name was called. "Uh-huh. I'm here."

"Roger, tell her how you thought you never measured up. How you worried all the time about what Dani thought of you, what her family thought. That's all we do, run around worrying about what other people think. So Roger there, he just overcompensated with everything. Travel, expensive gifts; he was devoted to her. After I followed them from the mall and dropped by The Post, I saw it with my own eyes. What a sad thing — this man lavishing attention on a wife who didn't care. Controlled by this idea he had to be somebody. He had to be someone he wasn't."

"You thought she was the unfaithful type."

Haig didn't respond. Images from the various crime scenes flashed through her mind: Danica Payton sprawled out in the golden broomsedge. Colton Archer's pale dead face staring up at the sky. Haig's own wife in a creek. Jessica Carter-Spence shot in the head and still breathing — still alive as he drove away.

"At least I take ownership of my true nature," he said. "I'm awake, not in denial like Roger, or like you, fighting against who you are. But I can change that. I'm going to help you, too."

She felt her blood run cold and was momentarily at a loss for words, dreading what he might be talking about. *Who* he might be talking about.

"Agent Roth, I've called you for one reason, and one reason only. I've been watching a family. Husband, wife, three kids. They seem like very nice people."

The words erupted from her in a torrent at the same time her mind screamed that she not admit to anything. "You don't have to hurt anyone else, you don't have to, you've made your point, just leave them—"

"Rick and Uschi and the kids — they're nice people."

Heart pounding, thoughts scattered, just a blind need to protect her family. Her blood.

"We're just caught up in this thing," Haig said. "This is fate — me and you. You know, you could say — this is destiny."

"You don't have to do it. You can change."

"You have a playbook to go by and I have to finish what I started."

"I'll stop you first." Emotions continued to flood her, recent memories — the smell of maple syrup in her brother's home. The toys in the living room. The hopefulness in Rick's eyes.

"Jane Goodall studied chimps," Haig said when she thought he'd already hung up. "I read about that, too. And when she was studying them, she'd watch as the chimps patrolling the edge of their territory would kill any other chimps that wandered in. Just rip them to shreds, violent and bloody. No mercy in it. So there goes the whole 'noble savage' idea. We forget that we're animals."

There was only one word that surfaced in the roiling chaos of her mind: "Don't."

"I'm hoping this is the one. You're smart. Can you let go of your brother? Or his wife and kids, do you think? Can you step up? Become a new sort of person?"

She could only breathe. *Don't acknowledge anything.*

"Or will you implode, like Ted Archer? Will you turn into a blubbering mess, like Brad Spence? Or a pliable drunk, like Roger Payton. What do you think?"

She felt grimy, weak. "What do you want?"

"I want you to do exactly what you're programmed to do. I'm so confident that you're a machine, that you're so limited by all your procedures and rules, I'm just gonna let you go, Kelly. As soon as we're done talking, you're free." He added, "So to speak."

She looked at Payton, still watching her from the doorway. "I'll arrest Roger," she said.

"He's fine with that. Aren't you Roger?"

Payton nodded. "Yes."

"This isn't going to work out for you," she said to Haig. But she didn't sound convincing even to herself.

"Yes it is. I know every move you're going to make."

He hung up.

As soon as Payton finished freeing her hands, she shoved him aside and untied her own legs, got to her feet too fast and felt dizzy. She steadied herself at the bedpost and dipped her head to get the blood flow back. When it passed, she glanced up, expecting Payton to have left the room. He stood there, looking concerned. "Can I get you some water? You gotta be thirsty."

She was parched. "Why are you doing this?"

"I've got bottled water or you can just drink it right from the tap, like Chief Broward. There's good water up here."

"Where's my gun?"

"It's in the other room." He picked up the cell phone from the bed and stuck it in his pocket.

"Show me."

"All right."

He walked out, banging against the doorway with his shoulder like he was still drunk after all. She let go of the bedpost and followed him.

Her gun and holster were sitting on the kitchen table. She grabbed her piece and popped the magazine and checked it and slapped it back home and checked the chamber and, seeing that everything was in order, pointed it at Payton who stood at the sink, filling a glass with water. She wanted to go check the back rooms and see if Broward was okay, if he was even alive, but she didn't want to let Payton out of her sight.

"Where is he?"

"He's gone." He turned around and held out the glass of water. When she didn't take it, he set it on the table.

Carefully, she walked over and pointing the gun at him with one hand she picked up the glass with the other and drank, not taking her eyes off him. She set the empty glass back down and gripped the firearm with both hands again.

"I'm really sorry," Payton said. "I mean I really am. I had to get drunk just in order to do it. He wasn't even supposed to be here."

Her legs were shaking. She needed her phone and she needed to call someone. Everyone.

He frowned. "You should use the bathroom. Maybe put something on that — it's mostly dried up but you're still bleeding a little."

"Where's my phone?"

"I got rid of it."

Everything was quiet, only the crackling of the fire in the other room. "Give me the one in your pocket. The one he just called you on."

"It won't help you."

"Give it to me."

"I'm not going to do that."

"If it won't help me, why not? He used a burner and blocked the caller ID, right?"

Payton leaned back against the sink and sighed and looked away. "You'll try to call your backup. Call an ambulance and all that. And it's not part of the deal."

"Roger. He killed Dani and now you're *helping* him. Why?"

His heavy eyes found hers. "This is the only thing. This is it. All of it. I'm done."

"If you hurt Chief Broward, we can deal with that. We can keep you safe. If you help me, if you work with me, I can help you."

He formed a sad smile. "Never gonna happen."

"He's talking about killing my family. That's my brother! That's his wife, that's their three little children. That's who he's talking about, Roger. That's who's next." She was shouting.

Payton just looked at her as her words sunk into the walls. He walked around the other end of the table toward the living room.

"Stop, Roger. I'll put a bullet in your leg."

"That's fine." He kept walking.

She fired. Payton tensed but then kept going. She had aimed wide, giving him a warning. He opened the door to the woodstove.

"Next one goes in your leg!"

She'd never shot anyone. It was harder than she'd imagined. She'd been trained at the academy like every other agent, shooting at pop-out targets in Hogan's Alley. The hesitation cost her — Payton threw the phone on the fire. She ran to the woodstove and reached for it, ready to burn her hand if it meant getting word out that Haig was targeting her family, but Payton blocked her way and slammed the door shut. She glimpsed the phone amid a red-hot glow of embers and flames and then it was gone.

She backed away, cursing, aiming the weapon at Payton's center of mass, her finger on the trigger.

He stuck his arms out, turned his hands over, palms up, exposing his wrists. "This way you don't have to call an ambulance. It's better, you can just call a hearse." He wore that sad expression again. The thing was, she thought the remorse was genuine, and it made her even angrier. She couldn't understand it. Couldn't understand him helping a sadistic killer. Maybe to endure his pseudo-psychological bullshit for the promise of revenge, but this wasn't that. Roger Payton just wanted to die. That was his end game. Suicide by cop.

"Keep your hands where I can see them and sit down in that chair while I call this in." She moved the gun to her right hand again while she glanced around for the landline phone.

"I disconnected the house phone," Payton said. He nodded to the woodstove. "Threw Broward's in there, too. Been cooking for about an hour." He lifted his shoulders and let them drop. "So. Here we are. There's no way you're getting me out of here. No way you're going to bring me in. I've aided a murderer. Someone who killed a pregnant woman. What are you going to do?"

Shaking all over, trying to control it, keeping the gun on him. "Did you know that his wife was pregnant?"

Roger's brow knitted together in confusion. "His wife?"

"His wife. Tammy Haig. Roger — do you know who you've been talking to?"

"He never said his name. He told me he would. He said I would know who he was after you came." Payton shrugged again and looked at her with his colorless face. "Now you have to kill me."

"I'm not going to kill you."

Payton wiped away the tears as his eyes narrowed to points. He started across the room toward her.

"I heard Jessica Carter-Spence was still alive for a little while," he said. "He couldn't get her alone with the kids, he was hurrying to get to your family, but he'd already put in so much time. That's got to really eat away at her husband — that she lived for a while. That she lay there all alone and breathed with a bullet in her head and she died slow."

Kelly fired.

∗ ∗ ∗

There was blood in the bathroom, in the sink, on the floor leading away, and a smear of it on the hallway wall. She followed the trail to the front door and went outside. The Mazda was still there, but no chief, and no radio to call for help in a rental. Where the hell were the state troopers? It had been an hour since she and Broward arrived, and she hadn't checked in, and Blanchett was supposed to be monitoring. Maybe something happened that was holding them up or maybe she was putting too much stock in getting backup and was on her own.

Back inside, she rummaged through the kitchen drawers until she found a flashlight. Standing back beside the driveway she played the beam over the lightless houses in the area, just a few of them, and then ran and knocked on the one next door but no one was answering and everything was locked up. These were summer camps, only Roger Payton was up here in early December. She used the butt of her gun to smash in a window, hoping for an alarm. When none sounded, she cleared away the glass and used the flashlight to hunt for a landline. Nothing. She left and ran along the road until she came to another cabin, feeling the night stretch out, time going too fast, like a dream she couldn't wake up from.

After crawling through another window and cutting her hand she found a phone and felt a jolt of hope, but realized it was a cordless, it's charging battery removed.

She hurried back to Payton's, her hand dripping blood, found plastic zip-ties in another kitchen drawer. She holstered her gun and rolled him over on the floor in front of the woodstove and, straddling him and linking the ties end to end, encircled his wrist and cinched them tight, then repeated the process three more times. She got off of Payton and pulled her weapon back out. There was blood everywhere from his wound and hers, but he was alive.

"Stand up."

He spoke with his face mashed into the rug. "I can't."

"What did you do with Chief Broward?"

"He wasn't even supposed to be here."

"Why? Why wasn't he?"

"You should have killed me . . . please . . ."

"Where is he?" she screamed.

"In the pond," he whispered.

She was running, not thinking, out the door and through the back woods, branches clawing at her, until she reached the edge of the water. The light from Payton's cabin was just enough to see the shape floating twenty yards offshore.

She removed her winter parka. Wading into the water brought a shock to her legs and soon turned them numb. Up to her hips, calling his name, and she was shaking, her breathing fast and shallow. If she swam out after him she was going to freeze to death but there was a chance he was still alive and so she went. Kicking furiously, keeping her head up and scanning and feeling the pain sink into her muscles and bone, pain from the cold that drilled down, the water a living thing that tore at her, more burning than frigid, catching her lungs on fire, crackling in her head until she reached out for him and had a hold of his jacket.

Scissor-kicking her legs and heading back for shore, a vision of Danica Payton came to mind. She saw an Olympic-sized swimming pool and a woman in a skintight cap who dove and cut through the water.

Kelly fought against the blackness circling her vision, her thoughts, and pulled Broward behind her. He was face down and floating and she touched down on the bottom of the lake and pulled him to shore, dragged him as far as she could through the wet sand and sticks and rocks until she collapsed, panting, feeling the water turn to ice on her skin.

Get up. Keep moving.

She yanked open Broward's soaking coat and started chest compressions. The warm salty tears carved through the mask of frozen pond water on her face. She pumped his chest and then she breathed into his cold lips but Rob Broward was dead.

PART THREE

Knowing these things, and that there is still choice,
makes what we choose all the sweeter.

CHAPTER EIGHTEEN

They drove out of the wilderness, no stores around at first, and then what was around wasn't open. She'd opted to put Payton in the front seat where she could keep an eye on him and had used more zip ties to link him to the seatbelt. She wore her parka and had the heat blasting in an attempt to thaw herself but it was barely enough and she knew she was hypothermic. A headache drove through her thoughts like a freight train. They bulleted east on route 30, splitting the dark countryside and she kept their speed at eighty miles an hour. They came into Lake Clear where the general store was closed, houses dark. She could start knocking on doors but that could burn more time than just continuing on to Saranac Lake. Less than ten minutes later she saw the lights of a twenty-four-hour gas station.

"Can I help you? You all right?" The clerk was a skinny guy in his thirties with a bad beard and a worried look on his face as she came rushing in.

"I need your phone." She slapped her ID on the counter, water oozing out from the leather seams of her wallet.

Before he could hand it to her, she heard the sirens. They emanated from deeper into the town, growing louder — maybe headed for Green Pond. She took the phone and realized she didn't know the number for Uschi's parents. "Do you have a phonebook?"

"Uh . . ." He looked out the window as a state police vehicle went rushing by, lights flashing and strobing.

"Your phone. Please let me see your phone."

The clerk dug into his pocket and pulled out his smartphone and Kelly grabbed it from him as a second state trooper vehicle hit the brakes and hooked into the parking lot. Must have seen the Mazda. She tried to Google Dieter and Mischa Drabenstott and get an address but she was shaking so violently she could barely hold the phone — her core temperature was still way down. Finally she found the number in the online White Pages and dialed. Walking to the windows fronting the street she saw two state troopers get out of the dark blue troop car and approach her Mazda. When they saw Payton, they both drew their weapons.

She knocked on the glass and a trooper looked around at her.

Someone answered at the Drabenstott residence in Lake Placid, sounding sleepy. "Hello?"

"Rick — it's Kelly. Is everyone okay?"

"Kelly . . . what?"

She raised her voice. "Is everyone okay?"

"We're fine . . . we're fine."

"You need to get out of there. He's targeted you. He probably tracked your car."

"Kelly, calm down, I can barely — who's tracked us?"

"Get out of there," she said, and the state trooper stepped into the gas station. "Hang on," she said to Rick, and she told the trooper what was happening and gave him the address. "People are coming," she told Rick. "You have any weapons there? Dieter have a rifle, something?"

"No, Kelly, I don't think — are you talking about *him?* Your case?"

Her vision was blurring around the edges, her teeth chattering. She leaned against the glass with her shoulder, and her legs began to buckle. As she slid toward the floor she said, "I'm so sorry, Rick. I'm so sorry . . ."

It had been a house fire started by paper jammed in a radiator, keeping the state police busy on the other side of Saranac Lake, putting them an hour away from Green Pond at the time Blanchett reported losing her signal. Two troopers stayed at the gas station, put Payton in the back of the troop car and waited for the ambulance while the other pair headed for Green Pond. She wanted to go to Rick, but for the moment she was wrapped in a thermal blanket and sitting on the curb outside the gas station, talking to Dixon on the phone, explaining about Haig's confession and his plan to attack her family.

"They weren't home this weekend," she told Dixon. "They were up at Uschi's parents' home in Lake Placid."

"First troopers just arrived," Dixon said. "Found everyone in good health, house is secure."

She closed her eyes and pulled in a tight breath. "That's good. That's really good."

"You sound hurt. Troopers said you're in bad shape."

"Broward's dead." Her eyes popped open and she felt the tears springing up. "I pulled him out of the lake behind Payton's house. Payton killed him."

"And the state police have Payton, I'm told."

"They're taking him in now."

"You put him in your car? Kelly you're something else."

"He's been communicating with Blake Haig."

"And he'll sign a statement? He's going to cooperate?"

She looked at him through the windows of the troop car, just a dark figure in the back seat. "He was hoping this would all be over for him. Tried to provoke me . . . I think he'll talk, but he didn't know it was Haig. Never met him in person. Haig was at Dani's funeral but they didn't speak then."

"Wait for the ambulance, Kelly. I want you to get looked at. You go with them—"

"I can't do that—"

"Kelly you go with them and let them check you out, you're no good to anyone if you're dead of hypothermia."

"It's my family."

"I know, Kelly. I know. We'll take care of them. We'll take care of them."

CHAPTER NINETEEN

Tuesday, December 4

When the FBI and Auburn police surrounded Haig's home at seven o'clock that morning, Kelly was riding in another state police car. They escorted her from the Adirondack Medical Center back down to Syracuse.

A prepaid phone had arrived for her while still in the emergency room.

"Haig came quietly," Dixon said over the phone. "Acted like he didn't know what the hell was going on, like there'd been some sort of big misunderstanding."

"I bet he did," Kelly replied.

"A first look at his phone shows no outgoing calls last night. He's got another one around, though — we'll find it."

"Or he destroyed it."

"Yeah, maybe. What else do we got that's solid besides Payton?"

"Was there a tracker on the car? On my brother's car?"

"Troopers checked, nothing they could find. They questioned your sister-in-law per my instructions. She doesn't recall seeing anyone suspicious, being watched or anything. If he was tracking them at one point, he got rid of that evidence, too. I got to be honest with you, Kelly — at this point it's not looking good."

She visualized the agents in their black armored vests, yellow "FBI" stenciling on the back, the local Auburn cops — Orzo there too, Dixon said — taking Blake Haig from his little white house with black shutters, Haig coming out and looking like Billy Bath had, showing no fear, no remorse.

* * *

At the US attorney's office in Syracuse she listened to Haig's first interview with Orzo with her eyes closed, focusing on the voice. Payton had hit her over the head and she'd blacked out — her medical examination concluded she'd been concussed. She needed to confirm it was the same voice she'd heard on the phone, with Starkey expressing doubts over her mental state. She'd awakened in Payton's bed and he'd put the phone down beside her on speaker. Her head throbbing, her mind going in a dozen directions at once, she'd listened to the killer. Now she was trying to match that tinny voice with one of the three men she'd interviewed, and it wasn't working.

She already knew it was Haig. He'd talked about his wife's affair. They'd talked about Grumett's book, and she knew his voice, it had to be him.

But she'd been wrong about things on this case — too many times to ignore.

Dixon stood arms folded next to Starkey and the assistant prosecutor, Giovanetti, plus Genarro, who'd flown in that afternoon.

"Did he ever say his name?" Genarro asked.

"It was him," Kelly said.

"Did he ever admit it to Payton?"

261

She ripped off the headphones and dropped them to the ground. They'd been over this half a dozen times already. "It doesn't matter what Payton says."

Starkey moved closer. "You're right, it doesn't. The defense will say Roger Payton is unreliable, a grieving alcoholic. We're the prosecution and we have the entire police force at our disposal, the FBI, acting as investigators, but all *they* need is reasonable doubt. Haig is in custody — on your word — and we've turned his home upside down, but there's no evidence of any crimes. There's still no gun, no vehicle, no DNA evidence, no phone, no crime scene witnesses. Unless we get proof of the affair — either Grumett changes his story or we find some trace evidence of Tammy Haig in his car, or we get a witness — we've got no motive for Haig. And he's got an alibi for every single murder — he's at work every time, logged into the system and occasionally even caught on video."

Dixon looked at the floor. "Grumett still says no on the affair. He's agreed to cooperate with everything — he's got a lawyer with him but he's submitting to swabs and fingerprinting."

Kelly said, "That won't tell us anything. That's why he's doing it."

"I know."

"Paternity test on Tammy's baby was positive for Blake Haig."

"Right. It's a dead end. The baby was Blake's, whether she was having an affair or not, and unless there's something he can't wriggle out of, Grumett's going to stick."

She thought about it. "What about Jason Sandaker?"

Starkey looked between Kelly and Dixon. "The co-worker?"

"He works at Xylem," she reminded them.

"Yeah. The one you rolled up on outside his house." Starkey walked to his desk and pushed some papers around. "Okay — right — you found him and Blake Haig and the Harbaugh brothers meeting at a diner. The Harbaughs we talked to — they say no way it was Haig. He's been actively investigating his wife's death for weeks."

"Because he did it."

The prosecutor's eyes were sharp. "That may be so. But right now, Russell and Matthew Harbaugh are on for the defense. They're now convinced Payton is the guy, and all the rest is smoke and mirrors. And the facts on the ground are, Haig claims he's innocent. I get the strong feeling from his counsel there's no way he's going to take a plea, because they hold all the cards. All we'd have at a trial is your testimony, and you're on the record as concussed — you were unconscious for approximately two hours. If it goes how I think it's going to go with this lawyer of his then we'll be lucky if they don't sue."

"Who's his lawyer?"

"A guy named Lance Tomlin, and he is a pit bull. Tomlin was friends with Haig's late father, so he's got family ties, he'll fight all the harder — he's even doing it pro bono. Bail hearing is tomorrow. We've thrown everything at this, but the evidence is underwhelming and Blake Haig's record is so clean there's a solid chance the judge will set bail low, or just ROR him, and that's it, he walks."

She felt crushed.

"The Harbaugh brothers must've seen something, heard something. Maybe we can turn them," Genarro said.

"They're already crowing about police entrapment," Starkey said. "Rabble-rousing about this being an instance of police ginning up a suspect — Haig — in order to close a case."

Blake Haig had gone to work on them, Kelly thought, just like he'd worked on Roger Payton and Ted Archer, getting into their heads, twisting things around. Maybe others, too.

"Sandaker did something," she said. "He's covering for Haig, lying for him. We need to find out everything we can about him. Maybe he does more at Xylem than operate a forklift."

Everyone in the room looked at her.

Genarro moved closer. "Kelly, you need more rest. You don't look—"

She brushed him away when he tried to get an arm around her. "Haig's got another vehicle somewhere. He's got a rifle. Let's look at his mother in Utica. Find all his relatives. And that book . . ."

The room was starting to spin, faces elongating and twisting. "That . . . goddamned book is . . . somewhere."

And then Genarro caught her as her legs gave out.

* * *

Alone in her hotel room she plugged in her speakers and opened iTunes, selected *Country Down* by Beck and flopped onto the bed and let the music wash over her. Dixon and Webber and the rest of them were out hunting for anything they could find on Haig while she was relegated to her room. She closed her eyes and thought about the memorial benches in Onondaga Park, thought about death, identity, and what it all meant to people.

Payton was probably now just finished processing into County and about to spend his first of many nights behind bars. And for what? Because he thought he deserved it? Payton was talking, admitting he'd been called and that he now believed it had been Blake Haig, but it was just one man's word against the other. And Kelly had been under duress, beaten and confused, incapable of sound judgment. If there even *had* been a phone call, the defense would say, it could have been anyone. Desperate to put a face to the serial killer, she'd chosen Haig. An unscrupulous attorney might even call into question her character and insinuate that Blake Haig reminded her of her attacker from when she was eighteen, that she held a grudge against men.

That seemed to be the point for Haig — demonstrate that free will is an illusion, that human beings were ruled by emotions, incapable of making truly free choices. Because he lacked any real empathy of his own, he thought people were reactive animals at the mercy of outside forces.

But he hadn't predicted Rick's last-minute trip to the Adirondacks — Haig had screwed that one up. He'd gotten cocky and sloppy. It was random chance that Rick's family had decided to take a long weekend away from home at the same time she'd chosen to visit Roger Payton.

As if there was a balance to things, a barter — sparing her brother and his family had cost Broward his life.

It was also possible Haig never meant to kill them and this whole thing was just a set up for her, a way to play with her like he'd played with Ted Archer and Roger Payton. See what she would do, study her like watching a worm writhe on a hook, get off on predicting how she would react.

After a little while, she fell asleep.

CHAPTER TWENTY

Wednesday, December 5

Kelly's small suitcase was on her bed, packed and ready to go. Dixon came in and dropped the papers and photos on her table in the hotel room. She looked at the photos and drew a fresh lungful of air that felt good to breathe in.

"White Jeep Cherokee. Found in Utica, parked in the space where his mother lives at the elder care center." Dixon fanned out the photos and pointed to one showing a jumper cable compartment in the back. "Winchester Model 94. Box of Federal Premium .30-30 150 grain Centerfire Rifle Ammunition, purchased at Walmart in the same city. Cherokee is registered to a relative down in Pennsylvania, so is the gun."

She bent and moved some more photos around as Dixon continued to narrate. "Those are latex gloves in his trash, that's a bottle of baby powder, probably used to keep his hands from sweating, but they also kept prints from sticking to the inside plastic. No prints anywhere on the gun, but then we've got three eyewitnesses from the

Utica gun range who will testify that Haig was there shooting, and he was shooting that gun."

She picked up a picture and Dixon said, "That's his computer, and he's wiped it, but he never added any new files to complete the wipe so we've got a partial search history and it's loaded with good stuff about game hunting and ballistics, plus a few YouTube videos that have you talking to that reporter, Oxley, then headlines from back when you had your assault. We found links to a website that sells tracking devices and an emailed receipt of purchase."

"No book?"

"No book," Dixon said. "Talked to some relatives, though, the uncle in Pennsylvania. He says Haig grew up mostly in Rochester, his dad worked at Kodak, mother who may've been a bit on the rambunctious side. Used to tell little Blake Haig he was an accident. So, I don't know. By the time they moved here the father was working himself to death and the mother was losing her marbles. Haig just kind of did his own thing. The uncle said he was smart."

They stood side by side and looked over all the papers and photos. Dixon said, "Problem with all this? Gun — registered to someone else. Vehicle — common, could be a coincidence. Internet searches on game hunting and even tracking devices aren't enough. Seeing him at a gun range — not enough. It may be what it takes for a judge to set bail today, but it's not what we need to convict." Dixon looked at her. "The only way this shakes out in our favor is with a confession."

"I know."

There was the faint suggestion of a smile on his lips. "I got one last thing, though. You're going to love this."

She waited.

He set out more paperwork — an employee profile for Jason Sandaker. She studied it for a few seconds, felt the hairs standing on the back of her neck.

"He's moved up in the world," Dixon said. "No longer loading and unloading trucks. He's their Information Technician at Xylem."

She picked up her gun and holster and strapped it on. "Let me talk to Sandaker first. And I've got one last request for you, if you're up for it."

Dixon held her gaze. "Anything you need."

* * *

In an interview room of the Cayuga County Jail, Kelly set out her coffee and her notepad on the table and crossed her legs. She had a bandage over the stitches on her forehead, another one on her cut hand, and her side still ached from crashing into Roger Payton's chair. But otherwise she felt pretty good. Orzo sat next to her, his cheek puffed out from the dentist, but wearing a snappy silver suit.

Sandaker sat opposite them. Pale.

"So," Kelly began. "You work at Xylem as their IT person."

"Yes ma'am."

"You went to school at SUNY Plattsburgh, got your degree in computer science while working at Georgia-Pacific."

"Yes."

"And as part of your job at Xylem, you deal with the facial recognition software the company uses to identify employees coming and going — is that accurate?"

"I'm responsible for upgrading the firmware, making sure everything is running, yes ma'am."

"It's possible to trick that system, isn't it?"

He swallowed and looked down. "Not really, ma'am, I mean . . ."

"Even if you can't, say, digitally alter a face, you can change the time code — the date and time of the video, so someone coming in on a Tuesday, say April twenty-fourth,

268

can be made to look like they were there on a Wednesday, April twenty-fifth. Isn't that right?"

"I wouldn't know. I don't think so." Sandaker seemed to go a shade paler, his eyes big and ringed red.

Kelly leaned forward. "Jason . . . Blake Haig *told* us you manipulated the video — you changed the time code so that what the police were looking at, to corroborate his alibi, it was not actually for the time in question. And that you did it again for him three other times. Why?"

He looked at her, his mouth working, like he was having a hard time dealing with his own tongue. "He didn't say that. You're trying to . . . he didn't say that."

"You admit to doing it, though."

"I'm not admitting anything. And I want a . . . I need a lawyer, please. I need my lawyer."

"You have a lawyer? Or you mean a public defender. Well, look, you're not being charged — you're here voluntarily. We could charge you, arrest you, and then at your arraignment you could seek counsel. Hopefully your wife doesn't have her baby while you're going through the system. How is she doing, by the way?"

"Charge me with what? I didn't *do* anything!"

"Well, there's this — obstructing a federal investigation. Otherwise we'll take you in on your pot plants. It's still illegal to grow in the state of New York, and as far as federal law is concerned, the charges carry a weight similar to heroin. So we can go that way, where you spend the next year or so of your life in county jail, fighting an uphill battle to keep yourself from going down for seven-to-ten years in federal prison. Or, you can cooperate with us, admit that you lied for your friend and co-worker Blake Haig, that you helped provide him with an alibi."

Sandaker didn't speak, just looked at Kelly and Orzo some more and then glanced at the camera in the corner of the room.

"You have a family," Kelly said. "Jason? Why risk all of that? Why lie for a friend, why break the law for a friend? Blake Haig is a multiple murderer. Whatever he told you, it's a lie. It's a manipulation. He probably resents you because of what you have."

Sandaker swallowed hard as some color worked its way back into his face, his blood coming up. "You don't know him. He's not a murderer."

"Did he threaten you?"

Sandaker turned his head, looking away. His lower lip was shaking. He kept quiet.

"That's your right not to talk," Kelly said. "I respect that, I genuinely do. Here's the thing, Jason — I don't want to see anything bad happen to you. I think you made a poor decision, but you had a reason. You were trying to protect your family. So, think of the other families out there. Think of what Blake Haig is liable to do again if he walks away from this, the more lives he'll take, the more he'll ruin."

"Think of what he'll do to me if I say anything." Sandaker's voice was wet and his eyes shone with stark fear. "He has no . . . I don't know. He's missing something inside of him."

Kelly eased back into her seat. "He can't do anything to you if he's locked up."

* * *

An hour later, Haig sat where Sandaker had been, only Haig had on navy-blue inmate fatigues. Tomlin, his lawyer, sat beside him in a dark suit, his eyes hooded and a nose that looked like it'd been broken more than once. Agent Dixon had joined her and Orzo.

"Mr. Haig," Kelly said. "Good morning."

"Good morning, Agent Roth." His voice gave her chills she attempted to ignore, his eyes glinted with self-satisfaction. "Like I said, anything I can do to help."

"It's very kind of you. Let's get right to it — what's the nature of your relationship to Mr. Sandaker?"

"We're coworkers."

"Are you friends?"

"Sure. I guess you could say that."

"I've spoken with Mr. Sandaker, who's admitted to us that he manipulated the video of you at work — he used video from a different date and altered the time code to fool the Auburn Police Department. He also covered for you the hour you were not at Xylem, on April twenty-fifth, and he did the same for the August and November dates."

Tomlin grunted and leaned toward Haig and whispered in his ear. Haig nodded.

"This is your game?" she asked after a moment. "Hiding behind your lawyer? Come on, Mr. Haig. I thought you had this all figured out — you know everything that's going to happen. You knew you were going to be sitting right here, right now — and this is it? Just deny everything? That seems like a shame. To do all of this, to set this whole thing up, to accomplish everything you've done . . ."

There was a smile playing at the corners of his mouth — he was enjoying her attempts to provoke him.

"If you beat this," she said, "then nobody will ever know. Isn't the whole point for people to understand? We're just programmed machines, playing out our roles?"

Haig yawned and looked away, like he was more interested in the cracks in the puke-green walls.

"I wonder if you even thought about this sort of thing before Adam Grumett. Before reading his book. Maybe Tammy was coming home, though, sharing some of those ideas herself. Did she read the book first? I bet she did. I know the two of you both liked to read," Kelly said.

The lawyer looked at Dixon. "How long are we expected to sit here and endure this? We have a bail hearing in less than an hour."

"Before you go back to hiding out," Kelly said, "there's something you might be interested in." She pulled out a clear evidence bag with a copy of *The Myth of You*, several pages marked by fluorescent pink tabs. She set the book on its face and read from the back blurb:

"*Healing, Grumett demonstrates, is possible when we stop heaping 'blame and shame' upon ourselves, but seek to understand the conditions shaping our lives.*"

She pulled out Archer's notes next and slapped them down. "And this is Ted Archer's recollection of the call he received from a man claiming to be his wife and son's killer: '*He says healing is only possible when people stop heaping "blame and shame" upon themselves. Keeps talking about the nature of suffering. Conditions shaping our lives.*'" She looked up. "Sound familiar?"

Haig allowed his cockeyed grin full form. "Are you saying that Adam Grumett killed my wife? Because that's what it sounds like to me."

"I could see how someone would make that connection." She patted the hardcover book through the bag. "But guess where I found this? Or — rather, where Agent Dixon did? At the Goodwill, right near here in Auburn."

Haig lost the smile and his lips parted as if to speak.

"So here's what I think — your wife is sitting there with Grumett's book, and you picked it up, curious. Maybe you wait until after she went to bed — she was pregnant after all; pregnant women need their sleep. Is that how it went?"

"That's great," Tomlin said, his gaze shifting between her and Dixon. "So you found a book."

She cut a look at him. "What happens when the lab finds matching fingerprints for both your client and his late wife Tammy? Given that he told me he never owned a copy of this book, never saw it before — what is the prosecutor going to think about a suspect lying about such a critical component of this investigation? What would a jury think, if this goes to trial?"

"That my client forgot he even had it because he simply got rid of it — along with a hundred other books — after his wife was murdered." Tomlin rose from the table. "We have a bail hearing to get to. If you'll excuse us."

She held up a finger. "But wait — let me read you the inscription: 'To Tammy, one of my brightest: knowing these things, and that there is *still* choice, makes what we choose all the sweeter. Adam.'"

"Thank you," Tomlin said, with mock cordiality. He slid his paperwork into a leather briefcase. "That's all we have time for." He reached a hand toward Haig. "Come on, let's go."

Haig didn't move. He stared at Kelly with hate. She was getting used to it by now.

"I think you suspected your wife was cheating and maybe you went to the school," she said. "You saw them. Where were they? By his car, having a moment? Did you follow them to a hotel? Or even his place?"

"Don't answer that question," Tomlin said, hooking an arm around Haig. He moved him toward the door and called for the guard on the other side.

She twisted around to watch as they waited for the door to open, remaining in her chair. "Instead of killing Tammy's teacher, you killed *her*. But it didn't satisfy you. No — it opened a door. You went to the mall and watched people and waited until you found what you were looking for — a beautiful woman, a beautiful family, men who would do anything for them. Instead of dealing with Grumett, you became him. At least, you tried to use the philosophies in his book to elevate your crimes. But they don't. Your crimes reveal you as a coward and a cuckold."

The lawyer pounded on the door. "Hello? Let's go!"

Kelly rose out of her chair and came round the table. "Did you want to get caught? Was the call to me a cry for help? You rushed through the Spence family once you knew about me. You saw me as a way to end it, you told me what you were planning — you said you knew what I was going to do next." She spread her arms. "Well, here I am, Blake. The world is watching."

He turned and faced her. "You have no idea."

"*How do you feel?* That's what you asked Ted Archer. It's right there in your texts — *how do you feel?* For a while I thought maybe you've been gauging the emotions of others because you don't have any. Because you don't know what it's like to feel. But you do have emotions. You have shame. You have hate."

"Don't respond to that," Tomlin said. He pulled on Haig's arm.

"You hated Roger Payton for the way he loved his wife. And you hated Ted Archer for the way he loved his wife and his son — especially since you'd killed your own child. But the thing is, I remembered something — Detective Orzo telling me how in shock you were. How you never even wanted to look at your wife's body, never read the autopsy report. And you know what I thought? I thought, that pain is real. Maybe he didn't know that the baby was his. Maybe he thought it was another man's. But no, it was *your* child, Blake. Your own son you killed."

Haig lurched for her. He grabbed her around the throat and shoved her back against the table and loomed over her. His lips peeled back in a sneer, his eyes wild. Dixon and Orzo grabbed him, tried to pull him off. "Fuck you," Haig spat at Kelly.

She wanted to fight back. Every instinct in her told her to knee him in the crotch, take out his eyes. The flashback to Craig Danner was remarkable, as if she was in both the past and the present, two worlds coexisting, two men pinning her down, spitting in her face. But she didn't move. She felt his fingers pressing into her neck, constricting her windpipe, her air supply, and she didn't fight.

"It's okay," she whispered. "It's okay, Blake."

The door burst open and the guard came in. Together with Dixon and Orzo they pried Haig off of her. An instant later, he was on the floor and the guard had a knee in his back and Dixon was mashing his face into the ground.

Kelly gasped a breath of ragged air and sat up and rubbed at her neck. She was okay — it had only been a few seconds — and she squatted down beside Blake Haig and looked into his contorted face as he blew hot breath against the dirty floor.

"I did you a favor," he rasped. "I showed you who you really were. All your pain, your first case — I saw you on TV and you didn't know if you could do it. You should be thanking me."

Tomlin cowered in the corner, half-lidded eyes searching the room as he calculated the damage Haig was doing to their case. Dixon and the guard got Haig up onto his feet and though the guard tried to get him toward the door, Kelly shared a quick look with Dixon. He got it, keeping Haig in the room where the camera and microphone were recording his every action, every word.

Haig spat on the floor and drilled into her with his eyes. "You chase me, you do this to me — you've got no more choice than I do."

She pushed herself standing and faced him. "We'll get you help."

"I don't need help. The rest of you do. I got them to do every fucking thing I asked them to. *That's* the world we live in, *that's* the reality."

The room fell silent, just the sounds of breathing, the odor of sweat and bile in the air. Tomlin stared at the floor. Orzo was slack-jawed, his tie askew. Dixon wordlessly prompted the guard and they took Haig out of the room.

* * *

Outside in the parking lot, Dixon caught up with Kelly as he put his phone away. "You okay?"

"I'm fine," Kelly said.

"Doctor checked you out?"

"It's nothing. Haig's a lightweight."

Dixon just stared, then cracked a wide smile and laughed. First time she'd ever seen his teeth. Then he gave her ensemble an appraising eye and said, "We going to the funeral service for Broward now?"

"Yeah — you're driving."

They got in the car.

"Sandaker just spilled his guts five minutes ago," Dixon said. "The second he found out that Haig flipped out, he admitted to everything. Said he wants to come out on the 'right side of things.' He messed around with the system at Xylem, he said, changed the time code and dates. Says Haig was going to blab about his pot plants and get him fired from Xylem if he didn't do it. The guy was in deep denial, though, swears up and down he didn't think Haig was the Park Killer, just cutting out on work, up to no good. Says he doesn't really watch the news, read the papers." He gave her a sidelong look as he navigated the traffic. "How did you know for sure?"

She looked at herself in the mirror and adjusted her blouse, moved a lock of hair behind her ear. "I didn't."

* * *

The sky was royal blue and cloudless and the uniformed police pointed their rifles into the air and fired their salute. Kelly saw a woman standing on the other side of the open grave with two little girls and figured her for Broward's ex-wife. They listened as the priest gave his somber eulogy. A wind picked up and harried the autumn leaves in front of it as the coffin was lowered into the ground.

Kelly caught up with the woman and her daughters as they made their way out of the cemetery.

"Excuse me — miss?"

The woman stopped and turned around, put a protective arm around her girls, who huddled against her legs in their little black dresses.

"I'm Agent Roth: Kelly."

"I know who you are."

The anger and hurt came off Broward's ex in waves. Kelly took a step back, offered a smile, then bent toward the girls. "I'm very sorry about what happened to your dad. He was a good man."

The woman jerked them away and hurried toward the line of parked vehicles in the street. Kelly watched them go, thinking about how this event would affect the rest of their lives.

A man approached as she went to her car. "Detective Faber."

"I heard he was pleading guilty," Faber said, lighting a cigar. "Not even going to risk a trial."

"That's what I've been told," Kelly said.

He blew some smoke out. "That's how it goes. Courts are overloaded, prosecutor stacks up the charges, defendant pleads to a lesser offense just so everyone can move on with their day."

"He's got five counts of second-degree murder. All that was lost in the deal was the premeditation, but it will still put him away for life."

Faber kept giving her the eye. "I also heard you did a little bit of fancy footwork in there."

She started walking, not caring if he kept up or not, which he did.

"Word travels fast," Faber said. "So you see what I'm saying now — a cop's got to do what a cop's got to do. You're learning. That's good."

She didn't reply.

"So what do you do now, right? You take it with you? You let it grind you down? No. You put the guy away, where he belongs — in a cage. That's the result, that's what matters. Someday you'll know it," Faber said as she opened her car door.

She looked across the car roof at him. "Take care of yourself, Detective."

He laughed, and the smoke rolled over his shoulders as he walked away.

EPILOGUE

Thursday, December 6

"I don't understand," Rick said.

"I'd like to spend the night with you and Uschi and the kids. What's to understand?" Kelly asked.

Rick got a big grin and took a drink of his beer. "That's not what I mean. I mean this guy told you he was coming after us. There were twenty cops in Dieter's house. But they ended up picking him up at his job, you said."

She nodded, took a drink of her beer. First beer she'd had in — God, she didn't know. It was good. "Swing and a miss. He didn't know you had left town."

Rick looked away. "Jesus."

"Don't tell Uschi."

"I won't — are you kidding? No way."

"Haig wanted to come out of this without a scratch. He thought he could — I don't know. I guess he thought he had it figured out."

Rick contemplated this a moment as the dog ran back and forth in the yard, tongue lolling. "This guy was married, though. Had a kid on the way. They're saying stuff — I've been looking online — he had this emotionally abusive upbringing. Neglected, things like that. The reporter, same one who had you on there, Sarah Oxley, she did a piece last night on the professor? Gromet or something?"

"Grumett."

"I guess he got fired. He was sleeping with the first victim, the guy's wife. Fuckin' A man. I mean, what causes someone to do that? Okay, I get it, you know — the shitty childhood. But a lot of us have shitty childhoods. Then his wife cheats . . ." Rick shook his head. "This guy put on the works, sounds like, even acted like he was trying to find her killer."

"Yeah."

It loomed unspoken, the idea of someone missing the most vital part of their humanity. It was what she'd feared because it was something you couldn't see coming, couldn't defend against.

The door opened behind them, making her jump. Uschi stuck her head out. "You guys ready to eat?"

Rick looked at Kelly and lifted his eyebrows. The sheer joy on his face pushed everything else aside, and she quickly turned toward Uschi as she knuckled away an escaped tear. "You bet."

* * *

It was a little lonely back in Nokesville. Her apartment had been a haven and a hideout and now it didn't feel the same. She dropped her keys on the counter between the kitchen and eating area, rolled her bag to a stop beside the bed in the main room and looked around.

Her little apartment, which had been enough for her before, felt empty.

She took off her thick winter parka and tossed it onto the couch. Maybe she would get a cat. That was a good place to start.

The End

T. J. Brearton
December 29, 2017 — September 7, 2018
Elizabethtown, NY

Acknowledgments

I'd like to thank my father-in-law, Oak Clement, for key Syracuse-area details and helping me to shoot straight on gun basics. Abigail Fenton, for her guidance in shaping a strong central character. Early readers, Wanda Downs, Charlotte Mack, and Michelle Stottlemyer McLagan—thank you for your willingness, your boldness, your insight. While I have taken minor liberties, criminal law accuracies should be credited to Steve and Mary Buzzell and Jennifer Bulkley. To my publisher and editor Jasper Joffe, thank you for agreeing once again to take me on and make me appear to be a better writer than I am. And to my wife, Dava, and to my three children, thank you for everything.

Thank you for reading this book. If you enjoyed it please leave feedback on Amazon, and if there is anything we missed or you have a question about then please get in touch. The author and publishing team appreciate your feedback and time reading this book.

Our email is office@joffebooks.com

www.joffebooks.com

ALSO BY T.J. BREARTON

HABIT
SURVIVORS
DAYBREAK
BLACK SOUL

DARK WEB
DARK KILLS
GONE

HIGHWATER

DEAD GONE
TRUTH OR DEAD

Made in the USA
Monee, IL
21 January 2020

20640320R00169